The Children of the Calder Sea

FIONA TORSCH

FOR MY FAMILY

My first readers. Thank you.

CONTENTS

CHAPTER 1

ARRIVAL

The train chugged its way into the station, the screech of brakes jolting Isla awake. Hamish was watching her. His eyes seemed even bigger than usual in his small face, white with tiredness and worry. His sandy hair was sticking out at odd angles over his ears. He needed a haircut.

"Are we here little owl?"

Hamish scowled, "I'm not little, and I'm not an owl." But his heart wasn't in the protest, he looked out onto the small platform they were approaching and clutched his bear close.

"I know, I know. You're getting bigger every day. In fact, I think you've grown an inch since we left London..." He wasn't listening but seemed to be searching out a familiar face amongst the handful of people on the platform. Isla noticed that along with the rather bedraggled bear, Hamish's fingers were clenched around a dog-eared photograph.

"What's that you've got there? Have you been going through my bag?"

He turned around, chin jutting out.

"No! It's mine! Mother gave it to me. She told me I had to look after it. If I keep it safe then Mother will be safe, and... and we'll find Aunty Marion, and then Mother will find us." Hamish's voice cracked slightly, and as he pressed his face into his bear, Isla heard him softly add, "Then maybe Father will find us all together and we can go back home..."

She leant back into the seat with a sigh. It had been a long journey, and she had finally succumbed to sleep in the last two hours after watching her brother drift in and out of an uncertain slumber for most of the way. The sleep she herself had gotten had given her little rest.

She replayed the conversation that she had had with her mother before they had left their little flat the previous day.

"Isla, you're far too young to be taking on so much responsibility, I'm so sorry I'm not coming with you. But you're my brave girl, you have your father's courage and your granda's smarts. I need you to look after Hamish. He's too little to understand. Let him be a child a little while longer – I've told him you're going on an adventure for the summer and seeing your father's sister." Her mother had paused for a second, as if searching for what to say next. "You'll be safe. That's all I want for you both. You'll be safe." Isla remembered her mother drawing her close, the scent of her familiar perfume. "I love you two so much. I need to stay here for when your father gets back... he will be back, we just don't know when." She'd shaken Isla slightly at that point. "He is safe still, don't you worry about that. We just need to make sure he can find us when he's back."

When she closed her eyes, Isla could almost smell her mother's perfume again. Almost.

Aunt Marion was a mystery to both Isla and Hamish.

The photograph that Hamish had in his hands, she could just make out, was of their mother holding Hamish as a baby. Marion was in the photograph standing next to her sister-in-law and tiny nephew. That photo was taken almost seven years ago, and Isla could just about picture that moment in time. She'd been seven, and she could vaguely remember the strange yet familiar woman who had come to stay. The only time Marion had ever left the island, that's what Father said.

She wondered if she'd be able to recognise her aunt now, after all this time. She hoped so.

The train shuddered to a halt and the steam rolled past the window, reluctantly giving way to reveal the station they had stopped at. The conductor's whistle blew. "Final station! Attention, all passengers."

"That's us Hamish, can you reach your bag?" Hamish looked up uncertainly at the luggage over his head. "I don't know if I can get it Isla," he turned to look beseechingly at his older sister. "Can you help me?"

"Of course I can. That's what I'm here for isn't it?"

The steam was quickly disappearing into the grey cloud cover which they had been met with since leaving Edinburgh. Hamish kept close to his sister, although his eyes were flicking around the emptying platform. He looked at his photograph, still held tight in his hand, and then back up at her with a frown. "I can't see her."

Isla looked around. True enough, the last of the passengers were disappearing with their greeting parties. The only other person left on the platform was the conductor. She walked up to him and tapped him on the shoulder. He jumped slightly and turned around, apparently astonished that there was anybody left.

"Sorry lassie, I didn't see ye there. Where's yer ma and

pa?"

Isla blinked at the strong burr of the unfamiliar accent. "They're not here. I'm taking my brother to visit our aunty. Do you know if there are any buses to Arraway?"

"It's not a bus ye need lass, ye need a boat."

"Oh. Well, where's the nearest boat?"

"I suppose ye'd need to get to the ferry point first off. That ye can get a bus to. But it won't come for another hour at the very least."

Isla shrugged; she could see the elderly Scotsman glancing towards his watch. "Thank you very much, we'll just wait here until the bus comes."

She glanced back over at Hamish, who looked particularly little when stood by himself. It seemed that his attention was now firmly fixed on the road, his brow furrowed in concentration.

"Isla, look, a car's coming. Maybe it's her!"

Isla looked over to the road. Sure enough, in the distance a car could be seen gradually getting bigger as it approached.

As she turned away from the train, she caught a glimpse of movement next to the carriage. When she looked back, nothing appeared to be out of the ordinary, but she couldn't help but think that she *had* seen something darting in and out of the shadows.

Hamish tugged at her arm. "Isla, let's go." She pushed the thought to the back of her mind and smiled reassuringly at her brother. "You're in a hurry, come on then."

The car came to a stop, and they could both see the woman inside lowering her sunglasses to survey the two children standing by the side of the train.

As the door opened, Hamish held up his photograph as

if comparing the likeness. He paused, and then for the first time since leaving London, he broke into a smile, and then a run. He threw his arms around his surprised aunt, and he cried out "Mother said I'd know it was you Aunty Marion!"

Isla wasn't surprised that her brother could recognise their aunt, despite not being able to remember the one time having met her. The likeness to their father was unmistakeable. Isla bore the same resemblance. Red, ringleted hair, high cheekbones. But grey eyes not blue and she looked more serious than their father, Isla thought as she approached at a cautious pace. Marion was missing the smile lines that her brother had.

"I take it you're Isla and Hamish? My, the last time I saw you laddie, you were a bairn. And Isla, you've grown so much! I hardly recognise you!"

Isla relaxed as she leant into the warm brogue of their aunt's voice.

"Hi Aunty. Thank you for coming to meet us."

"Of course I've come. I wouldn't miss meeting Duncan's bairns. I'm so glad you've come to... visit." She hesitated as she chose her wording, but the smile on her face was sincere.

Hamish was holding his aunt's hand firmly, and her smile deepened as she appeared to notice this for the first time.

"Come on then, we've got a wee bit of a drive yet. Hop in. Pop your bags in the back. You two must be exhausted! I'll get you a hot bath when we get back to the island."

As she brought her case to the car, Isla couldn't help but look back to where she had left the conductor. He had resumed his plodding towards the station office, apparently forgetting about the two children left on his platform.

Hamish bounced in the car, clambering up onto the

passenger seat next to his aunt, shouting out as he did so, "Isla, I'm big enough. Mother would let me go up front!"

"I didn't say you couldn't Hamish! But Aunt Marion might not want you up there...."

Marion closed the door to the car and adjusted her glasses. "Thank you for keeping me company laddie. It was a strange drive here by myself; it's been a long time since I've left my own island."

Isla broke in, "Father said that the first time you'd left the island was when Hamish was born. Is that true?"

Her aunt paused for a moment as she caught Isla staring at her in the mirror. "Aye, there was no call to before. I'd already met you as a bairn, but there was no way for your mother to bring you both up to my wee island after your brother was born." She laughed softly. "Such noise, and such a crowd! I'd never seen the like before. I couldn't stand to be away from the sea for so long again."

Hamish looked up curiously. "What do you mean your island? Do you own it? Are we rich?"

Marion laughed again, this time ruffling her young nephew's head as she did so. "Nay, I'm sorry to disappoint you Hamish. I just call the island my home, but it always seems to make more sense to call it 'mine'. We have an understanding, the island and me."

"Oh, so we're not rich?"

"Not in money perhaps but wait until you see the views from the cottage. No king could do better." With that, she started the engine, and the car coughed and whirred into life. Isla rested her head against the window, staring out at the green meadows passing them by. She knew she had been here once before, as a baby, but she could not remember any of it. The vividness of the wild landscape around them enchanted her, and she only half-listened to her aunt's stories of the history of the country that they had arrived to.

It was only when they turned a corner, and the shimmer of the vast expanse of water before them appeared, that the spell was broken.

"Oh!" she cried. "Look!"

Her aunt slowed the car and wound the window down. As she did so, the smell of salt on the air was carried into the car, and Isla inhaled deeply, certain that she had never breathed before. Hamish licked his lips uncertainly, unsure, and yet profoundly curious.

Marion looked at them, smiling softly as she did so. "You understand why I could never leave this?"

Isla looked around and nodded. She could.

It was strange, but she rather thought that the sea was calling to her. Pulling her closer. She shook her head quickly, pushing the thought away.

"Isla! Isla! Look!"

Hamish's excited squeals broke into Isla's thoughts.

"We're going on the sea! We're going to drive on the sea Isla! Mother would never believe this!" Hamish's squeals of delight pealed through the car, and Marion looked over to her niece with gentle amusement. "You can't miss the first crossing. Look and see where we are."

Sitting up, Isla took fresh stock of her surroundings. The car had come to a stop on the brow of a hill. From where they were perched, the hills of the mainland seemed to stretch endlessly behind them, and an almost unbroken expanse of sea was laid out before them. In the distance, an island beckoned to her.

"Oh, look at that Aunty! It's saying, 'welcome home'!" Isla burst out before she realised what she was saying.

Marion paused before she answered, a strange

expression quickly passing over her face. It cleared almost as fast, and she broke into a radiant smile as she surveyed her home.

"Aye, it does that indeed. That, my wee ones, is Arraway."

Hamish frowned darkly at his sister. "Isla, home is London.... Isn't it?"

At a loss for words, she couldn't reply. She didn't know what she'd meant when she'd seen the island for the first time. It had happened so suddenly. Of course she knew that London was her home. As she remembered the little flat they shared with their parents, a lump gradually formed in her throat. But, as Isla looked ahead to the land in front of her, all she knew was that, here, she'd found something that she didn't know that she'd been looking for.

"Hamish my lad, of course your home is in London, but for now I hope you both will see Arraway and my wee cottage as a home away from home. Just for a wee while. Think what adventures you'll have!"

Marion's words seemed to do the trick, and Hamish reverted to his happy chatter before Isla could finish processing what she was feeling. She looked up and caught her aunt's eye in the mirror. Marion gave her a quick wink, nodded encouragingly, and then started up the engine once more, announcing as she did so, "Right then, let's go and see Mr. Mackenzie about catching his ferry!"

Hamish rolled his window down and stuck his face out in the salty breeze, hollering and whooping as they picked up pace trundling towards the port below.

Mr. Mackenzie turned out to be a bear of a man. With a shock of reddish-brown hair, and a beard to match, he cast a great shadow as he approached the car. Alongside, keeping almost as close to him as his own shadow, was a tiny speckled four-legged creature.

Isla watched warily as he got closer. And then, his eyes crinkled into twin shining orbs as he broke into a deep belly laugh.

"Well, I'll be. Where've ye been for so long? Wee bairns with ye ma'am... Isla and Hamish I assume. Aye, we've been waiting for ye, so we have. We've heard all about the pair of ye, haven't we now!"

Hamish looked up at the giant in front of them, and almost in awe, whispered "You're really tall, Mr. Mackenzie!"

Mr. Mackenzie seemed to find Hamish's remark the funniest joke he'd ever been told.

Chortling, he responded, wiping tears of laughter from his eyes. "Aye, that I am laddie. It's this sea air. Aye, and oats!"

"Oats?"

"Aye, that's the breakfast for a growing lad such as yerself. Get your oats, and ye might grow up nearly as big as me."

He wiped his eyes again with the back of one massive paw. As he looked down at Isla, he softened his voice. "And what about you, lassie? First time on the island? But, no, ye've been here before, a long time back, is that nay right?"

Isla slowly nodded, at a loss for words as she regarded the friendly Scot in front of her. She looked down at the little creature and realised that it was a tiny puppy. Mr. Mackenzie saw where her attention was turning and smiled.

"That there is Tarn. She's only six months old. Found her all by herself so I did. Or, well, she found me more like. Here lassie, can ye look after her for me as I get the boat ready for crossing?"

Isla nodded; attention still focussed on the puppy. More delicately than she could possibly have imagined, the giant picked the animal up and placed her through the window to where Isla was sat.

"She's so tiny!" The soft, warm, furry body she'd been entrusted with wriggled, and she realised that the thumping against her arms was the pup's enthusiastic tail wagging at full pelt. This was soon accompanied by a few well-aimed licks to her face.

"She likes ye lass. That's a good sign. Ye've got a friend for life right there, so ye have."

"She's pretty," Hamish leant over the back of the seat, and tentatively brushed a hand gently across the dog's back. "What does 'Tarn' mean? That's a funny name."

"A tarn is like a small stream. That's where I found her, not too far from here. I think she was wanting to find a way over to the island. All the birds to chase over there... she's no fool that pup, she knows where the fun's to be had!"

Hamish looked up at his aunt. "Tarn can come and visit us sometime, can't she?"

Marion sighed, shaking her head in bewildered amusement at the dog and her newfound friends. "We'll see.... Mr. Mackenzie might not be able to spare Tarn to go visiting."

Hamish nodded wisely, "Tarn has to be a good guard dog here, right Mr. Mackenzie?"

"Aye, that's right laddie. But maybe there'll be chance she'll get to visit the island sometime."

The car creaked forward slowly up the ramp and onto the boat. Isla had been so engrossed in holding onto Tarn that she hadn't seen how Mr. Mackenzie had started up the small boat which they had now progressed up to.

"And we're off!" Marion cried. "Look at the sea... what a calm day for a crossing!"

Isla wasn't too sure that 'calm' was the description she would have chosen, but the bobbing motion as they made their way across the waves seemed to put the dog in her lap into a near-trance.

"Look, Aunty. Tarn's asleep!" Marion looked over and nodded approvingly. "That's a clever pup right there. She knows where she's safe. Remember, the sea will always keep us safe Isla. We're part of the sea here, and the sea is part of us."

Hamish crashed open the door of the car and bolted onto the deck.

Before Isla could shout for him to stop, Mr. Mackenzie had appeared as if out of nowhere. Throwing out one massive arm, he held Hamish back before he toppled over the side in his eagerness.

"Woah there laddie, are ye planning to swim across?"

"No! I saw something... Look! There!"

They all turned to look over to where Hamish was delightedly pointing. A great shape jumped out of the water, inches from the boat. As it landed back in the waves, the resulting splash poured over Hamish, drenching him from head to toe.

"What was that?!" he shouted, wide-eyed.

Mr. Mackenzie breathed a deep hearty chuckle as he answered "That's a porpoise. They're a friendly bunch, but we don't see them this close normally. Ye've got the royal welcome today and make no mistake about it!"

Isla turned to her aunt with shining eyes. "A porpoise? Are there lots? Can we see them from the island?"

"Aye, there are many. I never know how many exactly

because they travel all around the islands. But it does seem that there are some which prefer this island to all the others. I think I know that one, I've seen it before, I'm certain of it. Look, at the mark on its back."

Isla looked just as the porpoise jumped again, marvelling as it twisted mid-air. As she watched, the light reflected off its glossy back, and she saw that there was a dark patch along one side of the porpoise's back.

"What is it?"

"It's just a marking, the same as we might have, I suppose..." Marion replied, eyes still on the porpoise. "I can see them from the house from time to time, playing out in the waves."

"I think his name is Patch" Isla announced decisively.

Marion looked over to her, nodding as she considered. "It could well be. Why do you think that it's this one's name?"

"It just fits right. And, I've got a feeling, that's what he'd call himself." Isla leant back, closed her eyes, and thought about the porpoise jumping again. Her eyes still shut, she said, "Yes, it's definitely Patch."

When she opened her eyes, she found her aunt looking at her closely. Marion turned away and said "Well, you may well be right there Isla. It's as good a name as any, and it would fit that one. You'll have to keep a watch out for him around the island now that you've named him."

Isla nodded, watching her brother staring out to where the porpoise had disappeared to.

As they neared the shore on the other side of the strait, Hamish was guided back to the car by Mr. Mackenzie. "All back in, ready to dock now."

Hamish rushed back and jumped into his seat shouting, "I saw it first!"

The boat slowed to a gentle bob, and as Mr. Mackenzie busied himself with tying off the ropes that secured the boat to the dock, Tarn jumped off Isla's lap and through Hamish's open door onto the deck. She ran to her master and resumed her faithful shadowing duties.

Marion started up the engine, saying as she did so, "Welcome to Arraway."

CHAPTER 2

CALDER COTTAGE

The car rumbled off the rickety wooden planks Mr. Mackenzie used as a ramp, and onto the cobbles leading away from the sea. They gathered speed once they had traversed the village sat on the harbour's edge. Mile by mile they hugged the coastline, occasionally taking a turning which obscured the view for a few moments, but not more. Isla was entranced by the sight of the waves, sunlight dancing and sparkling off the white crests of foam. Hamish, equally mesmerised sat, huddled under a gigantic overcoat lent to him by Mr. Mackenzie. As their kindly ferry master draped it over Hamish through the car, he'd laughed at the sight.

"Laddie, ye've got a fair ways to go before that fits ye proper. Next time I see ye, ye might be fitting into it a wee bit more. Remember yer oats!" Chortling, but not unkindly, he'd waved them off as they departed his boat.

Now, Hamish was still shivering slightly from his encounter with Patch, and teeth chattering, said "Aunty Marion, why is the water so cold?"

"You mean the sea my wee bonnie one? And how else

do you think it should be?"

"Warm!!!" Hamish spluttered indignantly, "It's too cold for people to swim in!"

Marion looked down at her bedraggled nephew, and said kindly "And what if people weren't supposed to be swimming in it? That water down there, it's full of different types of animals, so many types of fish, porpoises like your Patch, seals, and so many types of plant life, and that's barely scratching the surface of what's in there!"

Hamish, scrunched up his nose as he considered, "You mean, they wouldn't be able to live there if the water was warmer?"

Marion looked thoughtful and said "Aye, some would be able to, but it's a fine balance you ken Hamish. If one group of animals were not able to adapt to new conditions, they might just fade away. And that would then have an impact on the other creatures who live with them."

Hamish thought for a moment. He piped up, "I suppose it's alright if it's not the best kind of water for me. I live on the land, and I've got the sun to keep me warm. Right Aunty Marion?"

Marion nodded as she said "That you do Hamish. Although, you might not find the sun quite as often as you did in London now that you're in Scotland!"

Isla looked out at the bright blue sky above her. She couldn't believe it wasn't always like this. "But it's sunny now, and warm!"

Marion laughed quietly, "You've been given a royal welcome, to be sure. But, best to be prepared now, you might not find days like this as readily as you might think. Best enjoy them when they come!"

As the car wound its way along the track that they now found themselves on, shadowed by hills on each side, Isla watched the landscape pass by. She wondered what her mother was doing now, whether she knew that they were safe. Whether she was safe, all by herself, waiting for their father in London.

Her father... where was he? Out at sea somewhere? On land and marching towards the next skirmish? Isla was no longer watching what they were passing, and she could no longer hear her brother's chattering, or her aunt's soft replies. Instead, unseeing and unhearing, she lost herself in her imagination, oblivious to all else.

After what seemed like hours, she felt the car slow, and roll to a stop. They'd come to rest on the plateau of a hill. She could see the waves crashing against the bottom of the cliff. Turning, her attention was drawn to the other side of the road. A neat path led to a small green wooden gate. Pink and white roses, honeysuckle, and climbing vines draped themselves elegantly over the gateposts, mixing their floral scent with the ever-present brackish note of the sea. Beyond the gateway lay one of the most inviting scenes Isla had ever set eyes on.

A whitewashed cottage stood in front of them, with a door as green as the gate before it. The roof was slate, housing not one, but three resplendent red brick chimneys. A trellis next to the doorframe supported arching roses and a climbing purple flower which Isla had never seen before. Full blooms gathered bumblebees and butterflies, a riot of colour against the white walls of the cottage.

Beside the house stood a peculiar domed frame. Isla heard a faint buzzing, and as she looked closer, she saw that the bumblebees were zipping backwards and forwards between the flowers and the dome.

The most amazing thing she thought, though, was the goat, tethered to one side of the fence. It had a large, bronze bell around its neck.

It bent to eat the grass at its feet, the movement catching the bell. A tinkling could be heard, merging with the buzzing of the bees and the crashing of the waves. It was an enchanting mix of melodies... which quickly gave way once the goat looked up and saw the car, with the trio inside.

Its loud 'baaah' made Hamish jump and hold tightly onto his bear, which had somehow found its way inside his arms once again.

Marion laughed. "That's Basil, don't worry, he won't bite!"

Hamish didn't look too sure, but instead kept a very wary eye on the goat as he followed his aunt towards the gate.

It was unfortunate at this point, exactly when Hamish turned his attention away from Basil to open the gate in front of him, that the goat decided to take a great interest in the coat that Hamish was still draped in. As it dragged along the floor, Basil seized his opportunity to take a great mouthful of the tantalising item. Hamish, still oblivious, shut the gate, and turned to catch up with Marion. The surprising strength of the goat's jaw, and the haste with which Hamish was moving, jerked him back with a jolt.

"Help! It's got me!" He yelled, frantically engaging in a fierce tug of war with Basil.

Isla clapped her hands over her mouth, as she stifled a giggle. A little way behind her aunt and brother, she'd watched the whole event unfold. She could swear she saw a wicked glint in the goat's bulbous amber eye.

Marion turned, and sharply she snapped "Basil! Leave it!"

To the children's astonishment, the goat appeared to

understand. At the very least, it slowly chewed the remnants of the cloth in its mouth and let the rest fall to the floor.

Hamish gathered up the coat in his arms and rushed to the front door as fast as his little legs could carry him, weighed down as he was by the sheer amount of fabric enveloping him.

"For goodness' sake Basil! That is not how we treat our visitors. We talked about this! Particularly not the children!" Marion continued to scold the goat, hands on hips as she sternly spoke. Isla watched in disbelief. Surely, the goat didn't really understand. It continued to placidly chew, looking Marion straight in the eye until she wagged a finger at him, and finally gave up with a sigh.

"Ah, what's the use? Such a stubborn, cantankerous mischievous billy goat there never was! I'll never know why I don't just put him in the cook pot."

Basil gave a baleful bleat, and promptly turned his back on all three members of his audience.

"There now Hamish, are you quite alright? You're not hurt are you laddie?"

Hamish was in the middle of examining the damage. He glared up, eyes narrowed as he cried out furiously, "It ate Mr. Mackenzie's coat! Look!" He held up a portion of the coat, and it was true, a sizeable hole could be seen winking back at them.

"I thought you said it doesn't bite?" Hamish groused, his pride far more damaged than the coat.

Marion sighed. "Basil's... well, Basil. You could say he's just a stomach on legs. He won't ever hurt you, but he does think everything is food."

Isla laughed. "You should have seen your face Hamish!"

Hamish scowled at her. "It's not funny! What am I

going to tell Mr. Mackenzie?"

Marion stepped in, "Don't you worry your bonnie head about that laddie. I'll patch it up, and it will look good as new." It was clear that Hamish didn't think this was possible, but he was more anxious to get inside than to try to argue with his aunt.

Isla made sure that all her attention was focussed on the goat as she opened and shut the gate, keeping her own coat well out of reach of its curious gaze... and vociferous appetite.

As she got closer to the front door, Isla noticed a woven doormat on the paving stone by the doorstep. On it was written, 'Calder Cottage'.

"What's that Aunty?"

"The door mat?" Marion asked, as she negotiated a big, bronze key ring.

"No, Calder Cottage. Is that the name of your house?"

"Ah, yes. Yes, Calder is an old family name we once had, many moons ago. It seemed to fit the house." Marion smiled, and that was the end of Isla's line of questioning, as the front door key had now been identified, and was making its way towards the lock.

Marion fitted the key into the lock with a well-practised click, and the door swung open. She looked down at her two charges, and ushered them in. Hamish, wide-eyed, bounded forward into the cool interior. Isla hung back for a second and looked back towards the car.

"Isla are you coming?" her aunt asked her kindly, as she held the door ajar.

Isla swallowed as she nodded. Taking a deep breath, she marched forwards, and took her first steps into the cottage.

She blinked as her eyes adjusted to the light inside the hallway. Then, she blinked again. The hallway sprawled out in front of them, with doors and corridors peeping out from all angles. It appeared to Isla that surely the cottage that she'd seen outside could not hold all the rooms that this hall seemed to suggest!

At the very end of the corridor stood the most magnificent staircase that the children had ever seen. It appeared to have been carved from one single tree, its boughs now forming the stairs. Under the elaborate staircase lay an alcove. Through the round window all that could be seen was a shimmer of green.

Hamish hopped from one foot to the other, desperate, it seemed, to start exploring. He pulled a face at his sister, unsure if he was allowed to.

He tugged at Isla's arm, and whispered, "Can we look around?"

Marion heard the whisper. "Yes of course! But listen. One rule, my room is at the top of the stairs on the left. Yours is on the right. You're welcome in any part of the house, but I'd prefer it if my room is private. Will that be alright?" Marion's voice held a tone of finality that the children both knew brooked no argument. They nodded, and she smiled once again.

"Excellent. Now we all know where we'll be, I'll give you the same promise. Your room is for you, and I won't disturb you there. Now, go on, explore!"

The two children bounded off, needing no further encouragement. Hamish was first, peeking into the first doorway leading off the hall. He put one hand against the sturdy wooden door, then said in surprise, "It's heavy!" Isla saw her brother put all his weight into the attempt, and she shook her head. "Honestly, Hamish, you're tiny! Let me help." She put both of her hands against the door, and together, they pushed the door open. Not sure what to expect, they tiptoed inside.

The room was a deep turquoise, a colour so rich the children had never seen the like. However, it was what lay inside the room that drew Hamish's squeals of delight. It was apparent that Marion had been preparing for their arrival.

A model train track was set up in one corner of the room, along with tin soldiers, bags of marbles, a slingshot and, to Hamish's utter astonishment, a pair of boots with wheels attached to the bottom. He picked them up, "They're my size Isla!"

On the other side of the room, a large dollhouse stood, and even from where she was standing, Isla saw that it looked remarkably like the cottage which they were now in.

Beyond the dollhouse lay a fully stacked bookcase. Running over to inspect it, Isla spied several old friends already waiting for her along with many books she had never before heard of. Finally, her eyes settled on a similar pair of wheeled boots to the ones that Hamish had already found. Tentatively, she picked them up.

Marion had followed the children in. "Are they the right size?" she asked.

Isla was surprised to hear a tinge of apprehension in her aunt's question. "They're... perfect" she breathed. She turned slowly on the spot, surveying the entire room. A cheerful brick fireplace was snug to one wall, and a large bay window gave them a thoroughly unrestricted view of the sea.

"Is this all... Did you do this for us?" Isla asked, unbelievingly. It was so much more than she had ever imagined.

"As long as you're here, I want you to feel at home," Marion answered softly. "I didn't know what you might be able to bring with you, or what you might like... I hope that you like it."

Hamish let out a great whoop of delight. He scurried over to his aunt and flung his arms around her waist. "Mother won't believe this. Thank you, Aunty Marion!"

Marion smiled fondly down at her little nephew. "It's my pleasure." As she looked over to Isla, she saw that the girl was still lost in her discovery of the room.

"Isla, look over there." As Isla followed her aunt's gaze, she came across a little desk tucked behind the edge of one of the floor-length window drapes. A small chair was nestled beside it. On top of the ornately carved wooden surface of the desk, Isla spied a sheaf of paper. She picked up a single sheet. It was heavy and silky to the touch. A fountain pen was in an inkpot next to it.

"I thought, you may want to write to your mother..." Marion began. She stopped as she saw that Isla's eyes had flooded with tears. "What's the matter? You don't like it? I can move it..."

Isla shook her head, and then moved over to hug her aunt, just as her brother had. "It's perfect. It's all perfect. Thank you so much Aunty Marion. Can I write to Mother now? She'll want to know that we got here."

"Of course you can Isla, lass. I'll get some tea ready. Hamish, you can keep looking around if you'd like to, or you can help me with dinner?"

Hamish had already raced out of the room, keen to keep on exploring. Marion turned to Isla with a smile and a shrug. "I asked Mr. Mackenzie to send a telegram from the mainland to let your mother know you both had arrived safely. The post won't go until tomorrow from the island, but I'll make sure we get it sent before the next post goes out."

"Thank you, Aunty."

"Come and find us when you're ready." Marion put a gentle hand on top of Isla's head, and then quietly left the room.

Isla sat down on the velvet plush cushion of the chair and took hold of a leaf of paper almost reverently.

She had always loved rushing to the letterbox with the clatter of the postman's offerings. As time went on, and especially after her father had enlisted, the excitement increasingly turned to a nervous anticipation. Hamish had never shared the interest expressed by his sister in the correspondence appearing through the letterbox, but even he had begun to feel the tension radiating from both his mother and sister every time a letter arrived.

Isla picked up the fountain pen, tapped it against the inkpot, and began to write. She lost track of time, as she concentrated on not letting the ink smudge over the paper.

She folded her letter up, popped it into an envelope, and then went to find her brother. As she wandered through the house, she noticed for the first time that along the edges of the walls, dainty shells were fixed. On impulse, she leant forward and tilted her head to the shells. To her surprise, she heard a noise. A faint hum was all she could make out at first, and then she gave a start. The sound of waves crashing could clearly be heard, and she rather thought that the noise was coming from the direction of the shells. She stepped back and shook her head, clearing the sound from her mind. Clearly, she was too tired to think straight. With a last glance at the seashells lying still and quiet along the wall, she pushed the closest door open, and peered inside.

This door was much easier to negotiate. It swung open and revealed a light and airy room within. A roaring fire crackled merrily in the open hearth, and a low, soft armchair faced it.

"Aunty Marion?" The pop of the fire was the only answer she received. Isla pulled the door to on the empty room, and softly made her way down the corridor.

Suddenly, a loud clatter made her jump. She turned towards the noise and heard the unmistakeable sounds of Hamish's chortling laughter. Following the sounds, she made her way around an unexpected corner of the corridor, and soon found a peculiar doorway. It seemed to be split in two, horizontally. A circular handle was attached to an iron latch, and tentatively she lifted it. The door swung open.

Inside, a scene of utter chaos awaited. A small white monster was running around the kitchen, and a white cloud was gradually clearing to reveal Marion doubled over with laughter. Hamish, Isla realised, was the little figure running around, with an upturned flour bag covering his head, and he was covered head-to-toe in flour. Indeed, the flour seemed to be everywhere. It covered the floor, the large kitchen table, the countertops, and even Marion's flame-red hair was now a diluted coppery white.

The rising flour in the air made Isla sneeze violently. Marion looked up and waved her in, her eyes still streaming with tears of laughter.

"Isla! You found us! We've been cooking." Hamish ran excitedly up to the door, and then Isla realised, she was safe from being flour-caked herself, as the bottom half of the door that she had opened was still firmly shut. Only the top half had opened. Puzzled, but glad of the barrier to the bedlam in front of her, Isla shook her head in amazement.

"Why, Hamish Roland Gelder. What have you been doing?!"

"It's alright, lassie. I put the flour too close to the table edge, and my wee enthusiastic helper here helped it right over the side." Still smiling, Marion shook her head in amusement. "I've been saying I wanted to redecorate my kitchen... but I hadn't thought of using flour before!"

"We were making bread Isla! But... I made a mess." Hamish's face fell, and his lip wobbled as he surveyed the scene around them.

"Not to worry laddie, there's still enough flour and some nice rolled oats here to make a bannock. Plus, there's next to no time to wait in the cooking. Let's see, we'll tidy up a wee bit here, and then I'll show you both how it's done. I'll bet you're hungry! Isla lass come on in, you just have to push on the door."

Hamish had found a broom and was vigorously stirring up the flour on the floor, creating a second whirlwind of white dust which made him sneeze loudly. Isla, having worked out the quirks of the door, seized the broom from him. "Why don't you grab a cloth Hamish? You can wipe down the sides a bit... The broom's too big for you."

Hamish was still sneezing too much to overly protest, so he did what he was told, and grabbed a dishcloth from the side of the sink.

As they worked, Isla curiously looked around the broad kitchen that they were slowly uncovering. The walls were white, and the window frames a dark wood. A large oven with several doors was stood in the recess of a large chimney. The chimney didn't look to be connected to any sort of fireplace, but instead, there were shelves running all the way along the sides of it, and what seemed to Isla to be hundreds of cookbooks lining those shelves. Up and up they reached, forming a staircase of books, until they reached the cupboards on either side of the chimney. On top of the stove a pot was bubbling away, and a delicious aroma wafted gently upwards. The sound of the children's grumbling stomachs made Marion smile.

"Hurry up, we're nearly done! Whilst you two pop those last bits away, I'll get the bannock ready."

Isla turned to put the broom away but was immediately distracted by the sight of the long low window on the far side of the wall. Looking out on the horizon, everything at first seemed still. However, as she looked closer, she saw waves rippling, blurring the skyline. The more she looked, the more she felt it was drawing her closer. Mesmerised, she didn't hear Hamish's whispers until they grew more persistent.

"Isla, Isla..." She looked down, seeing her brother's earnest eyes... along with a newly white handprint on her cardigan. She brushed it off with a sigh. "What?!"

"Look, she's putting the bread on top of the stove. Mother never did that..."

With a smile, Marion looked over at the children. "Hamish, come and have a look. Do you want to turn it for me?"

Curious, they both hurried over, drawn in by the comforting scent of the grain cooking. Pops and crackles were coming from the pan, and a rich, nutty, comforting smell accompanied the cooking. As they got closer, Isla saw that the 'bannock' was a round, flat bread; the crust crisp with oats as they slowly browned in the bubbling golden juices of what Isla soon recognised was butter.

"Butter! Is that real butter?" Isla was astonished. "I can't remember the last time we had real butter!"

Then with a flourish (and a guiding hand from Marion), Hamish flipped the bannock over in the pan, revealing a lightly browned base.

"Now, watch carefully Hamish!" Marion quickly grasped the bannock and lifted it from the pan. She brought it next to Hamish's ear, and tapped the bannock on the underneath, so that he could hear.

"Now, what do you hear?" Hamish looked uncertain. "I don't know... it sounds hollow?"

Marion beamed down at her nephew. "Excellent, then it's ready! I'll grab the stew. Isla love, would you take the bannock to the table?"

Marion set the stew on the table, and both children ran up, sniffing the air appreciatively. Isla put the warm bannock next to the pot of stew, and lingered there for a moment, her mouth watering from the fragrant aromas of the meal in front of them.

"Alright you two, take a seat. Now, let's see what you make of a real island supper." Ladling the stew into the bowls laid out, Marion handed each child a bowl and broke off a wedge of the bannock as she did so. "Go on then, no standing on ceremony. I know you're hungry. Grab some of the bannock, aye, there you go Hamish. Careful, mind, it's hot." Hamish needed no further instruction and dived straight in, spluttering slightly as the heat of the stew reached his mouth.

Isla, cautious of the steam rising from the bowl in front of her, inhaled the rich smell of the food, familiar and yet not at the same time. Licking her spoon, she looked up and caught her aunt's eye and smiled. Calder Cottage, she realised, felt like home.

CHAPTER 3

DUNCAN

The waves lashed against the ship, stinging spray sluicing over the sailors huddled in their positions of the watch. A lightning fork flashed across the deck, and the men shrank back, for one heart-stopping moment believing themselves struck. As soon as it had appeared, however, it vanished, leaving scorch marks in its wake. The sailors shaken, drew their overcoats closer and gritted their teeth, wondering if they would last the night.

And so, they waited. Peering out into the gloom, they kept watch. The driving wind and rain blistered the hands of those pulling at the ropes, but so numb were they that they barely noticed. Howling gales caused the ship to buck and heave. Crossing themselves, they gathered what they could and anchored themselves to the dubious safety of the ship's rail. Abandoning their post for the safety of the cabins within was not an option they were permitted to consider. For out in the darkness, the enemy lay in wait.

The simple oil lights had burned down low, and dark shadows obscured everything but the frightened faces of the boys closest to the lanterns. The youngest of them peered over to the figure resting on the bow of the ship. Standing apart from the others, his stance gave the boy courage. Straight-backed and tall, he exuded defiance in the onslaught of the sea.

As the boy watched and the lantern flickered, the older seaman's face was briefly illuminated. He thought for a moment that he was seeing the depths of the sea from within the sailor's eyes. The chance trick of the light stuttered as the lantern finally gave out, and the illusion disappeared when shadows once again masked the man's features.

Duncan remained still and alert, aware that he was being watched. His face was weathered, but not yet wholly lined with age, and his vision was as sharp as it had ever been. Identifying the source of the scrutiny, his thoughts returned to his family. Safe on land many miles away, he knew that his own son would be tucked up in bed, fast asleep. His daughter would be helping her mother in or out from her shift on patrol. At thirteen, the girl was growing up fast. This sailor boy and many others on this ship, he guessed, would be little more than five years older than her, perhaps less. The thought was sobering. So many young lives, eager to join the war effort and take their turn in becoming heroes. And look at them now, scared by the sounds of the creaking deck.

And why shouldn't they be frightened, Duncan thought, as he glanced away. They joined up seeking adventure, ready to do their part for King and country. And yet, here they were. Waiting in the dark to come to blows with an enemy that cared little for the innocence of youth.

He thought again of his wife and children. He would do

anything to protect them, including joining a fight that was not his own. He had hoped to be able to turn the tide away from his homeland, his family, his people... He wondered, not for the first time, if he had made the right decision.

The ship's siren abruptly pierced his thoughts.

Within seconds, the red warning beacon was pulsing urgently, throwing the sailors into mayhem. Skidding and sliding as they ran into position, the men jostled each other as they found their places by the artillery weapons with which they had become unavoidably familiar.

As they sought to make out any sign of movement in the darkness, the shouts of the officers directed them, above and below. From the sky came a furious torrent of more than just rain; heavy lead raked across the ship's deck. Duncan sensed, rather than saw, the missile speeding towards the ship in the seething waters below. He opened his mouth to shout a warning, but his voice was lost in the force of the impact. The collision itself sent men flying, but it was the gaping hole punched in the ship's hull which decided the vessel's fate.

The order was given to abandon ship. In the chaos that ensued, it was only the young sailor boy who realised that the man he had been watching was nowhere to be seen.

Pulling himself along the steep angle of the ship's balustrade, he heaved himself closer to the side. In the midst of the melee, he did not notice the tentacle retracting swiftly and stealthily, having achieved its sinister purpose. Frantically, he scanned the roiling water beneath him. Illuminated now by the tongues of flame escaping from the interior of the ship and growing steadily higher, the sea spoke its own tale.

The man's lifeless form was rapidly disappearing from

sight. The boy saw the body being flung up onto the crest of a wave, and then down, down, down. Finally, it was lost from sight, and the depths welcomed it into their embrace.

CHAPTER 4

A QUESTION OF PORRIDGE

The bright sun and the call of the gulls woke Isla the next morning. She shook her head, groggily. Her sleep had been broken. Her dreams skittering around a darkness she could not quite place. The memories faded quickly as she looked around, blinking as she got used to the light.

The room was airy, soft carpeting running along the floorboards. A large skylight was positioned in the middle of the ceiling, through which Isla had been amazed to see thousands of stars as she drifted off. Now she watched bright rays of sunlight chasing errant clouds along the sky. In the distance, Isla could just about make out the wheeling of the gulls.

On the other side of the room, Hamish's bed lay flush against the wall. His bear was wrapped up in the sheets, but Hamish was nowhere to be seen.

Throwing on the dressing gown which was laid out next to her bed, Isla set off in search of her brother. She paused as she came out onto the landing and saw the door at the other end of the gallery. That must be Aunty Marion's room, she thought.

The door was firmly pulled to, and Isla remembered that Marion had specifically asked them to keep out of her room. Isla fervently hoped that Hamish had also remembered. She crept closer to the door, listening out for any sound. And then, 'CRASH'. She jumped, and then despairingly shook her head. "Oh Hamish, what have you broken now?" she muttered to herself as she navigated her way down the winding staircase.

Following the noise, Isla reached the kitchen and, bracing herself for what she might find within, she opened the door. To her surprise, everything seemed normal. Hamish was sitting at the table, his legs dangling off the ground. In front of him was a bowl of what seemed to be... porridge?

"Morning Isla!" Hamish beamed up at her from around a spoonful of his breakfast.

"Morning. What time did you get up? And... what was that bang just now?" Isla realised that her stomach was grumbling as she watched her brother wolfing down the food in front of him.

"Not too long ago. I got up when I heard Aunty Marion downstairs. But then I got here and didn't see her. But there's breakfast! Look!"

Isla turned to where Hamish was pointing; behind her on the countertop next to the stove were three pans of porridge.

"Why are there three? And, honestly, Hamish, did you break something? What was that crash I just heard?"

"No! I didn't do anything! Aunty Marion is doing something outside, I think. Oh, and those pans all taste a bit different. I just got the one I liked."

Isla shook her head at the mumbling her brother was making as he talked through a mouthful of his porridge.

33

She dipped a spoon into the first pan of porridge. It was...
odd. "Salty?!" She exclaimed. Hamish nodded, "Yep. I
didn't like that one. The one on the other end is the one I
liked."

Isla tried a spoonful of Hamish's preferred choice.
"That is *so* sweet Hamish! Of course you'd go for that one."

"Nobody said I couldn't," Hamish muttered defensively.

Tentatively, Isla tried the middle pan, and then smiled.
Creamy, oaty, warm and slightly sweet. She filled a bowl
and then went to sit next to her brother.

"How come Aunty Marion made three lots? And why
would anyone want to put salt in porridge?" Hamish shook
his head, bewildered. "Honey is so much better! I bet you
Aunty Marion made the honey."

"People can't make honey Hamish."

"Yes, they can so!"

"Bees make the honey. But you're probably right," Isla
backtracked as she saw Hamish's face turn red. "Probably
Aunty Marion's bees made the honey."

At that moment, their aunt entered the kitchen,
through a side door which neither of the children had
noticed up to that point, so much did it blend into the
walls.

"Good morning! I see you both found some breakfast.
How did you sleep?"

"Really well, I didn't hear anything, then the seagulls,
and it was morning! I can't believe I slept so long."

"Aye, that'll be the sea air. It'll do it every time. And
what about you laddie?"

"I thought I heard you downstairs this morning, so
came down, but I didn't see you. I found the porridge
though!" Hamish proudly showed Marion his thoroughly
empty bowl.

"Aha, so you did. I was out milking the goat."

"Milking Basil?" Isla exclaimed. She couldn't think of many things stranger than salted porridge, but milk from a goat was an extraordinary idea.

"Och no, that would never happen with Basil! No, Basil has a friend who you've not met yet – "Wilhelmina" is her name, but I call her "Billie". You probably heard her outside just before, big noisy thing she is. Kicked the milk bucket right over." Marion then muttered darkly, "be a good thing maybe when *she* kicks the bucket."

Isla laughed, but Hamish either didn't seem to hear or understand. Instead, he was looking aghast as his aunt ladled a bowl of porridge for herself – from the salted pan. "You're eating the salty one?" he asked incredulously. "Yuck!"

Marion ruffled his hair as she joined them at the table, "It's how we like it up here on the island."

Isla was struck by a thought. "But how did you know what we like?"

Marion smiled and shook her head. "I didn't. Must have been the brownie."

Hamish asked immediately, "What's a brownie?"

"It's a little creature, a helper around the house. They're very shy creatures, so they work when everyone else is asleep. Early in the morning or late at night, the brownie will come out and do any sweeping up that needs to be done or washing or cooking. Even lighting a hearth fire when he has the mind to."

Isla thought back to the previous day and her exploration of the house and living room. Then, she shook her head as Hamish asked "But where does it live? How did it know how we like our porridge? I want to see it!"

"They're not really real Hamish!" Isla scoffed in

exasperation. "It's a fairy story!"

"Ah, now then lassie. Why are you so sure? Magic little folk they may be, but real enough they are too. Now then, Hamish. They live in little nooks and crannies, somewhere in the home. I've never looked for the brownie of this house, as they really are very shy, and happy to be left to their own devices."

Hamish was wide-eyed with excitement. "Maybe," he whispered, "maybe I'll find it."

Isla whispered back, "It's just a story."

Her brother clenched his fist into a little ball and said determinedly, "I *will* find it Isla."

Knowing how stubborn Hamish could get, Isla let it be. At least, she thought, it would be a good distraction for him.

"Alright you two? All finished? Why don't you get dressed, and then, if you like, I can show you the island and the village."

They needed no further encouragement. Jumping up, Isla and Hamish dashed out of the kitchen and both hurried to get ready. Racing each other down the stairs, they came to a sudden stop by the front door.

"Right, shoes on, and then we'll be off! As it's such a fine day, I thought we'd not take the car." Opening the door, Marion showed them what was waiting outside. "Your mother wrote to me in one of her letters that you'd both learnt how to ride a bicycle?"

Whooping with joy, Hamish ran up to the three bicycles lined up by the front door. The smallest was evidently meant for him. Isla took hold of the mid-sized bicycle, enchanted by the wicker basket sitting on the handlebars. Hamish grabbed his bicycle and, wobbly at first, cycled down the garden path to the gate.

"Look at me!" He shouted gleefully. As he turned back towards the house, he spied Basil peeping around the side of the cottage.

"Och, you've no worries there Hamish. Basil doesn't go for anything on wheels." Hamish didn't look convinced and decided the wisest course of action was to stay as close as possible to the gate, ready for a quick escape.

Basil bleated triumphantly and trotted out, a wicked gleam in his eye. Marion scolded him, with a firm tap on his rump.

"Now then Basil, you best mind your manners. Now, get on with you."

Basil turned to look at her and gave a bleat, before turning away and doing something quite inexcusable on the garden path. Isla giggled into her hands as her aunt shooed the belligerent goat away with a broom.

"I don't know why I bother! Might as well try to teach manners to a barnacle! You dirty goat, go on now. Shoo!"

Basil darted away, and Marion and Isla joined Hamish at the gate. Dusting her hands off, Marion climbed onto her bicycle and cycled down the road, her loose hair streaming in a fiery wave through the air. She looked back to make sure the children were following. Hamish, now steadier on his bicycle, pedalled fast to catch up.

Isla paused, then followed at a slower pace. She wished that they could have gotten to know their aunt in different circumstances. She wondered what her father was doing now, where he was. Her mother, she supposed, wouldn't have received the telegram yet, but, if Mr. Mackenzie really did send it today, then surely it wouldn't be long before they heard from her.

Isla's legs began to ache as they covered the distance to the village. She noticed that Hamish had slowed a little too; just as they approached the first of the houses that signalled the beginning of the village she saw his head raise a bit higher, and legs pedal faster as he rushed to race to the village first.

Marion ushered them over to leave their bicycles at the side of one of the buildings. "We'll leave these right here, they'll be safe enough. Everybody looks out for each other here on Arraway, so we don't have to worry about that," she answered when Isla asked her about whether they should leave their bicycles in a safer location

"But, oh my, look at the pair of you!" Marion exclaimed as she looked them over, both standing red-faced and slightly out of breath.

"Well now, I'll wager that after a few weeks here you'll be racing around the place with no troubles. Some good island food and island living. That's what you two need. Fine city folk that you be! Now, Hamish, no use standing around like a limp lettuce! Come on, let's go!"

They trudged through the village, forgetting their tired legs as they followed Marion, listening to her commentary of their new surrounds.

"So, this is Burnside. It's a small place, most folk here have always lived on the island. Not many new faces in these parts, so you'll get to recognise folk soon enough I shouldn't wonder. There's a wee stream that flows down through the hills and comes out somewhere near the town; that's where the town got its name. Round these parts, a 'burn' is what we call a stream.

"Legend has it that the river folk got fed up with the island's first inhabitants always using their river, for water, for washing and the like. They gave the stream to the villagers with the promise they wouldn't bother their river anymore. But the river still flows; you'll find it on the other side of the island, and I daresay the folk of Arraway still use it a fair bit. Plenty of fish, and good swimming spots too! I'll take you sometime."

The houses they were passing had cheery, brightly painted doors in every different colour, brightening the grey stonework from which they were all constructed. Isla was about to comment on the unusual village they were walking through when she saw Hamish's downcast face. Swimming, she supposed. Their father had promised to teach Hamish how to swim this summer. To distract her brother, she jokingly asked Marion, "These river people, are they the same as brownies?"

Her aunt stopped and looked at them very seriously. "No," she said darkly. "The river people are very different. They're proud, and spiteful to boot. They give a gift and if the terms of their gift aren't met, they get angry. Trust me, you would never want to encounter an angry river person. Over the years, they've been called many things, "water goblins", "hobgoblins", "kappa", and others. Tricksters, but malevolent with it. No, not at all like a brownie."

Hamish forgot all about swimming, and looked up at his aunt with a quick question, "But what do they look like? How will I know if it's a brownie or a river person?"

"Well now, a brownie is a small, wee thing. A good head of hair on them, and quite brown and wizened. They're a good creature, but you must always be kind to a brownie. I leave a pot of cream out for our brownie. And never say a mean or ill-spirited word to a house brownie. It will leave a house forever if it feels itself to be insulted. Now, a water goblin, or a river person, is a trickier beast to spot. Some have the ability to take on the form of another, some have the power to persuade, and others have the power to bewitch. The most powerful, and the most dangerous of these will have an assortment of these enchantments at their fingertips. So, to look at, you may never know. It's the characteristics that will give the game away. A brownie, at its heart, is generous to a fault, and will do anything for its house. All it does is to be a helper. A river person, on the other hand, is selfish and all of its actions are self-serving. It is never wise to try to befriend a river person. At all costs, you must try to avoid them."

Despite herself, Isla asked, "But, if there are river people, and they gave the village a stream as a gift, then shouldn't something bad have happened to the people who still use the river?"

Marion stopped to consider, "Aye, you'd think there would be a consequence from the river people. Many folk no longer believe in them; it has been many years since a river person has been seen on the island. Perhaps they left the island once their conditions were broken, perhaps they have faded to be merely folklore, or perhaps they are simply waiting. Some of those who still believe say the river people are the reason why there are no children on the island."

She paused, then chuckled. "The population is low, but I'm not certain if I believe that."

When she saw Hamish's eyes, wide as saucers, she smiled and said kindly, "Not to worry laddie, I've been here for many a year, and not seen hide nor hair of a river person."

Marion stopped for a moment to greet a passer-by, and Hamish ignored the adults' exchange for a moment as he whispered to his sister, tugging at her sleeve anxiously. "How does she know she's not seen one if they can change what they look like?" Isla whispered back, "It's just make-believe Hamish, they're not real."

Hamish whispered back furiously, "But Aunty Marion

said!"

"It's just a game, Hamish. Honestly! It's just a story."

Their near silent exchange was cut short when they heard Marion say, "This is Isla, my niece. And this is Hamish, my nephew. Duncan's bairns."

They looked up and saw that Marion was speaking to an old lady. Her grey hair was pinned up under a tartan bonnet, and her stooped frame was covered in a tightly knitted woven shawl. Despite the mid-morning sun, she looked like she was preparing to do battle with the sharpest of winters.

"Och, why hallo children. Isn't it just a wonder to finally see ye? Bonnie, that's fer sure, the both of ye. Aye, I can see Duncan right enough, Och, a chip off the auld block so ye's are."

She smiled, and Isla could see that the woman had hazel eyes which twinkled as she did so, and a little dimple appeared next to a line in her cheek. Isla decided that she liked her, although it had been a task to concentrate to understand what she had said. She looked to her aunt for an introduction.

"This is Mrs. MacGregor. She's the post mistress here in Burnside."

"Now, where are my manners? Ye're right about that lassie," she burred pleasantly to Marion. "Aye, ye'll find me over yonder, in the wee shop across the road." She gestured, and all three turned to look. Sure enough, a small building stood with a red 'Post Office' sign swinging gently from the front.

Hamish spoke up, frowning, "It looks like a house, not a Post Office."

Merrily, Mrs. MacGregor replied, "Well, where are we to get a fancy big post building from on this island, wee man? It's a wee auld house aye, lad, but the Post Office still the same. Post Office in the front, and I have my quarters in the back."

"We'll be by before we head back," Marion said to Mrs. MacGregor. "The bairns will be looking forward to seeing the Post Office, being so different from the big city, isn't that right?"

Isla smiled and nodded, and nudged Hamish, who reluctantly did the same, albeit keeping one eye suspiciously on the post mistress.

Marion led the way onwards through the village. As they walked along the cobbled pavements and passed the curious shops and houses, Hamish tugged at his sister's sleeve once again, and frowned up at her. "I think she's a water goblin."

"Who?" Isla laughed.

"Mrs. MacGregor."

"Oh, don't be silly Hamish. She's just a nice old lady!"

"She asks too many questions, and Aunty Marion said they could look like anything."

"Yes, but she also said that they're not nice. And Mrs. MacGregor is nice."

"She sounds funny," Hamish muttered.

"Everyone sounds like that here Hamish!"

They started to walk back up the high street. Isla took more note this time as they wound their way back. A greengrocer's, a butcher's, the rectory and the church were all on one side of the village high street, alongside a few houses dotted in between. On the other side stood the post office, a bakery and another assortment of houses. She stopped suddenly and asked, "Aunty Marion, are there really no other children on the island? Do we have to go to school?"

Marion sighed and said, "Aye, lass, there have been no children on the island for a long while. Those that were went over to the mainland with their families, and the schoolmistress has long since gone too. I cannae see why anyone would move away from the island, there's no place safer than Arraway, particularly in these times. I cannae tell you whether we'll see any children your age on the island now. If you do, they are likely fisher folk over from the mainland. They tend to keep themselves to themselves. Not overly sociable folk. It takes a long time for some of them to warm up to who they see as outsiders."

"But Mrs. MacGregor was really nice," Isla protested (Hamish looked dubious), "and," she continued, "you're not an outsider. You've always lived on the island, haven't you?"

Marion paused. "Not always, no. But long enough, that is true. I'm more or less an islander now. But I like my own space on the island, so, I don't suppose I'm too worried if not everybody sees me as one of their own. Besides, Mrs. MacGregor and the folk here are islanders, not fisher folk. There's a difference. You'll see it when you come across it."

They paused outside the Post Office and Marion said, "As for school, well, shall we see how the summer goes? And then, let's see." Hamish whooped. "No school! Yay!" He punched the air, and Isla put her hand on his shoulder. "Shush, Hamish."

Marion said, "Like I said, we'll see. Who knows what will happen in that time? The whole summer is ahead of you. But now, let's forget about that. We've got Mrs. MacGregor waiting for us."

Marion pushed open the door in front of them, red like the pillar boxes Isla was used to seeing back home. The bell above the front door tinkled as they walked into the cool, shaded interior.

Cabinets full of envelopes, stamps, boxes and more lined the walls. Behind the counter stood Mrs. MacGregor and shelves and shelves stacked high with all manner of glass jars, each containing a different type of sweet.

Isla recognised sugar mice, liquorice all sorts, strawberry pencils, chocolate limes, lemon sherbet, jellies, white chocolate coins, milk bottles, and so it went on. Any sweet she could think of, it seemed, was in the Post Office's treasure trove. Hamish's eyes lit up. Suddenly, he didn't seem so disgruntled to be meeting Mrs. MacGregor again in such a short space of time.

"Aye, Mr. Mackenzie was in early this morning, ye ken. He brought in a letter I believe ye had ready to be sent to London, lass?" She asked Isla kindly. Isla nodded, wondering when her mother would receive it.

"He asked for it to be sent first class, or as quick as it could go. It's been sent express, so it may arrive by tomorrow morning perhaps." She nodded at the counter. "But if any telegrams get sent, I'll be here with them, aye, that I will. So, if ye're ever in the village, come along by, and ye may find yerselves a wee message. Of course, they'll come to ye, won't they sure enough, but this is the first stop."

"Here ye go laddie. A chocolate lime." Mrs. MacGregor gave one of the sweets to Hamish who devoured it greedily, stopping just long enough to say, "Thank you Mrs. MacGregor, they're my favourite!"

"Ah, who'd have thought. Certainly not me, the rate ye've been eyeing them up!"

As they said their goodbyes, Isla having been given a sugar mouse, Hamish looked up at Isla and whispered, "Probably not a water goblin after all." Isla smiled, and shrugged. "Probably not. And, also, they're not real!"

Finding their bicycles safe where they had left them, the trio started their journey back to the cottage. As they cycled, Isla wondered at her aunt. She seemed to be so sensible in so many ways, warm and welcoming, and full of good cheer, but at the same time, why would she keep bringing up the strange folklore of the island? "Maybe it's a distraction technique for us, if she thinks that we'll not miss home so much" she reasoned to herself. And, she thought, it certainly seemed to be working as far as Hamish was concerned.

The rest of the day, Isla and Hamish spent exploring the garden and fields beyond the house. Marion just let them roam, for, as she said, there was nothing about for miles and miles.

The children returned home later that evening, muddy and grinning. They recounted their adventures to their aunt as soon as they spilled through the doorway.

Marion welcomed them with a smile and laughed at their dirt-caked faces. "You must be starving! Go on, wash up, and then we'll see about some supper."

Hamish ran charging off, with Isla close behind. Upon their return to the kitchen, their hungry eyes ate up the sight of what seemed to be a feast in front of them. A large joint of ham sat in the middle of the table, with heaped fluffy mashed potato alongside it, a large terrine of green beans, a loaf of freshly baked bread, and a creamy, golden block of butter all stood on the table.

"Is this all for us?" Isla exclaimed. They hadn't seen such a spread since... she couldn't remember when.

As they sat around the table, Marion, ladling food onto

their plates, said, "Well, what we don't eat tonight will be supper tomorrow." Isla buttered her piece of warm bread and watched as the golden spread liquified and seeped into the soft crust. A silence descended on the kitchen as they ate. Marion smiled. "The sign of a good supper", she said.

Hamish looked up around a thick piece of ham and beans and muttered something unintelligible. Isla frowned at him, and he said, swallowing, "It's really good!" After a moment, he looked up at his aunt, and said cautiously, "Aunty Marion, can you teach me how to cook?"

She blinked, clearly surprised, and Isla looked disbelievingly at her brother. "Since when did you want to do anything helpful in the kitchen?" She laughed.

He flushed, and looked down at his plate, mumbling, "I want to cook Mother a dinner like this when she gets here."

Immediately, Isla's eyes welled up, and she looked at her brother, embarrassed that she hadn't had a similar thought. Marion cleared her throat and said briskly "Of course you must learn how to cook laddie. And Isla too, if you've a mind. It can be a good skill to have. So, if you'd like to learn, I'd be happy to teach you."

They washed the pans in relative silence, each caught up in their own thoughts, the children suddenly exhausted by the day's adventures.

They filed up to bed without complaint and slipped into sleep as soon as Marion bid them goodnight.

CHAPTER 5

THE LOCH

Isla had been dreaming that she was out at sea, amidst the crashing waves. But, strangely, she had not been frightened. She kept her eyes closed and she could almost feel the spray of the waves and taste the tang of salt in the air. Then, gradually, the memory of the dream dulled and faded, and she opened her eyes to find sunshine once again flooding the room. And, once again, Hamish's bed was empty.

She tiptoed downstairs to find Hamish, not in the kitchen as she had expected, but instead, peering through the crack between the two halves of the kitchen door.

"What are you doing Hamish?" She whispered loudly. He jumped and wheeled around.

In an angry whisper he replied, "You scared me! I'm trying to see the brownie! But you probably scared it away."

Isla rolled her eyes, but before she could reply, the kitchen door opened in front of them and Marion stood there, surprised as Hamish all but fell through the door.

"Well, now, good morning! And what might you be up to I wonder?" She laughed and helped Hamish to his feet.

"I was trying to see the brownie, Aunty Marion," he said earnestly.

"I see! Well, it may be that you're not quite early enough. I do believe brownies are notorious for their early rising and working."

He frowned. "But what do they do for the rest of the day?" he asked.

"Now that, Hamish, is an excellent question. I suppose sleep for some of it, as they're up in the wee hours. But nobody rightly knows."

Hamish quietened after that, but as they got their porridge, again each to their own tastes, Isla could see that he was deep in thought, and she was sure that he was up to something. Before she could try to find out what he was planning, there was a knock on the door, and they could hear Basil and, they supposed, Billie, bleating angrily outside.

Marion went to answer, and for a few moments Isla and Hamish could only make out the muted sounds of a conversation taking place in the hallway. Then, the kitchen door opened, and a familiar face appeared in the doorway.

"Good morning, Mr. Mackenzie," Isla said brightly.

"Ah see ye've found yer oats laddie," Mr. Mackenzie chortled. "But ye've a ways to eat before ye grow a mite bigger I'd wager. Eat up, eat up! And good morning to ye too, lass."

Marion smiled and said, "Mr. Mackenzie is acting as the new village postman this morning. Penny has written to you both."

Isla rushed up from her chair, and Hamish was not far behind. "Aye, I'd reckoned that ye would be wanting a letter delivered as soon as it arrived," he said, handing over an envelope to Isla. She recognised her mother's handwriting on the address and began to rip it open. "I bring the post over from the mainland," he continued. "I don't believe Mrs. MacGregor will be too upset if I saved her a job this morning."

Hamish shouted, "Isla! What does it say?"

Isla said, "It's from Mother." She unfolded the letter and began to read aloud.

"Dearest children,

I received the telegram saying you had arrived safely and were now at Calder Cottage with your Aunt Marion. I couldn't wait to write back, to tell you how glad I am that you are both safe, and I know that you will have the most wonderful time. I miss you more than words can say, but I know that you will be my courageous soldiers up on the island. Make sure that you do lots of exploring, and have many adventures, so that you can write and tell me all about what you are doing, so that I might imagine myself there with you.

"I do miss you terribly, but I am so glad that you are away from the city, for it is not a place where children can play freely any longer. Most of your friends have been sent away to relatives in the country, and I know that Mrs. Rogers is taking Daisy and Daphne to their grandparents' in a matter of days. I must remain a little longer, as I'm needed in the hospital. There are new faces every day, and each must have the care they deserve.

"There are not so many nurses or doctors as there should be for all of the patients. But, as these soldiers are doing, and as your father is doing, I must do my part and help where I can. I wait to hear news of your father, and although I have not yet had word, I expect to very shortly hear that his ship has docked. I will let you know when I receive news.

"In the meantime, my darlings, be good and be brave. Tell me all about your adventures, and Isla, you must teach Hamish how

to swim! Hamish, be a good boy, and help your aunt as she asks.

"Marion, I thank you beyond measure for looking after my two children. I know you will all have a jolly time together, and I am sure that I will see you soon. These times will draw to a close, I am certain of it. In the meantime, I send you my love, and my blessings.

"Your very loving Mother (Penny)."

Isla finished reading, with a slight tremble in her voice, and said, "Mr. Mackenzie, do you think she received my letter?"

He replied gruffly, "Aye, that I do lassie. Perhaps she will receive it today, and it will be a grand surprise for her. I'd wager she sent that letter before she received yer own."

Hamish darted out of the room and was gone for several minutes. He returned, slightly out of breath, and handed Mr. Mackenzie a folded piece of paper, through which Isla could just make out her brother's untidy scrawl.

"Mr. Mackenzie, could you please send this to Mother?" he asked stoutly.

"Aye laddie, that I can. I might just need an envelope if ye have one?" From behind his back Hamish drew out an envelope, already addressed.

"I did it already."

"Then, in the post it shall go. I will see to it that Mrs. MacGregor sends it as soon as she can. Lass, do you want to write anything?"

Isla shook her head, "It's Hamish's turn."

As Mr. Mackenzie left, Marion showing him out, Isla turned to her brother and asked, "What did you write?"

He looked down at his feet, shuffling his socks along the tiles, then muttered, "I told her about the loch that we found, and that Marion will teach us how to row the boat and... just things. I wanted to let her know that we're alright."

Isla laughed and ruffled his hair. "I'm sure that will make her come up here faster. But you didn't say that Aunty Marion is going to teach you how to cook?"

He looked up defiantly. "That's a *surprise*, Isla! And don't you tell her either," he added furiously. She held her hands up, "I won't, I promise! It's your surprise, I won't ruin it!"

Marion came back through the door, announcing as she did so, "Right then! The sun's out again! So, why don't we all head to the loch? Time you learnt how to row a boat!"

Isla and Hamish cheered, and ran to put on their shoes.

Marion led them along a stream and eventually they came across the loch which they had discovered the previous day. There, a little rowboat lay moored up by a narrow wooden jetty. As they neared, Isla saw that two wooden oars lay in the bottom of the boat. Marion showed them how to navigate their way onto the vessel. "Now, make sure the boat is balanced. You don't want to be tipping your way out, and into the water if you weren't planning on taking a swim. Isla, watch your brother."

When they were all in the boat, Isla and Hamish on the back bench, Marion in the middle of the front bench facing the children, she showed them how to pick up the oars.

Hamish said in a surprised voice, "You're sitting backwards Aunty Marion."

"Aye, Hamish, but that's how you set about rowing. You see, you pull the oars back, like so, and then away you go. You see, you both are going forward? Well, we are all moving forward, but to do so, it takes a person sitting backwards as you row. Now, Isla, lass, would you like to try?"

Isla nodded shyly, having never taken her eyes off the motion of the oars. Carefully, she manoeuvred her way across to where her aunt was seated, holding her arms out to steady herself.

She swapped places with her aunt who sat beside Hamish. "At the moment, Isla has longer arms Hamish, and knows how to swim. When you've learnt, we'll see how long your arms are, and see if you can take the oars yourself. Aye, that's it Isla. Now, both together at the same time, or else we'll be going round in a circle."

Surprised at the weight of the oars, Isla pulled, trying to move each oar in time, leaning her body forward, and then drawing herself back as she pulled back on the oars. Sure enough, the boat glided along as she continued to row.

As they approached the other side of the loch, Marion called out, "And now, pull to your right to turn, Isla." She followed her aunt's instructions, her arms beginning to tire, but pulling hard to the right none the less. Her fatigued hold slipped a little, and the oar hit the water with a splash, dousing her brother and aunt who cried out and laughed as the cold water hit them.

The boat turned, sure enough, and Isla gratefully exchanged places with her aunt, who took the oars from her.

Isla turned and looked across where they had come from, and for the first time realised that the loch was not, in fact, a perfect lake. There was a narrow outlet which had become visible now they had reached the far shore.

"Where does that go to, Aunt Marion?" she asked, pointing. Marion looked and then said, "That's just a wee river. But, children, you are to stay on this loch alone. The water moves faster out there, so you are not to go out by yourselves down that stream."

They nodded their understanding, and they made their way back to the other side. When they arrived, the sun broke out from behind a cloud, and surprised them all with the sudden warmth it brought.

"It's a fine day to learn to swim Hamish," Marion said, looking up at the sky. "What do you think?" Suddenly, he looked nervous, and stammered, "But, I don't have my swimmers. And the water looks cold... and really deep!"

Brightly, Marion replied, "Well, once we learn to swim, we won't know how deep it is. And, if you keep moving, the less cold you'll be. I think we can go in with our clothes on, there's a change of clothes waiting for all of us back at the cottage. It's a warm day after all. Make the most of it while it's here!"

"Come on Hamish!" Isla shouted. She'd hopped out of the boat as soon as they landed at the jetty, and needing no further encouragement, kicked off her shoes and jumped, summer dress and all, straight into the shimmering waters of the loch. Ever since she had had her first taste of swimming with her father, she had loved it, and felt as at home in the water as on land.

She disappeared, out of sight, and Marion and Hamish looked on aghast. They had no sign of her for several, long moments.

Then, suddenly, she bobbed up on the other side of the boat. She spluttered a little, and said through slightly chattering teeth, "Come on in!"

Hamish's face turned a bright red and he shouted, wiping away tears which had sprung to his eyes, "Isla don't do that! I thought you'd gone!" Marion put an arm around her young nephew's shoulders and soothingly said, "Now, there, look see, Isla's part fish it would appear. She's safe as safe can be. Look at her."

Isla could now be seen almost at the far edge of the loch, where they had previously been with the boat. She had surprised even herself with the ease she had found taking those first strokes across the water. By the time she realised that she had left the boat far behind, she had practically reached the shore. She realised that she was no longer cold, and the aches in her shoulders from rowing had all but vanished. In her element, she kept her eyes wide open as she dived under the surface. The world took on a whole new dimension. Suddenly, the colours of what lay within the loch were no longer murky or distorted, but bright and clear. The sunlight dappled the blues and greens of the water and the reeds, and what looked like seaweed glistened as it drifted, catching the sun. Small fish darted in and out of the rocks, not seeming to fear her, nor were they overly interested in the new visitor to their home. Isla watched, and followed as they swam, both behind and above them, immersed in the new sights that surrounded her and the thrill of being underwater. She felt free.

When a shadow loomed over her, she looked up, and saw that she was now directly under the hull of the boat. She had swum the entire distance of the loch underwater as she had followed the fish. She swam up, kicking hard, surprising herself again at the speed and strength that propelled her upwards.

She broke the surface of the water, blinking in the bright sunlight which now filled her vision. As her eyes adjusted to the change in her surroundings, she saw Hamish leaning over the side of the boat, his face pale and drawn with worry. She then heard her aunt's voice speaking to her, but it seemed to be far off, as if she was waking from a dream. "Isla, why don't you stay close to the boat for a time, so that Hamish knows that you're alright?"

Isla looked up at her aunt, and saw that Marion was looking at her with a very curious expression. As Isla met her gaze, she blinked and looked away. Isla couldn't be certain of it, but she had, just for a moment, thought she'd seen a glint of recognition in her aunt's vivid grey eyes. The moment passed, and Isla noticed that Hamish now appeared agitated and somewhat anxious, clinging to the side of the boat as if his life depended on it.

"Come on Hamish," she wheedled. "It's not really cold. Look, I'm not blue!"

"Aye, Hamish, let's go in," Marion coaxed in turn.

But he would not be moved. He stubbornly held onto his seat in the boat, no manner of persuasion or cajoling convincing him otherwise.

The only movement which he decided to make was to get out of the boat, trotting back along the jetty. After much consternation, Marion had thrown her hands up in the air and said, "Well, that's it for today. I ken you'll have a grand time when you decide to make up your mind to do it, and I have no doubt you'll be just as much a natural in the water as your sister. But, if you've a mind not to, you've a mind not to. And that's that. Just as stubborn as your father."

They trooped up back to the house, Isla drying quickly in the sun and sea breeze which picked up as they made their way along. Hamish was quiet the whole way back. Isla tried to talk to him, but each time she did he would either grunt or shrug off her hand when she put an arm around his shoulders.

Isla decided to leave it. Hamish could be as obstinate as an ox, and she had learnt in the past that it was only Hamish who could change his own mind. Perhaps, she thought, they would have some swimming lessons in a few days', or maybe even weeks', time.

Once they reached the door to the cottage, Marion clapped her hands together and announced, "If I'm not mistaken, there is a freshly baked ginger parkin waiting in the kitchen for you. Hamish, why don't you go check to make sure?" Hamish brightened immediately, straightening his scrawny frame, and kicking off his shoes in a bid to race to the kitchen.

Marion stopped Isla, and said quietly, "You've got a gift lass, and take it from me, not everybody has the same ability that you seem to have in the water." Isla flushed, and mumbled, "It feels different here, the water... it's different." Marion nodded and replied, "Aye, the water's in your blood Isla. Your father gave you a gift right enough. Up here, once you know the water, the water accepts you. So, you have my permission, lass, when the weather is fine to go and practice your rowing, or swimming, and I'll keep an eye on Hamish until he's ready to go back to the water."

Isla nodded. She was excited at the idea that she would be able to slip away to the loch any time that she chose. And yet... she felt a pang of guilt at the thought of leaving her brother behind. Almost as if she had read her thoughts, Marion said gently, "He's not ready Isla. But he has a keen interest in the kitchen, so we'll have some cookery lessons, Hamish and I. Myself, I only learnt how to cook when I was feeling alone, with not much familiarity of the island. So, if it helped me, I'm certain that it will help him also."

Together, they entered the cottage, and as Isla heard Hamish's delighted squeals over the sweet treat that he had indeed discovered waiting for them, she looked at her aunt and smiled. She knew that Marion was right. Hamish looked up as they entered having, Isla noticed, cut himself a very sizeable wedge of what appeared to be an immensely dark and sticky cake.

"Aunty Marion, this cake is the best!" He mumbled through an exceptionally large mouthful. "It's got oats in it?"

"Aye, it's a parkin. And I'll thank you to wash your hands once you've finished inhaling that slice," Marion said as she tapped Hamish's sticky hand.

He laughed and licked his fingers enthusiastically, at which both Isla and Marion chuckled. Marion threw a tea towel at him. "Go, shoo!" she exclaimed. His spirits evidently lifted, Hamish ran to the bathroom and did as he was bid.

The rest of the day passed with little care or concern, and no mention was made by either child of Hamish's fright on the boat. Cycling up and down the lane, learning how to collect honey from the bees, and identifying and gathering various herbs from Marion's abundant garden, they occupied themselves until suppertime.

The cold cuts of ham accompanied fried patties of the potato left over from the night before. As they ate, the children falling ravenously upon their food, all three felt, rather than heard, the weather change.

Suddenly, the wind rattled the windows, and large raindrops beat down with ferocity. It sounded to Isla as if buckets of glass were being thrown over the cottage. Streaks of rain lashed at the walls and at the windows. Amazed and scared, Isla and Hamish pressed their faces against the glass to try to see what was happening.

Marion, all the while, had remained calm and sighed, "I'd best be seeing to Basil and Billie. No such luck as they'll be washed away."

Isla exclaimed, "But, look at it! It's raining!"

"Aye, lass. But you've come to Scotland you know. This is what we call a summer!"

Hamish crinkled his nose in disgust. "Well, I *don't* call this a summer!"

"Oh, aye, it's a wonder it's been so fine for you both up until now!" With a shrug, Marion got up and threw on a heavy raincoat from a hook on the back of the kitchen door. She slid her feet into a pair of very heavy-duty shoes which were bulky, but completely covered her feet. The children cowered as she opened the door, shocked both at the rage of the storm outside and how fast it had set in.

A few moments later, Marion reappeared, her hair now muted into a sodden caramel stream. Trickles of water pooled by her feet, and she grumbled, "Both goats already safely tucked up in the barn. Bah, the goats. I'll just leave them to it next time. Right royal pains."

Hamish lost some of his fright as she closed the door, and said hopefully, "If you don't like them, can't you get rid of them?"

Marion wrung her hair over the sink and grimaced. "Believe me, Hamish, I've thought about it many a time. Ornery creatures that they be. But I sell some of the cheese that I make from Billie's milk, and their value outweighs their temperament. Besides, they're good guard creatures."

"Oh." Hamish disappointedly turned his attention to clearing the pots.

"So, tomorrow," Marion continued. "If the weather holds out like this, it'll be a day for being indoors. Remember, my room is out of bounds." The children both nodded, and Isla was astonished to see that Hamish's chirpy personality was resurfacing. He whistled as he washed the pots, and Isla nudged him.

"What are you up to?"

He raised his eyebrows innocently. "I don't know what you're talking about Isla."

"Yes you do, little owl. You're planning something."

"No I'm not! And I'm not an owl!" He shot back with a glare.

"Fine, have it your way. But stay out of Aunty Marion's way!" She shrugged and turned her attention back to drying up. If Hamish wanted to keep a secret, then as far as she was concerned, it was all his if it kept him happy.

Later, Marion lit a fire in the living room which Isla had spied on the day of their arrival. With steaming cups of hot cocoa, they whiled away the time by playing cards; Marion teaching them new games as the evening wore on. When Hamish began to yawn uncontrollably Marion gently ushered them both to bed. Again, worn out from the events of the day, Isla welcomed the comfort of her bed. Drifting off, she thought she saw Hamish furtively checking his watch by the side of his bed. Closing her eyes, she instantly forgot all about it.

When she opened her eyes again, a muted grey light filtered into the room through the clouds which filled the skylight above her. By force of habit now, she looked over to Hamish's bed and saw that it was once again empty. She rolled her eyes, exasperated that here he found no trouble in rising early, whereas back home she and her mother had had to prise him from his sleep. As she began to get up, she caught the sounds of a light tapping at the window. It took her a moment, blearily rubbing her eyes, to realise that the sound was in fact a light drizzle of rain pattering against the glass.

Shrugging on her dressing gown, she wandered downstairs. Of course, Hamish was in the kitchen, this time yawning into his porridge. She giggled as she caught him nodding off; head propped in his hand, drooping dangerously closer and closer towards the half-filled bowl in front of him.

"Morning Hamish!" She called out brightly, startling him awake. "How long have you been up for?"

He yawned. "I don't know... two hours?"

Isla laughed, "Are you still looking for your brownie?"

Hamish avoided her gaze and began shovelling his porridge into his mouth in what seemed to be a bid to avoid answering her.

"All right, have it your own way." She helped herself to porridge, and then went to get dressed, leaving her brother still yawning at the table.

With the rain maintaining a steady beat against the cottage, neither Isla nor Hamish felt overly drawn to further outdoor exploration. Isla busied herself with some of the new books left out for her in the playroom. Hamish, meanwhile, seemed determined to conduct a thorough examination of the entire house. Isla caught him opening every cupboard door and cabinet in the kitchen, even lifting up the rug in the living room.

"On a treasure hunt, Hamish?" she asked sweetly. He glared at her and again made no reply. Isla laughed to herself, amused at Hamish's determined investigations. He clearly believed himself to be stealthy in his sleuthing, but Isla could clearly hear which room of the house he was in according to the numerous bangs and crashes which invariably resounded.

It wasn't until lunchtime that Isla realised that they had not yet seen Marion. She called out to Hamish as he crept past the playroom door.

"Have you seen Aunty Marion today?"

He shook his head, clearly in a hurry to continue in his mission.

"You're keeping away from Aunty Marion's room, right Hamish?"

"Yes, Isla! I promised!" He ran off before Isla had the chance to quiz him further.

Following the grumbling of her stomach, Isla made tracks to the kitchen, where she found a loaf of crusty bread and cold cuts of chicken waiting out on the countertop. Next to a bowl of bright red tomatoes lay a note. Isla recognised the elegant script of her aunt's penmanship.

"I've gone out. I'll be back later this afternoon. Chicken and tomatoes are for sandwiches. Love, Marion."

Isla picked up a tomato and pressed it thoughtfully in her hand. It was firm and had the wonderful smell of having been freshly picked from the garden. She wondered where her aunt had gone to, and how she hadn't heard her leave.

She soon forgot about her aunt's absence, however, as she turned her attention to the ingredients and busied herself with preparing sandwiches. She placed each on a plate and cut them precisely down the middle, as she'd seen her mother do so many times before. Calling her brother, she sat at the table. She couldn't contain a laugh as Hamish made a rather grubby and dust-covered appearance. Sneezing several times in succession he eventually asked, "What's for lunch? I'm starving!"

Isla looked him over. "Where have you gotten into?! You look like you've been underground!"

Hamish sneezed again. "I found an attic. Achoo! There wasn't much up there. Just a lot of dust. HACHOO!"

Isla shook her head. "Wash your hands and your face.

We've got chicken sandwiches for lunch." Once he was relatively clean and half a sandwich in, Hamish looked around.

"Where's Aunty Marion?"

Isla showed him the note. "I guess she's gone out for a bit. I don't know where."

Hamish chewed thoughtfully. "Oh. Ok. But it's wet!"

Isla shrugged. "I guess she's used to it if it really is like this so much here."

Amidst the tapping of the rain on the windowpanes, they gradually picked up an unusual sound coming from outside the back door. Hamish looked up. "Is that a... goat?"

They pushed back their chairs and got up to investigate.

Having opened the back door a smidge they saw, to their astonishment, a most unexpected sight. Basil and, they presumed, Billie each held in their long, crooked teeth the seat of a pair of trousers. The trousers in question belonged to a little old man who was hopping up and down on the spot with rage.

Isla imagined that his face was usually not quite so red as it was now; his livid complexion only heightened by the tufts of white hair which seemed to sprout out of unusual places. An equal growth of hair appeared to be found in his ears and out of his nostrils as on the top of his head.

"Get ORFF me ye horned, cloven-feeted monsters. ARGHHHH!"

With a wicked gleam in his eye, Basil gave one final wrench of the fabric he had latched onto, and an unmistakeable ripping of cloth could be heard. That appeared to be the cue for Billie and another rip was made, resulting in the seat of the unfortunate gentleman's trousers tearing clean off in the jaws of the victorious goats.

The man gave a yelp and clapped both hands to his backside.

"Don't ye know how to teach yer goats any manners? They should be locked up, or, or... put in a POT!"

Isla and Hamish both had their hands covering their giggles, and Isla recovered long enough to attempt an apology.

"We're really sorry. They're our aunt's goats.... We don't know much about them. If you let me know your name, I'm sure Marion will pay for your trousers to be repaired?"

The man spluttered, dots of white speckling his enraged countenance. "Aye, and what a greeting it is. I'm the new milkman to the village, coming to make enquiries of folk for orders. Glenn's the name. But I'll not be troubling YE anymore. Good day to ye both!"

He staggered backwards, hands still clutching his buttocks, moving as fast as he dared. He disappeared around the corner, and they just about heard his racing footsteps recede in his eagerness to leave the cottage in his wake.

Once they heard the click of the gate latch, Isla turned to Basil (Billie now having retreated into the barn), with her hands on her hips saying, in a tone mimicking Marion's, "Basil you are in so much trouble when I tell Marion!"

The errant goat bleated, unapologetic, and trotted into the little barn, head held high.

Hamish looked up at his sister and said doubtfully, "He didn't look like a milkman."

Isla remembered the jolly, whistling flat-capped milkmen of home, and replied, "Well, maybe that's what they're like up here. Oy, where are you going?"

Hamish had managed to envelop himself in a waterproof and slid on his aunt's outdoor shoes. Much too large for him, they drowned his feet and he clunked around, looking for something.

"I'm going into the barn," he announced bravely. "I just need a.... aha! I'll use that." He grabbed the broom from beside the door and raised it in front of him.

"Just in case Basil gets any ideas."

She rolled her eyes. "Your funeral."

Hamish stuck his tongue out at her and inched out of the door to the barn.

"Shout if you need rescuing from Basil!" Isla called after him, but he studiously ignored her, intent on his mission.

Isla sighed and shut the door behind him. She brought her book into the kitchen, just in case Hamish got into a sticky situation. Isla read for the next few hours. Hamish eventually reappeared, bedraggled, with bits of straw sticking haphazardly out of his unkempt hair. He did not look particularly triumphant, Isla noted.

"Not uncovered any buried treasure then, Hamish?"

He sighed and flopped into a chair. "It's just a barn. Lots of hay. And it smells."

Isla scrunched up her nose. "So do you! You smell like a third goat! Go take a bath."

He must have been fairly cold and quite tired, as he did as his sister said without putting up a fuss.

Marion made an appearance not too much later, walking in through the kitchen, blinking when she saw Isla there.

"Isla, lass, did you find everything you needed today?" Isla nodded, curious as to where her aunt had disappeared, but not yet confident enough to ask. By all appearances, Marion had been out in the rain, but was not at all bedraggled as Hamish had been. Instead, she seemed invigorated, colour in her cheeks and a sparkle in her eye.

"I lost track of time, sorry about that. I went for a walk, and then for a swim!"

Isla looked outside, unsure of whether her aunt was joking or not. "But it's raining!"

Marion laughed. "I was already soaked through, so why not?"

Isla wasn't sure what to make of that, so instead she filled her aunt in on the events of the day, including the unexpected visitor they'd had.

"Well, I didn't know that old Michael was no longer the milkman. Mayhap Basil did a good job of guarding the cottage... for once," she added darkly. "But still, I'll find out whether that is the new milkman or no. Glenn was it? Sounds like he won't be in a hurry to deliver out here even if he is!" She shook her head, smiling ruefully. "A sight to see, I'm sure. I'm sorry I missed it!"

Once Hamish reappeared, looking (and smelling) all the better after his bath, they ate supper and all headed off to bed, the sound of the rain discouraging anything livelier for the evening.

Isla didn't hear her brother creep out of bed in the small hours of the morning.

The next few days remained grizzly and damp. Isla got fed up with being cooped up indoors and, during one of her aunt's excursions, took it upon herself to head to the loch. Hamish refused to come when she asked him, looking furtive and excited all at once. Isla put it down to his cooking lessons with Marion, and hurried out, anxious to be near the water and practice rowing the boat, despite the lack of sun.

She practiced and practiced and, after a few days, her arms were aching less as her endurance increased, and she rowed herself around and around the loch. Repeatedly she passed the outlet of the loch and resisted the urge to explore further, heeding Marion's warning.

One day, on her return to the cottage, she noticed that Hamish was acting incredibly oddly. Or, she reasoned, more oddly than usual.

He was tiptoeing down the hall, on his way from the kitchen with a large glass of milk, and a bowl of tomatoes. He seemed to be on his way to the living room. He jumped guiltily when he saw his sister watching him.

"What are you doing Hamish?" Isla asked, pointedly looking at the bowl of tomatoes.

He changed direction almost immediately and walked into the playroom. "I was hungry," he said defiantly.

"Aren't you cooking dinner with Marion?"

"Yes! We're having chicken and leek pie – I made the pastry myself!" He looked immensely proud of himself. Isla continued, "So, you're eating the tomatoes, now?"

Hamish looked confused for a second, then seemed to search around for an answer. "I wanted a snack..."

His eyes opened wider, as they always did when he was trying to maintain his innocence. Isla knew his ploy well, but just laughed and said, "Whatever you say little owl," ruffling his hair and dodging his angry retort as she ran upstairs to change.

As she rounded the staircase, she looked back down into the hallway, and saw that her brother was now changing tack again and tiptoeing again towards the living room. She rolled her eyes.

When she came back downstairs, Hamish and Marion were both in the kitchen, and Marion was slicing up a steaming, thickly crusted pie onto plates.

"That smells amazing!" Isla exclaimed.

Marion put a hand on Hamish's shoulders. "Hamish made this nearly all by himself!"

Isla looked at her brother in astonishment.

"Mother is going to be so impressed! And Father won't believe it!"

Hamish flushed and bowed his head, clearly embarrassed, but pleased with himself. Isla went to sit at the table saying, "Well, I can't wait to try it! I'm starving!"

"You've been out for hours," Hamish looked at her. "You've been out on the loch, haven't you?"

She nodded, "I think I've cracked the rowing Aunty Marion."

Marion smiled and said, "I wouldn't wonder, with the hours you've been out for lassie! You'll have to show me soon!"

Once they were all seated at the table, the plates in front of them, silence descended as they began to dive into their dinner. The flaky, buttery pastry melted on Isla's tongue. Then, as she scooped up a large mouthful of chicken and gravy, she tasted it and pulled a face.

Not wanting to embarrass Hamish, she gamely kept eating. Marion noticed, and tentatively tried hers also. She paused, silently poured a glass of water for herself, and then kept eating.

Hamish, meanwhile, had polished off his pie crust appreciatively, and then tried a heaped mouthful of the pie filling. Immediately he pulled a face and shouted, "It's so salty!" Isla and Marion put their forks down and each had a gulping drink of water.

Isla said, "How much salt did you put in it?"

Marion replied, chuckling, "I think we need to work on

our tablespoons and teaspoons, eh Hamish?"

Hamish pushed his plate away, "I can't eat it."

"Not to worry, I think I can do something with it. Leave it to me." As Marion busied herself with her attempts to rescue the remainder of the meal, Isla yawned and excused herself, the long hours in the boat catching up with her. She took a book upstairs to bed, but barely managed two pages before she'd fallen asleep.

In the early hours of the morning, she awoke, a ferocious thirst consuming her. She looked over to Hamish's bed and, in the silvery moonlight, saw that his bed was empty.

Confused, bleary-eyed and thirsty, she crept down the stairs to get some water from the kitchen.

She paused outside the kitchen door. Listened. Was that a noise coming from within? Slowly, quietly, she pushed the door open, and stopped, shocked. She rubbed her eyes, and then opened them once more.

There, sure enough, was Hamish.

Sitting next to him, was a brownie.

CHAPTER 6

HOB

At least, she thought, the creature perfectly matched Marion's description of a brownie. Tiny, it perched on the countertop, its full height appearing to be merely half of Hamish's torso. As the name suggested, it was a nut-brown colour, and was so wrinkled, it reminded Isla of a picture she had once seen of a walnut. Spindly arms and legs protruded from a small shirt and shorts held together by a pair of miniature braces. The brownie was barefoot, and its long, thin, knobbly toes were remarkably similar in appearance to its twig-like fingers.

Suddenly, the brownie looked up, saw Isla, dark brown eyes widening in shock. With a shriek, it dived behind Hamish.

A half-eaten tomato rolled away from where it had been sitting.

Hamish wheeled around, at once looking guilty, exultant and defiant.

When he saw that it was only Isla standing there, he relaxed, but only fractionally. He whispered angrily, "What are you doing here?"

69

Isla blinked. "I was thirsty. But what are you doing? And WHAT is that? Is that really a..."

Their hushed whispers sounded loud to Isla's ears in the quiet of the house. She closed the door behind her and stepped further into the kitchen. Hamish moved with her, blocking the creature from view.

"His name's Hob," Hamish whispered, a tad possessively, Isla thought. "*I* found him, Isla. ME!"

"I know, but what exactly is Hob?"

He snorted. "Hob's a brownie. Obviously."

"Oh. *Obviously.* But they're just a story!"

The brownie's eyes narrowed as they peeped over Hamish's shoulder at Isla.

"Shush! You'll make him angry!" Hamish hurriedly whispered. "You can't insult a brownie, or else it could leave and never come back!"

Isla held her hands up, and looked over to the brownie, well, what she could see of it. "I'm very sorry... Hob, is it? I don't know much about brownies." The creature seemed to relax, and sidled closer into view, remaining close to Hamish.

"He's very shy," Hamish reported, importantly. "Hob's a young brownie. Not even one hundred! Well, that's young for a brownie. Apparently, they're allowed their own houses when they reach ninety, but they aren't considered fully grown until they're at least one hundred and fifty! And they're not really supposed to be seen by people."

"Oh!" Was all that Isla could think to say. Then, "But, how did you find him?"

"I looked all over the house... NOT in Aunty Marion's room, and in the barn. EVERYWHERE! But I didn't find anything. But I know that Aunty Marion never makes the porridge in the morning, because I've never heard her once downstairs, and I've been up early ever since we got here. So, I slept in the kitchen a few nights ago, and then," he beamed proudly, "Then, I found Hob!"

Hamish turned to the brownie, and whispered, "Can I tell her? We can trust her."

The creature's eyes settled on Isla, and for an uncomfortable moment Isla felt she was being measured. To her surprise and relief, the creature finally nodded.

"Hob lives in the chimney!" Hamish announced. "Look, see?"

He got up, and pointed to the brickwork of the stove, where the books lined the higgledy-piggledy bricks. Hamish pressed the side of the left-hand corner of the middle brick in the chimney arch. Immediately, the brick swung outwards, as if on a hinge, leaving just enough space for a brownie to enter and exit.

"The front of the chimney is hollow!" Hamish pointed out, "And, look, it's amazing!"

Hob the brownie puffed out his chest proudly, and clambered up the chimney, to show them inside. Isla grabbed a chair to stand on, and then peered inside the gap in the brickwork.

Inside was indeed a hollow chamber, in which a miniature bed, candle and chair were all to be found. A small mat lay on the floor. She stepped back. "It looks very cosy. You made it all yourself?" Hob nodded, bashfully.

"And do you do all the tidying, and make us breakfast... and bake?" Isla guessed. Again, the brownie confirmed by nodding his head.

"And in the daytime, you like to sit by the fire?" On a hunch, Isla remembered the lit fire in the living room on the first day of their arrival. Hamish pouted, put out that his sister had figured out one of his secrets.

Isla suddenly remembered the reason why she had come downstairs in the first place. "Oh, I forgot. I came to get..." She stopped, as Hob shyly presented her with a full glass of water. She hadn't even seen him move to get it.

"Oh, thank you!"

She yawned and rubbed her eyes. "Well, it's been lovely to meet you, Hob. But I do need to get back to bed. I'll see you soon I hope?"

The brownie gave a neat little bow and squeaked out "Goodnight!" She jumped, for it was the first time she had heard him make a sound.

"Goodnight Hob. And, Hamish, are you staying up all night?"

Hamish shook his head. "No, but Hob said he'd show me how to make porridge. I got hungry."

Hob nodded earnestly and busied himself with getting pans out and ready.

The whole encounter was so surreal that Isla simply nodded and walked back up to bed, half-convinced that she was dreaming.

In the morning, she woke up, looked over to Hamish's bed, and to her astonishment, saw that her brother was actually in his bed. Beside him, on the table, was a bowl of half-eaten porridge.

Looking around, up, and out of the window, Isla could see nothing but thick cloud. Even the calls of the birds appeared muted by the heavy grey blanketing the sky. She wandered downstairs, and through the kitchen window saw that the clouds were not just confined to the sky. A thick white fog was creeping over the ground, covering almost everything in sight. She strained her eyes, and could just about make out Basil, who, it appeared, had seized his opportunity to sneak some of Marion's roses. He chewed contentedly, swishing his tail as tendrils of mist encroached upon him.

Marion entered the kitchen at that moment, spying Basil immediately. She grabbed the nearest object to her, which happened to be a teapot, flung open the window, and threw it at the wayward beast with all her might. Sensing real danger, Basil instantly dropped the remnant of the rose as Marion's furious cries chased him into the barn. He did not re-emerge.

"Morning, Aunty Marion," Isla said cautiously. She was met with a grunt.

"That was my best teapot and all. Wretched animal!"

Isla grabbed a piece of bread and decided to make a hasty exit herself. Her aunt's mood did not seem to be showing any signs of improving.

And so it lasted, for the days which followed. The spirit-sapping mist seemed, to Isla, to be doing exactly that to her formerly cheery aunt. Marion would disappear for hours at a time, the children never knowing when she was or wasn't in the house. Her withdrawal was not merely physical, but she appeared absent even when she was in the same room as them. For all of Isla's attempts to draw her into conversation, or make her smile, the most common response was a nod, or a non-committal answer.

Hamish, caught up in his newfound friendship with Hob, took little notice. Isla and Hamish, in their aunt's absence, frequently spent time with Hob in the living room, learning more about their unusual housemate, or playing cards.

Hob lost some of his shyness and recounted many stories of the land and island that they had come to; stories which Isla would have been sure were myths and folklore if the teller himself had not stepped out of one such fairy tale. She noticed that Hob only told humorous tales, of the mischief and mayhem which brownies of old had wreaked upon the houses they had occupied, especially where the unfortunate humans had caused insult to their brownie helpers.

His lilting voice reduced them to tears of laughter on a number of afternoons. As he told one particular story, of a fisherman whose boat always seemed to spring a leak whenever he didn't finish his breakfast, Isla realised that she hadn't paid a visit to what she now considered 'her' boat in several days. She and Hamish had come to an agreement that they would not tell Marion or their mother, through the letters which they sent back and forth, about their discovery.

"After all," Isla said, "They probably would just think that we were playing games."

Hamish nodded sagely. "*You* didn't believe me until you met Hob, so I don't think that Mother will... Marion would, I think, but..." he tailed off. It hadn't appeared to bother him that they had been left more and more to their own devices, but Isla knew that it was Hamish and Hob who prepared their supper most nights. Occasionally they would be joined by Marion, who ate, but did not appear to notice what it was that she was eating.

Isla asked Hob about the fog which had come in, as it showed no signs of leaving.

"A sea fret," he squeaked. "Not always this long. It hurts them as need the sea. Drowns it out, so it does."

Isla wondered at that. Marion had always said that she couldn't bear to be parted from the sea.

It was true, the fog muted almost all sound of the waves on the rocks below, and the gulls were silenced by the thick cover of cloud. Even the tang of salt in the air seemed to be diluted.

"Do you mean Aunty Marion?" she asked Hob, curiously. Surely, if he had been at Calder Cottage for ten years, he would know more about some of the mysteries which surrounded their aunt.

"I haven't told ye about the story of Figan and Drudle!" he exclaimed with a laugh, ignoring her question.

"Aye, Figan was a cousin of mine, five times removed, and he's a wee bit aulder than me, by aboot a hunnerd years or so. Anyways, Figan was never a broonie who was fond of the broonie way of life. He never foond a hooman house fer hisself, no laddie, that he did not.

"Drudle was a wee tyke from the hamlet that used to be over the sea crossing. Aye, he was desperate for a broonie to live in his hoose, so'n that his mather would leave him alone fer the dishes. So, he crossed over to the island, aye, that he did. Crept up to the hollow that Figan was living in, and set him a trap, so he did.

"Figan wasnae wise to the tricks that Drudle was fond of, so the wee lad caught him right enough! He took him, tied him in a sack, kicking and pinching, all the way back to his hoose over the way.

"He let him oot and promised Figan that he would always be polite and kind to him, if he'd only be their hoose broonie. Figan gave a wicked grin and agreed.

"Drudle's chores were to do the dishes, sweep the hearth and the floor, and to milk the coo.

"Well, that first night, Drudle went to bed, feeling right proud of hisself. Aye. In the morn, he got such a hiding from his mather. The dishes were washed, aye, but they were each in pieces in the sink. The floor was swept, but all the coals from the hearth had been swept across the room, blacker than the groond ootside. And, oh aye, the coo had

75

been milked, but it had had such a fright that the milk had soored inside her, and it was months before it was right agin!"

The brownie squawked with laughter, slapping his knee, chortling. He wiped a tear from his cheek and continued.

"Drudle couldnae load Figan into the boat quick enough. He set him back in the hollow from which he'd taken him and begged him to never come back to his hoose agin."

Isla and Hamish rolled on the floor laughing, Hamish laughing so hard that he had to clutch his sides as he gasped for air.

As Isla regained her composure, she asked innocently, "What other stories do you know about the fisher people and sea tales, Hob?"

He wouldn't be pressed, however, and it soon became clear that Hob was far more interested in telling stories about his own kind, and the island, than anything else. Isla gave up, and listened to the tales that he would tell, not making any further requests.

The talk of the boat stayed with Isla, however, and the next day, she resolved to go out to the loch, even though the fog was as thick as ever. It was difficult to make out the path, but she closed her eyes and listened to the sound of the little stream as it gurgled along. Opening her eyes again, Isla walked gingerly, guided by the sound of the flowing water. It took her double the usual length of time to find the boat, but when she did, she stepped in, sat down, and knew that it didn't matter that she could no longer see clearly. The familiar rocking of the boat nudged the oars into her hands in a practised motion. As she began to row, her concentration focussed solely on the rhythm of the oars.

She leant into the oars, pulling her shoulders back and felt the boat slip smoothly across the water.

After a while, she noticed that the boat's motion had subtly changed. It was no longer gliding but maintained a gradual bumping across the water. She was also moving faster through the haze, but her rowing pace had not changed.

She frowned. She should have reached the opposite shore by now.

Gradually, she noticed that she was now able to see more clearly; the thick cover of fog was dissipating. Tendrils of mist curled, beckoning her onwards. As her vision improved, so too did her other senses. She smelled and felt the salt of the spray now hitting her face. The water had changed again, waves forming against the bow of the boat. Cries of the gulls filled the sky.

With a start, she realised that she had taken the boat through the loch and had followed the outlet to where she now saw was the mouth of a river. The sea was mere metres ahead. She gulped, thinking of the caution that her aunt had given her. But it was too late now.

The thought struck her that it was peculiar that she and Hamish had not been allowed to explore the shore of the island, or even shown how to get to the sea – such a big fixture of their aunt's island home.

She jutted out her chin. She *would* explore the coastline. It was their home now too, after all. Marion had said so. Besides, she reasoned, she could see clearer here than she could before. She would just go a little way... and then she thought, Hamish! He would want to see the sea. She chuckled to herself. No swimming required! With an effort, she turned the boat around, realising the reason for the quick progress of her voyage downstream was the strong current which had propelled her. The journey back up stream was far more challenging. Adrenaline spurred her on, and she forgot about her aching arms as she reached the jetty. She moored up and headed back to the cottage as quickly as she could, back along the stream. She snuck in the cottage quietly, jumping when she heard Hamish come through from the kitchen with a bang. She pulled him into the playroom, shushing him as he protested.

"Shhhh," she whispered. "I've got something to show you. Tomorrow morning, we're going out."

Hamish grinned, nodding his head enthusiastically. Discovering Hob had instilled in him a new sense of adventure, she thought proudly. Her brother had grown so much in the short time that they'd been away. Not quite the shy, anxious boy she'd arrived with on the train from London.

The next morning, the children were up at the crack of dawn. They grabbed a thick slice of flapjack each, made by Hob, and munched the warm, oaty squares as they walked. Hamish stuck close to Isla, scared of losing his way in the mist.

"We're... we're not going swimming are we Isla?" He whispered, his teeth chattering slightly, although from cold or nerves she wasn't sure.

"No, don't worry. Shush. It's a surprise! Look, here's the boat, hop in!"

Tentatively Hamish edged his way into the rowboat, clutching his sister's hand all the while. Once they were both in, Isla took up the oars and began to row. She followed the same trajectory as the previous day, and sure enough, even with the limited visibility around them, they continued to move.

"Hey, this isn't a surprise!" Hamish grumbled. "I've already been on the boat."

"Hush, Hamish! You'll see!" Isla shook her head at her brother's impatience. Watching all around for signs they were reaching the river mouth, she finally said, "Alright. Close your eyes. Listen." She watched as her brother reluctantly did as he was told. As he strained his ears to hear, she saw that he realised they weren't on the loch anymore.

"But that's the sea! How did we get..."

"Look, open your eyes!" The fog had once again lifted, revealing the river mouth that they were travelling down.

The vast expanse of sea lay ahead.

The crashing of the waves against the shore gave Isla the idea to row out a way beyond the shoreline itself. The current was not so strong, and the bobbing of the boat spurred her on.

"But, Isla, Aunty Marion said we weren't supposed to..."

"Honestly, Hamish. How long have we been here? And we've not even seen the sea properly! At least, not the beach. Didn't you want to see the beach?"

He nodded, still uncertain.

"And, besides, I've been practising. We'll be fine. It's calm out here today anyway."

And it was. As they joined the body of water which took them out away from the shore, they looked back to the island. They could see a heavy blanketing of fog still enveloping the land, but it stopped at the sea line. The grey water reflected the colour of the sky, but beyond the occasional lapping wave against the boat, the surface was still. As they went along the shoreline, Hamish gained interest, pointing out the new sights along the way.

"There's sand over there! And now it's pebbly! And

look at the birds! They look like they're fishing! And see, the little black ones with the orange beaks. They're strange!"

Isla laughed; her brother's excitement was infectious.

"Hey, where are we now?" He asked suddenly.

"We're off the island still Hamish!"

"No, I mean, are we close to the cottage? Do you think we have a beach near Aunty Marion's?"

Isla shrugged, unsure. She hadn't seen a path to the sea, or any sign of one, but they hadn't fully explored yet. "I don't know. We can look tomorrow."

Isla realised that she'd been rowing for what seemed to be a long time. And, they still had the return journey to make.

"Sorry Hamish, I thought we'd be able to get around the island, but it's bigger than I thought it would be!"

"Are you getting tired Isla?"

She nodded but kept a cheery smile on her face. "I'll be alright, just time to head back I think."

As they turned, Isla's arms straining as she tried to coax the boat around, she was certain that she felt a bump against the boat. The boat swivelled, and they found themselves facing in the direction to head back to the island. Hamish jumped, face pale.

"What was that?"

Isla kept a smile on her face. "I think I just caught the boat with my oar Hamish. Honestly, don't be so jumpy!"

He relaxed and looked sheepish. "Oh, right. Sorry. I thought we were going to be eaten by a sea monster or something!"

Isla laughed, but kept an eye on the water around them as she rowed, aching arms now forgotten.

As they coursed towards the inlet heading back to the

loch, neither Isla nor Hamish noticed the small grey creature slipping through the waves, following them as they rowed. It stopped only when the boat had reached the mouth of the river. The children's chatter drifted back on the wind, oblivious to what lay in the waters behind them.

CHAPTER 7

TELEGRAMS

The fog lifted the next morning. Isla awoke to a clear sky, and heard the waves mingling with the cries of the birds. She smiled. But then, as she stirred, she groaned. Her arms and shoulders were tight, muscles knotted. She raised them, slowly, stretching. The previous day had tired her more than she had expected, but the sunlight pouring in through the window warmed her and, gradually, her aching muscles began to relax.

The change in the weather appeared to have not only brought the sea back to life, but she found Marion singing to herself when she went into the kitchen.

"And good morning to you Isla! What a fine morning it is too! Do you not agree?"

Having barely seen or spoken to her aunt for the many days prior, Isla was astonished at the transformation she saw in her aunt. The colour was back in her cheeks, and she almost danced as she moved around the kitchen.

"Um, yes. Lovely." She looked around, hoping to find her brother.

"Hamish is out in the garden, looking for strawberries. I

don't get many here, but he was sure he saw some ready! We've just made some scones. You can't beat a warm scone with strawberries!"

Isla saw the golden domes cooling on a wire rack, and as she inhaled the sweet scent of the freshly baked goods, her stomach grumbled loudly. Marion laughed and put a scone on a plate for her. Just then, Hamish rushed in, jubilantly waving a bowl of freshly picked berries.

"Look what I found! There were loads, Aunty Marion!" He frowned up at his aunt. "You mustn't have looked in the right place."

Marion ruffled his hair with a smile, "Aye, I suppose I missed them. Well done lad, just in time. Isla was about to taste one for us."

She pulled out a blue earthenware pot from the icebox and placed it on the table alongside the strawberries and scones. "We can't have scones and strawberries without fresh cream, now, can we? I popped to the village earlier for it. I met Glenn... I can't say as I'm all too surprised Basil didn't take a shine to him!"

They laughed, but silence descended as they savoured the scones in front of them. Sweet, buttery, flaky; the taste reminded Isla of one of her earliest memories. She was sitting in a park with both of her parents in summer, eating scones and strawberries. She must have been two, she supposed. Back where there was no talk of 'the front', when her father was at home with them, and when her mother still smiled.

She took another bite, smiling wistfully. Her mother used to love baking scones... On reflection, Isla decided that it was probably because it was one of the few recipes which she could actually make. She wondered when they would next all be sat around the same table again, making jokes at the expense of her mother's cooking; her mother scolding them all but joining in good-naturedly once she herself had tasted what she'd put in front of them

"Tuppence", her father would declare. "Ye're the love of me life, but by all that's holy, I need to learn how to cook!" He would always kiss their mother's hand as he said it, and she would tartly reply, "Well, maybe I'm just waiting on the day you do!" Isla and Hamish would laugh and pull faces as their parents cheerfully bickered and kissed.

Isla sighed. It seemed like a very distant memory.

As they finished scooping up the last crumbs on their plates, Marion asked, "So, what have you in mind for today?" Isla looked up. "Oh, we thought we'd cycle inland a bit, and explore that way more. The road, it goes that way doesn't it?"

Hamish looked confused, and Isla kicked him under the table.

"Aye, where the road forks, the left fork takes you to town. The right fork will take you further in. By all means, go, explore! There's not a whole heap there, mind, but it's a fine day. And you'll see plenty of the island. If you go in far enough, you'll even see the mountain!"

Hamish asked, disbelieving, "The mountain?"

Marion smiled and shook her head. "It's not an actual mountain as such, but it's what the island folk like to call it. Really, it's just a big hill, but it's the only one such on the island. You can see it in the distance from the back of the house."

They said their goodbyes, and as they were putting their shoes on in the hallway, Hamish asked, "Why did you say we were going inland?"

Isla put a finger on her lips, motioning for him to be quiet.

When they were outside, Isla said in a hushed whisper, "I don't think Aunty Marion wants us to go to the sea. She's never said we could. I didn't want to say we were going to explore to find the beach by the house."

"Oh. Well, she won't be angry with us, will she Isla?"

"Not if we don't tell her! Ok, come on then Hamish. Race you!"

Springing on her bicycle, Isla pedalled off, letting Hamish catch up with her once they reached the road. Taking the left fork, they looked all around for any paths or possible routes down to where they knew the beach lay below. They even got off their bicycles and walked about, peering over the edge of the rocks, but saw only a sheer drop below.

After an hour of fruitless searching, Hamish got bored and started tugging at his sister's dress. "Isla. There isn't a way down. We've been sitting here for ages! Can we go back?"

She recognised the whiney tinge to her brother's voice and realised that they wouldn't be finding the beach that day. Avoiding a full-blown tantrum was always preferable, she thought.

"Well, we could actually go inland like we told Aunty Marion we would?" Her suggestion appeared to appease Hamish. His face lit up immediately.

"Yes! I want to see the mountain!"

They cycled back up the road, and past the fork; this time turning right.

Their legs were stronger now. The good island food and daily cycles to the village appeared to have toughened their muscles. For two hours they cycled, the ascent gradually increasing until their legs strained to pedal and maintain their momentum. At last, they reached the pinnacle of the hill, and saw ahead of them a craggy series of peaks which they were nearing. They turned a corner and saw that what they had at first taken to be several peaks now revealed itself to be a solitary, albeit lop-sided, hill. If they had not been informed otherwise, the children would have classified it as a mountain.

They cycled up to where the road arched around the side of the hill and saw several paths which looked as if they had been made by sheep.

Pausing to peer up at the height of the hill looming over them, Hamish didn't argue when Isla suggested they come back another day to explore the soaring paths further.

As they embarked upon the return leg of their journey, the children had little knowledge that it would be some time before they returned.

They knew that something was wrong as soon as they returned to the cottage. Marion was sitting on the front step, her eyes red with tears. In her hand was a white slip of paper. A telegram. Isla recognised it immediately. Her heart sank, and she felt her stomach flip over. She pushed her bicycle aside, grabbing Hamish and propelled him through the gate. He looked bewildered.

"What's wrong Aunty Marion?"

Marion dashed a hand across her eyes and pulled her small nephew in for a hug. Isla hung back, watching, waiting. Finally, Marion released Hamish who looked at her, still confused.

Gathering her composure, Marion said to them both, "Here, take a seat my lovelies." She patted the step next to her.

"We've had a telegram from your mother. From Penny."

Hamish's lip quivered. "Is she alright?"

Marion sighed, "Ah, laddie. She sent news. Your father is missing, he's been lost at sea."

Isla froze, her blood running cold. "Can I see that?" she whispered, holding her hand out for the paper.

Marion handed it to her, and Isla took it with trembling fingers.

"DUNCAN LOST IN TORPEDO FIRE. SHIP SUNK. MISSING. PRESUMED DEAD. PENNY."

She read it to herself, not recognising her mother in the static missive. Numbly, she looked at her brother, fearing his reaction. In her frozen state, it took her a moment to notice that he didn't seem to be upset.

"Hamish, do you understand?" She spoke slowly, taking her brother's hand.

"I know what Aunty Marion said. But you said, Aunty Marion, that he was at sea. Father loves the sea! Just like you! He'll be alright, won't he Isla? They just haven't found him yet. He's too good at swimming." His sure voice jolted Isla out of the state of shock which she'd been drifting into. It was true. Their father was the best swimmer she knew. Yet, doubt plagued her. He couldn't really be gone, surely? "Presumed dead." That didn't mean it was real. She squeezed Hamish's hand.

"You're right little owl."

Marion gave a watery smile and drew them both in for a hug. "Ah, you two are a gift. Duncan is safe in the sea, I'm sure. We just need to keep an ear out for news."

Isla said, "But Mother won't know we know that Father isn't really gone." She couldn't bring herself to say, "dead".

Marion hugged her tight. "Aye lass, and it'll be that much harder for your mother having you wee ones away from her."

Hamish piped up, "We'll go to the village first thing tomorrow to send her a telegram, right Aunty Marion?"

She nodded. "Aye, that we will. It may be that there is some further news by tomorrow."

That night, the children said their prayers, remembering both of their parents, as they did every night. But their father was most prevalent in their thoughts.

As Hamish finished, "...and please keep Father safe at sea, or on land, and don't let Mother be upset," Isla bit the inside of her cheek to keep a sob at bay.

Hamish turned and sleepily mumbled, "It doesn't feel like he's really gone, does it, Isla?"

She blinked back her tears. "No, it doesn't. I'm sure he's fine. Just somewhere where he hasn't been found yet. Now, go to sleep Hamish."

The next morning, they all cycled over to the village. Mrs. MacGregor greeted them with sympathy, but there was no letter or telegram awaiting them.

"Och, right sorry I am for ye wee ones. Aye, and yer poor mather. Must be sick with worry I shouldn't wonder. Ooh dear, the poor woman." She tutted and Hamish glared at her. Isla thought she distinctly heard him mumble "water goblin" under his breath.

Marion rebuked the postmistress, but not unkindly, "Come now, Mrs. MacGregor. Nothing is certain. We are just waiting to hear more."

Mollified with a sugar mouse apiece, they left the post-office otherwise empty-handed.

And so, for the next few days, they followed their new routine. Up, breakfast of porridge, cycle to the village, and straight to the post office to see if any word had come. Isla noticed Hamish slip out of bed most nights that followed, off to play cards with Hob, or listen to the brownie's stories. She was glad that he had a friend of sorts.

On the fourth day, their visit to the post office was different.

Mrs. MacGregor greeted them at the door with a sealed envelope in her hands.

"It's addressed to you, dearie," she said to Marion, handing her the letter. Isla caught a glimpse of the handwriting. It was unfamiliar to her.

She busied herself by browsing the limited shelves and displays in the shop; she'd already memorised each article on every shelf. She looked up when her aunt placed a hand on her shoulder. "Isla love, it's from a doctor in London."

Her aunt's soft voice stirred up a dizzying course of emotions in Isla. Hamish's freckles became more prominent as his face grew pale. "What did the doctor say, Aunty Marion?" He tried to put on a brave face, but his fingers gripped Isla's like a vice. Slowly, Marion read aloud.

"Dear Ms. Gelder,

"I have been reliably informed that you are Mrs. Tuppence Gelder's next of kin, and currently looking after her two evacuee children.

"Allow me to introduce myself. I am a physician in Harley Street. Mrs. Gelder has very recently been referred to my care and observation. I fear that great distress has caused lasting illness, and it is my belief and professional opinion that the lady will require ongoing care for some time.

"The full impact of the news of the loss of her husband, I fear, may not be wholly known for some time.

"Mrs. Gelder is not responding to the usual courses of treatment.

"With events unfolding in London, I am loath to keep her in

my care, but write to you, Madame, to recommend that her care be transferred to the country. It could be that fresh air and the company of family would work a cure that I, at present, cannot.

"If you would be agreeable to receipt of my patient, please send a telegram at your earliest convenience.

"Your faithful servant,

"Dr. M. Byrne."

Seeing that Hamish looked bewildered, Isla said to him, "Mother's not very well, Hamish. She's coming to stay on Arraway with us, right Aunty Marion?" Checking herself, Isla realised that Marion had not yet confirmed whether their Mother would be cared for on the island.

To her relief, Marion answered immediately. "Of course, lass. Penny will be made as comfortable here as can be. Family sticks together. I will send a telegram directly."

As she turned to Mrs. MacGregor to arrange the message, Hamish tugged at his sister's hand. "Mother is coming to see us, Isla!" he whispered exultantly.

"She can meet Hob! She'll have to believe me if she sees him!"

Isla smiled weakly and nodded. It didn't sound as if their mother were in a condition to be introduced to fairy tale creatures, but she didn't say any such thing to Hamish.

The next two days were filled with making arrangements for their mother's arrival. The train was due on the third day.

Marion arranged the living room, transforming it into their mother's bedroom, and busied herself with bringing in flowers and greenery from the garden into the room. "Plants have wonderful healing properties," she responded to Hamish's questioning. "And they're cheerful to look at, besides."

"If your mother is having a bad day, and can't get to the outside, well, we'll just bring the outside in!"

The day of arrival dawned. Marion organised for Mr. Mackenzie to help her meet their mother at the station and bring her back to the island.

"I don't know how Penny will be after such a long journey, but it may overwhelm her to have a large party meeting her on the mainland. Can I ask you two to prepare the house for when we bring her back? The nurse is travelling only as far as the station, so I will need to help your mother perhaps on the journey back over to the island."

Hiding her disappointment, Isla nodded. She knew that it was likely to have been a tiring journey. Hamish didn't mind at all, it turned out. Instead, he happily got to work preparing a meal for their supper with Hob's help once Mr. Mackenzie had come to fetch Marion. Mr. Mackenzie left Tarn with the children to 'look after them' as he said, so Isla spent the next few hours playing with the excitable pup.

Her excited barking signalled their return. Isla and Hamish ran to the door then stopped cold in their tracks. The figure being led up the path towards them, supported on either side, was almost unrecognisable.

She was gaunt and frail. Pale and pinched, her face had taken on new lines and shadows which had never been there before. She barely glanced up as her children greeted her in subdued tones, shocked at what they saw. The light had gone from her eyes.

Hamish gave her a quick hug, and then rushed inside as it wasn't reciprocated. Isla looked to her aunt.

Marion spoke in a hushed voice. "She hasn't said a word, Isla. Not responded to anything. The nurse said that she's been like this ever since word of Duncan. Isla, love, she's protecting herself, that's what it is lass. The pain of losing your father, well, I think she's just switched everything off."

Isla said fiercely, "But we haven't lost him! They just don't know where he is!" She shook her mother and said furiously, "Father isn't dead! It's alright! They just haven't been able to find him yet!"

Her mother just looked at her blankly, withdrawing and shrinking into herself. She didn't seem to recognise her daughter.

Marion took Isla's arms away from her mother's shoulders gently. "Isla, she's not there. She'll come back, but it's not your mother at the moment. We must remind her who she is. Who we are. Come, now lass. It's been a long day for her. Let's make her comfortable inside, shall we?"

Isla wiped a tear from her cheek with the back of her hand. It was true. She didn't recognise her mother at all in the person who stood before her. She fought back her tears angrily. She clenched her jaw. It *was* her mother, and she wouldn't let herself, or her mother, forget. She was still here, after all. So, she must be still in there, somewhere.

As they led Penny inside, Hamish emerged out of the kitchen, tightly clutching a bowl of chicken broth. He brought it into their mother's newly arranged room and insisted on feeding it to her. He refused point blank when Marion suggested she do it. Both Isla and Marion took it as a good sign when Penny complied, silently, with no interaction, but at least she was eating.

So became the routine over the weeks that followed. Isla would bring her mother fresh flowers every morning from the garden, or fresh heather from the moors by the mountain. Then she would spend time telling her mother stories, stories about their family, about life in London, and about the island.

Both she and Hamish told their mother about brownies, and about Hob. Each story they told was met by the same silence and blank expression of indifference.

Hamish's cooking, however, was making a difference to their mother's physical health at least. Her cheeks filled out once again, the impact of rationing removed, and the trembling cough she had held for years living in the smog of the city eventually disappeared. Marion put it down to the fresh sea air and the honey which her bees had made.

Hamish cooked practically every meal for their mother and wouldn't let anyone but himself feed her as she still made no effort to feed herself.

When the sun shone, Marion would help Penny outside to the garden bench where she wouldn't stir for hours. Occasionally, Isla saw her mother close her eyes as if enjoying the warmth and the scents from the garden, but any such reaction was so few and far between that she didn't set much store by it.

To the children's surprise, Basil and Billie showed no signs of antagonism towards Penny in any way but would come up to her from time to time, gently nibbling her fingers. They became her unacknowledged companions in the garden.

Isla eventually lost hope that their mother would improve quickly. As Marion pointed out, "The problem isn't with her body. It's her mind. We can only do so much, lassie."

Isla took to swimming in the loch when her mother was in the garden and the sun was out. The boat lay untouched for a time.

However, when she did join her mother in the garden, her gaze was drawn time and again to the long stretch of blue out beyond the cliffs. Often, she would see the dorsal fin of a porpoise in the distance. She confirmed it to be Patch to her impassive mother, explaining his tell-tale markings. Each time her attention was drawn to the sea she felt an unfathomable pull out to the water.

She ignored it, becoming restless, feeling a sense of being penned in. She felt herself to be frequently on edge, and she began to avoid the cottage more and more, roaming out towards the hills and lochs of the island, uncovering new streams and waterways to swim in and explore, finding that the water dulled the lure of the sea.

Marion and Hamish increasingly took on the care of Penny, and nothing was said of Isla's frequent absences. Even Hob took to looking after Penny as she slept, building the fire when it was cold, or opening the windows when it was not. He was always careful to keep out of sight, however.

Then, one day, Isla's resolve failed. She made her way to the loch near the cottage and unmoored the rowboat from the jetty. As she began to row, a sense of elation filled her, and she set a course for the passage to the sea.

CHAPTER 8

THE STORM

The rush of the current drew her faster and faster downstream. Exhilaration flooded her. She didn't know precisely where she was going, or why. She just knew that she couldn't bear to watch her mother be so unlike herself. It wrenched at her, and her heart ached as she remembered the happy, fun-filled summers of old.

Her joy at being on the water dimmed, and as she made her way out onto the sea, she looked around at the vastness around her and finally felt all of her emotions hit her at once.

She leant into her oars and pulled as hard as she could. All her sorrow went into her rowing, all her anger, all her sense of futility and hopelessness of seeing the mother she knew come back to her.

The calm exterior that she wore at the cottage dissolved and a rage the like of which she had never before experienced consumed her. The fear of the loss of her father and the anger she hadn't realised, until now, towards her mother crashed over her. *Why* had she abandoned them so completely? Why couldn't she just *be* there for her children?

The grief she had been hiding along with the worry, duty and fear she felt both for herself and Hamish made her throat throb. Hot tears streamed down her face; all she wanted to do was scream, but no sound emerged. Her arms kept working, well-versed in the motion of the oars. She threw herself into the movement of the boat; so inwardly focused that she took no notice of the direction that she was heading in. Thoughts occupying her, her eyes half-blind with tears and salted sea spray, she finally tired.

She stopped, leant back in the boat, and when her tears finally ran out and her sobs receded into nothingness, she lay down and let the waves gently rock her. She felt tired, empty. Her anger had drifted away as if she had cast it out by sheer force. All that remained was exhaustion.

How long she stayed like that, she wasn't certain. With her eyes closed, her mind drifted as she listened to the lapping of the water against the edge of the boat. She could have been there for moments or hours. And so she stayed until the sky darkened overhead. She opened her eyes at the precise moment a drop of water hit her face with startling force. Then another. And another.

She sat up just as the heavens opened. The air around her was heavy with water, both from above and below. The raindrops were so fierce they bounced back from the surface of the sea.

Isla searched wildly for the oars. She grabbed at them, nearly knocking them out of the boat in her panic. Clutching the handles tightly once she'd captured them, she looked around.

She didn't recognise where she was. She could only barely make out the fact that there was land somewhere to her left. Or was there? The rain was coming down with such weight that all she could see was water. It dashed in her eyes, and she bowed her head against it.

Chilled to the bone, she felt and saw the wind lift in mere moments. The little rowboat was now being buffeted by the waves, and as the wind howled violently, the sea increased its vehemence.

Up, up, up, the boat bravely rode the waves as they built. Then, it crashed down as the wave it was being propelled on broke, smacking the boat against the sea's surface.

Isla was terrified. She had never been out in a storm. Not like this. She felt vulnerable, exposed. She tried to row, but her efforts were to no avail. The sea had her at its mercy.

She could feel the boat being inched out, further from where she thought she'd glimpsed the shadow of land. Helpless, she clung on to the boat and the oars with all her might, as it pitched and bucked. The wind howled and the rain, horizontal now in its strength, drove at her.

Shivering uncontrollably, she gathered the oars in and hugged herself in a desperate bid to retain some warmth. She didn't know what lay beyond the island, but she had a sinking feeling that she would soon find out.

She gritted her teeth. Without warning, a crash of thunder resounded, rumbling so loudly that it made Isla jump. Involuntarily, she let go of the oars.

Screaming, she managed to save one, but with absolute horror could only sit and watch as the other slipped away, sinking down, down beneath the waves.

Fear froze her. Her mind went blank. Her means of getting back to the island had vanished into the depths.

Suddenly, a shadow formed. She looked up.

A towering wave was rearing, poised to strike. She

shrank back and watched as it loomed. She knew that when it hit, she would likely be cast into the sea.

But it didn't break. Not on the boat. The tower of water collapsed, but metres from the rowboat. Isla couldn't believe her eyes. She *knew* that she had been right below it. She didn't understand. The swell of the broken wave rocked the boat backwards. Then, she realised, the boat was continuing to move.

She wondered if it was the current. But no. The sea was moving against her, but the boat continued its gradual, jolting retreat away from the heart of the storm. Disbelieving, she cast her gaze all around, even standing up gingerly to look, before being plonked unceremoniously back into her seat by a rolling wave.

The rain seemed to be lessening, she thought. Her eyes adjusted as the deluge became first a steady drizzle, and then a light mist. Now, she could make out a shape in the distance! It was growing closer. Land!

The boat continued its progress, and now, peering into the waves around the boat, she finally spotted the reason for her inexplicable rescue.

There, gliding through the water in front of the boat was a sleek, dappled grey creature. It had a shiny grey fur, flippers and a long body which ended in a tail? No, two flippers again. The flippers were working hard, rapidly propelling both the animal and the boat towards the land. She thought she recognised the creature from an encyclopaedia of animals she had once read... it was... she cast her mind back... a seal? She had never seen one in real life before. She was sure of it.

Astonished, she looked out towards the animal's head. From what she could see, it was round, and the seal's jaws appeared to be clamped around the rope used for mooring the boat onto the jetty. It was pulling the boat, and Isla, away from the eye of the storm.

She didn't have time to dwell on her unexpected rescue, or on the mysterious creature in the water, as the boat then gently slid onto a pebbly beach which she had not, up to that point, noticed, so curious was she in watching the seal.

Relief flooded her. She clambered up, out of the boat and pulled it higher onto shore. The mist prevented her from being able to make out the size of the land which she had shored up on, and whether it was Arraway or not. As she pulled the boat up further onto the beach, she saw a hollow in the rocky outcrop further up the beach. Isla looked around for the seal which had led her to shore, but there was no sign of it. Intent on securing the boat, she had let it out of her sight. Now, it was gone. There was no trace of it.

She made her way to the cave she had spotted. It was large enough for her to be able to walk inside. It stretched back a distance, but it got darker the further back it went, and she shivered, not wanting to venture further. She decided to take shelter in the front of the cave, where she could still see the boat. It was surprisingly warm, protected from the wind and the mist. She sank down, her back against the wall of the cave and waited for the mist to clear. Exhaustion caught up to her.

The rawness of her emotions, the storm, it had all been too much. Her eyelids grew heavy, soothed by the lullaby of the gradually calming waters breaking on the shore. Just before she closed her eyes she thought she saw the figure of a girl, standing by the boat. She struggled to open her eyes to take a second look, but she couldn't. A deep and dreamless sleep overwhelmed her.

Warmth from the sun woke her. She started, looking around, unsure for a moment of her surroundings. Then, she remembered.

She was stunned to see that no trace of the storm remained. Instead, the smooth surface of the sea glistened and glinted as it reflected the sunlight.

Isla got up and went to look outside of the cavern which she had sheltered in. She didn't recognise where she was. She could see that it was an island, but it was not Arraway. That, she knew for certain.

It was rocky and small; she was sure that she would be able to walk around it within an hour if she had the mind to.

Looking outwards, towards the sea, she spotted it in the distance. Arraway. She peered out and could just about make out the details of the cliff edges which she and Hamish had spotted from their illicit boat trip.

She jumped. Hamish! He must be so worried about her, she thought. She realised she had no idea of how long she had been gone for. She needed to go back!

It was then that she remembered that she'd lost an oar. Frustrated, she kicked a pebble and watched it skip down towards the sea. She followed its progression down to her boat.

There, lying inside the rowboat, were both oars. She stopped, amazed. "But how?" she whispered. She thought of the seal which had pulled her to shore, but surely not... Then, Isla remembered the image which she'd thought she'd seen just before she fell asleep. The girl.

She looked all around, even wandering up to the top of the rocks in which the cave was hidden. But there was no sign of anyone, or anything. No creatures, no people.

She knew she needed to go back to the cottage. Pushing the boat offshore, she scrambled inside, taking up the oars, keeping a firm grip on each. As she increased her distance from the island, she saw, again, the figure of a girl. Isla stopped rowing, calling out to where the girl had materialised from. But just as quickly as she appeared, she vanished again.

Isla scanned the shoreline, but the girl was nowhere to be seen. Uncertain of whether she was hallucinating, she began to row again. Soon after, she saw a seal close to the boat. By its markings, it was the same one which had rescued her. As she rowed, it kept pace, keeping a safe distance from the boat. Every now and then, Isla caught a glimpse of the animal's face, and she could almost swear that she saw an impish gleam shining from its large eyes.

She didn't understand. Why was the creature following her? And who was the mysterious girl on the island? And why did the seal want to rescue her in the first place? The questions raced through her mind as she closed the gap between the boat and the island of Arraway.

She didn't get the feeling that the seal meant her any harm. After all, it had saved her from the storm. And it looked friendly enough, she thought. Almost playful.

As she got closer to the shore, a familiar creature jumped out of the water and over the boat, splashing Isla as it landed. "Patch!" she called out, before realising that it wasn't likely that a porpoise could understand what she was saying. Both the porpoise and the seal kept her company as she rowed towards the inlet which would take her to the loch.

Making her way up the river mouth, she watched the two animals grow smaller in the distance. Then, she gasped. At the estuary, at the point where the river met the sea, the seal abruptly vanished. In its place was the girl which she had seen on the rocky island.

Again, Isla stopped rowing, staring, mouth agape. The girl in the water smiled at her, and the same mischievous look which she had seen on the seal's face was now replicated within the girl's expression. She waved Isla goodbye.

"Who... who are you?" Isla called, stuttering as she did so.

The girl's lilting voice floated back to her across the water. "Come back tomorrow, and you'll see."

She dipped under the water, and the next thing that Isla saw was the seal swimming back through the waves, re-joining the porpoise.

Stunned, Isla sat for a few moments in disbelief, unable to make sense what she'd just witnessed. She was fascinated, yet scared, at this inexplicable turn of events. Lost in her thoughts, she eventually picked up her oars and returned to the loch.

Mist dimmed the air once again, but, as she reached the jetty, she thought that the fog did not seem as thick as it had during the sea-fret. Although, it did appear to be getting darker. Isla realised that dusk was setting in. She tied the boat up to the jetty in a panic. She had been out all day! She ran back, knowing that she would find herself in a great deal of trouble if her aunt were to discover where she had been. But why didn't Marion want her to be out on the sea? Her mind racing along with her body, she didn't think it was purely because of the dangers of storms. What was she hiding from them?

As Isla approached the cottage, she resolved to not tell her aunt where she had been or what she had seen. For one, she knew that she would be forbidden from going out on the loch anymore, and surely nobody would believe her!

She crept through the doorway, tiptoeing. The house was dark. She called out a tentative "Hello?", to which there was no reply. She pushed open the living room door, and there a fire was lit. Her mother lay asleep on the sofa next to the fireplace. Softly, Isla pulled the door shut again and then peeked first into the playroom, and then the kitchen. Neither her aunt nor Hamish were anywhere to be seen.

Puzzled, she crept up the stairs, gingerly testing each with her foot, trying to avoid the squeaks of the protesting floorboards. The room she shared with Hamish was empty. She looked around, finding no clue as to where her brother might be hiding.

Venturing back out to the hallway outside of her room, she looked to where her aunt's room lay at the other end of the corridor. Cautiously, she walked towards it.

Marion had said that the children were not to go into her room, but surely... if it was merely to see where she was?

Isla knocked softly at the door. "Aunty Marion?" she whispered loudly. There was no answer. Drawing a deep breath, she knocked once again, louder. Still, she was met with silence.

Steeling herself, Isla put a hand to the handle, and, slowly, turned it. The door swung open noiselessly. Scarcely daring to breathe, she tiptoed forward. Curiosity propelled her into the room once she saw it was open. Isla didn't know what she had been expecting, but it wasn't this. There were no great mysteries apparent in the room. It was a simple bedchamber, clean, bright and airy. A bed stood in one corner of the room, and a closet at the other end. A desk lay against the far wall by the window, facing out towards the fields. Underneath everything ran a thickly woven rug. It was beautiful, Isla thought. The only striking object in the room, it was rich in colour; dark blues were splashed and highlighted by thick golden threads which scrolled along the edges of the rug.

Without thinking, she walked slowly over the rug towards the desk. She didn't know why she was lingering but linger she did. She wondered if there was more to discover about her aunt. Running a finger lightly over the wooden surface of the desk, her hand brushed over an elegant, creamy white comb, which sparkled lightly as it moved. Looking closer, she saw that it was not quite white, but rather, it contained a myriad of colours sheening from different angles as it caught the dimming sun. 'Mother of pearl', that was it. She'd seen it once before, this material, on a brooch which her mother had once worn. That was a long time ago, when her mother still owned trinkets; it had long-since been pawned off to buy food as the war carried on.

She noticed that there were little drawers in the desk, set equal distances apart. Out of sheer curiosity she opened each one-by-one. There was nothing in the first two drawers. Disappointed, she drew the third open slowly. There, she found a necklace with an elegant locket threaded onto the silver chain. She picked it up. The locket was delicately made, an elaborate filigree looping over its curves. She frowned, unable to recall seeing her aunt wearing any jewellery, let alone this locket.

She opened the clasp carefully, prising the edges apart. Inside, a single ringlet of brown hair lay. Isla touched it carefully. There was no inscription, no photograph. So fixated was she on her discovery, she didn't hear footsteps approach from behind.

"So," Marion said quietly. "It seems you're back."

Isla jumped, hastily snapping the locket shut as she wheeled around.

"I'm sorry, Aunty Marion... I was... I was..."

"Snooping?" Isla didn't recognise the cool tone which her aunt was speaking in.

"No! I was... I was looking to see where you were."

"Aye lass, and we were out looking for *you*, Hamish and I."

"I... I got lost. The fog set in, and...." Isla said lamely, desperately searching for an explanation which she could give.

"You were gone for *hours*, Isla. All day! No note, no clue... We've been out searching all over. I've had Mrs. MacGregor looking in the village, and Mr. Mackenzie out over the hills! Hamish was so worried! Aye, and so was I!"

"I'm sorry." Isla hung her head. "I was... just, I needed to get away. But I got lost. I just found my way back. I'm so sorry Aunty Marion."

Marion's stern expression softened. However, when she noticed what Isla was holding, her gaze grew considerably colder.

"I'll thank you to not be looking through my belongings, young lady." She held out her hand, and Isla flushed, dropping the necklace into her aunt's waiting palm.

"I'm sorry, I didn't mean to... I just, I was just looking for you, and, well..."

"And you thought I might be hiding in the wee desk there?"

"I... no... I..." Stumbling, Isla didn't know what to say.

Marion gently, but firmly, put a hand on Isla's arm, drawing her out of the room.

"From now on lass, 'out of bounds' means 'out of bounds'. This is my own space, and so I'd like it to remain."

Blushing, Isla nodded. However, she couldn't contain her curiosity, and she ventured to ask, "Aunty Marion. The locket...who...?"

"That is my own concern, and none of yours Isla. There will be no more talk on the matter. Is that understood?"

Marion's tone brooked no argument. Isla recognised the warning in her voice. She nodded, meekly.

"Now, Isla, let's go find your brother."

They headed into the kitchen where Hamish was sitting at the table. His pale, anxious countenance was back, Isla saw with a pang of guilt.

"Hello there Hamish," she smiled weakly.

"Isla!" Her brother rushed up to her, and nearly toppled her with the ferocity of the hug which he threw upon her. He began to cry, jerkily sniffing "you were gone for hours and hours! It was getting dark... and the fog... Isla, I was scared!"

Remorse flooded her. "I'm so sorry Hamish. I just went out for some... change of scenery. But I'm back now."

He squeezed her tighter.

"You *can't* leave me Isla. Not you, too. Promise!"

"I promise," she whispered, tears of her own dropping onto her brother's face.

He wiped them away and then gave a watery smile. "I'm glad you're back."

"Me too, Hamish, me too."

Marion cleared her throat. "Let's have some supper then, shall we?"

They nodded. Isla realised suddenly how hungry she was.

Their dinner of beef stew and dumplings was demolished in near record time. All three cleared their plates in relative silence, Hamish trying occasionally to tell his sister about how he'd made the dumplings. She smiled and nodded at different intervals, studiously avoiding meeting her aunt's watchful eye.

At the end of the meal, Marion hesitated, then said, "I think it's best that we all stay close to the cottage whilst the fret is in. Best to not go wandering off until the weather's right."

Mutely, Isla nodded. Then, she remembered. The girl in the water! She *had* to get back to the sea. But how?

As Hamish went to give their mother her supper, Isla wandered into the playroom, absently making her way to the bookcase. Distractedly, she ran her fingers over the books on the shelves, lost in the day's events. Then, she stopped. On the cover of one of the books, she spied an image of the same creature which had rescued her. A seal. The book was titled, "Scottish Myths and Legends." Isla flicked through the pages. There it was. "*Selkies.*"

"*Selkies can transform themselves from their seal form to human form...shedding their sealskin, otherwise known as a selkie skin, to do so...*"

Isla skimmed through the pages, her eyes darting from word to word in excitement. She had never heard of a 'selkie' before. Even as a fairy tale. But it must be real! Not just a myth confined to the pages of a book. She thought of Hob. Folklore was not just a story, not here.

Pushing the book back on the shelf where she had found it, Isla fled to bed in a daze. She had to know more. She resolved that she *would* find the girl again. She just had to work out how.

Slipping into an uneasy sleep, thoughts of the sea and

mythical creatures filled her dreams.

CHAPTER 9

DISCOVERIES

Isla was awake and alert far before Hamish the next morning. Excitement and nervous anticipation made her jittery and, unable to sleep, she tiptoed out of bed and down to the kitchen. It was so early that she even managed to see Hob before he retired for his morning sleep.

"Mornin' to ye, Isla. What be ye awake fer at this time?" the brownie asked her as it ladled her up a steaming bowl of porridge.

"I don't know... I couldn't sleep."

Hob looked at her astutely. "Hamish was a mite worried about ye yesterday. Aye, and the lady, too."

Isla looked down at her slippers.

"I know. I didn't mean to be gone for so long."

"Aye, well, a storm can have that effect, I don't doubt it."

She looked up at him quickly. "What do you mean? I got lost in the fog..."

Isla looked outside; it was indeed just as grey now as it had been the previous evening.

Hob stopped and looked her straight in the eye. "Mebbe

that's what you want to let on to the lady. Dinnae be tellin' Hob any untruths, now. Besides, Patch already told me."

Isla flushed. For the first time that she had known him, Hob's temper began to show through. She remembered what Hamish had said about the consequences of insulting or angering brownies.

"I...I'm sorry, Hob. I didn't mean to... well, yes, I did. I just don't want Aunty Marion to know."

Then, Isla realised what Hob had said. "Wait! You said Patch told you? But how do you know Patch? And how did he tell you... And what do you know about..." she lowered her voice to a whisper, "...selkies?"

Hob raised his eyebrows and turned away, yawning, "Up here, we all know each other. But there's some things that we're not allowed to talk aboot, us broonies."

Isla's curiosity was piqued. "Who says what you can and can't talk about? The selkies? Patch?"

"That's broonie business." Hob said importantly.

"Please, Hob?" Isla wheedled. She could feel that she was on the cusp of learning a great secret.

But the brownie was not to be swayed. As he made his way to his hidden sleeping quarters, the only thing that he would say to Isla, as he pressed the secret brick, was "The hoose will tell ye all ye need to know."

The chimney swung shut, and Isla was left with her porridge... confused and annoyed.

What did he mean, "the house will tell you"? Houses couldn't talk. But then, neither did porpoises... and brownies belonged in fairy tales!

Feeling silly, she ventured, quietly, "Hello house? Can you tell me about the rocky island I was on... and what lives there?"

Isla was greeted with silence. And then, a soft sniggering

came from the chimney where Hob had just disappeared into.

"Fine then!" she huffed, leaving the kitchen feeling entirely foolish.

She peeked into her mother's room and closed the door quietly back to as she saw her, peaceful at least in sleep.

She ducked into the playroom. She made her way to the bookshelf again and browsed through the titles intently. Picking up the Scottish folklore tome, she couldn't find any others which looked as if they would give her the answers she sought.

"Mythical creatures which resemble seals in the water, but assume human form on land... Gentle souls... Wild yet playful... They capture the spirit of the sea, yet have an undeniable affinity to humankind..."

Isla skimmed the pages again, drinking in what was written. But the description was confined to a mere few paragraphs; no explanation was given of why selkies, if that was indeed what she had seen, would have any interest in her.

Disappointed, she began to look through the rest of the book, hoping to find anything to do with the information that Hob had given her. The little that he had given her, rather. Here was nothing to be found relating to 'Porpoise', yet Isla felt sure she had seen an illustration depicting a creature like Patch during one of the times she had skimmed through the book's pages. She started from the beginning once again. There, she spotted the image she remembered.

'Dolphin'

A short summary lay alongside it.

"Considered by many to be messengers of the seas, dolphins are sacred creatures. They connect the earth-bound to the underwater world."

Isla closed the book thoughtfully. Surely, 'dolphins' and 'porpoises' were not too dissimilar. She wondered if Patch was such a messenger, and if so, how did Hob communicate with him? And where did Hob go, to communicate with him?

Isla shook her head, laughing over her thoughts. Over the fact that she was trying to make sense of something that truly did not make sense! But she knew what she'd seen yesterday. She'd *felt* the storm's rage, and she *knew* she'd been pulled to safety. But why?

She slid the book back on the shelf once more, and wandered, absentmindedly, about the room. Not watching where she was going, she didn't see one of Hamish's skates, left where it had been strewn in the centre of the room.

"Oomph!" she tripped over it, landing inelegantly at the foot of the dollhouse. She got up, dusted herself off muttering angrily in the general direction of her brother. She stopped suddenly. She turned her attention fully on the object in front of her. When she'd first seen the dollhouse, on their first day on Arraway, she'd noticed that it bore a resemblance to Calder Cottage. She had not really played with it since. But now that it was directly in front of her, Isla saw with realisation that the dollhouse was not just a similar representation of the cottage that she was now standing in, but was, in fact, what appeared to be an exact miniature replica of Calder Cottage. It mimicked everything, from the flowers arching over the doorframe, to the three chimneys jutting proudly from the roof. She smiled, even Basil and Billie had their own tiny replicas hidden behind the house. She wondered that she had not noticed this before.

Then, a thought struck her. "*The house will tell you...*"

Surely Hob hadn't meant *this* house? But what if he had?

With trembling hands, she began to explore the dollhouse in earnest. The front hall was as she knew it to be, it even boasted the window at the base of the staircase, which itself was just as beautiful in miniature as the full-size staircase mere metres away.

Isla examined the bathroom, faintly disappointed that the little sink and bathtub did not actually produce any water when she turned the taps (which did, surprisingly, turn). Tracing her finger through from the bathroom to the living room, she noticed that the room had been staged with the fire lit, as on the day that they arrived.

That got her thinking. Hob had lit the fire that day... So, if the fire was taken as a sign that Hob was in the house, then maybe... She took a closer look at the room in which a miniature kitchen was housed. There, everything was as she knew it to be from the full-scale version. But surely, not *everything*?

She gasped as the same brick in the dollhouse revealed the very hidey hole that Hob was now napping in. Her mind raced. How did the maker of the dollhouse know about the brownie hole?

She wondered whether the upstairs rooms of the dollhouse would reveal as much. If there was, in fact, anything to reveal. Opening the door to the room that she and Hamish called their own, she examined it thoroughly. There was nothing remarkable about it, she thought with a sigh.

Hesitantly, she waited a moment before examining the miniature version of her aunt's room. Her aunt's rebuke still fresh in her mind, Isla wondered whether Marion would consider the dollhouse inspection an intrusion. She brushed the doubt away, reasoning that Marion wouldn't have given her the dollhouse if she hadn't intended her to play with it. And perhaps she didn't know all the secrets which it harboured!

Isla looked inside the room with great interest. The desk was as Isla had found it only hours before, but the drawer handles didn't open the drawers to the replicated version. The bed was in the same place, and even the carpet was as she had seen it. She noticed that the room was rather plain in its style, unlike the detail which had been adopted in the rest of the house. She wondered why that was. Curiosity led her to open the doors of the closet, but there was nothing to be found within. Sighing again, she shut the miniature closet door, and knocked the little structure accidentally with her hand. The side panel of the closet swung open.

"Oh no," Isla groaned, inwardly kicking herself for having broken it. "Aunty Marion can't see this; she'll be so angry with me!" Hurriedly, she tried to push the panel back in place, but to no avail.

It was only after a few moments of fiddling with the panel side that she realised that the closet wasn't perhaps broken after all. Acting on a hunch, Isla slid the panel... It clicked into place. Eagerly, she pressed the side of the closet. Again, the panel swung open. Her thoughts raced.

If Hob's hiding place was shown in the dollhouse, then maybe this closet panel was the same as the real closet in Marion's room. Isla tried to peek inside but could see nothing. All she felt was an empty space, but her fingers were too big to feel if the space led anywhere.

"Maybe that's how we never heard Aunty Marion leaving the house," Isla whispered to herself. She had a suspicion that the sliding panel was actually hiding a secret passageway, but she didn't know where it led. She didn't dare go back into her aunt's room again to test her theory.

But, surely, that wasn't what Hob had meant. There must be something else – something that could provide an answer to what she was looking for. Then, it dawned on her. She ran as quietly as she could upstairs, and shook her brother awake.

"Shush! It's alright, just me" she whispered as he started.

"What do you want? Isla. Go away," Hamish mumbled, pulling the covers higher over his head.

"No! It's important! Come on Hamish!"

"What?!" Grumpily, he half-opened one eye.

"When you were looking for Hob, you looked all over the house, right?"

"Yessss..."

"*All* over?"

"Not in Aunty Marion's room, Isla. I already told you!"

"I know, I know. I'm not asking that. You said you found an attic, right?"

He looked up at her blankly, convinced, seemingly, that she had lost all sense. "Yes... but Hob wasn't in there."

Isla impatiently brushed his comment away. "No, I *know* Hamish. But where is the attic?"

"Here."

Isla looked at him as if he were now the simple one. "What do you mean, 'here'? This is our room."

Angrily, Hamish jumped out of bed. "No, I mean *here*,"

he groused, pointing at his bed.

Isla shook her head. "I still don't understand..."

"Watch!"

Stomping over to the foot of the bed, Hamish pulled the piece of furniture towards himself, away from the wall. Now Isla could see what he had been pointing to. A hatch in the wall had been hidden by the bed. Hamish opened it.

"See? The attic!"

Isla peered inside. It was dark and smelt dusty. "Did you go in there?" she asked, impressed at her brother's sleuthing.

"Yes, but just enough to look around a bit. There's nothing there! Besides, Hob would never want to stay anywhere so dusty and dark. He likes clean places."

"Never mind Hob. Come with me."

"Hey, Isla! Ow! Let go!" Hamish grumbled as Isla pulled him out of the room.

"Shhh, just follow me. Be quiet!" she hissed. Reluctantly, he obeyed, but he still didn't look happy.

When they got to the playroom, Isla led him to the dollhouse.

"I don't want to play with dolls, Isla!"

"Oh, don't be silly. Just watch. Look at it. What do you see?" Isla waited as Hamish gave the dollhouse a cursory once-over.

"It's a toy house."

"No, look again. Look. At the chimneys. At the bathroom."

Hamish knelt on the floor to get a better look. "Hold on. This is... this is Aunty Marion's house!"

Isla nodded. "Look in the kitchen. See anything unusual?"

Hamish examined the layout of the miniature kitchen

and shook his head. "It's just the same as the one here, but..."

"No, look!" Impatiently, she showed him the hidden brick revealing the brownie hole.

Hamish looked up open-mouthed.

"But how did it know?"" he asked, uncertain himself of who or what he was referring to.

"I don't know, but there's more. Look. This is Aunty Marion's room. And this..." She showed him the closet. "...is what the dollhouse shows the room to have." She pressed the side of the closet, and the panel slid open again.

Hamish looked dumbstruck. "Is that another brownie hole?"

Isla shrugged. "I don't know. I don't *think* so. Here. Give me one of your marbles."

He did so, and she placed it in the space which the sliding panel had revealed. "Alright, let's see what happens."

She gave the marble a slight push with her finger, and they both watched, entranced, as it disappeared. They followed its progress by the sound it made trundling through the house, but they couldn't see where it had gone. Then, it re-emerged, outside of the house to the left of the cottage.

"Look," Hamish said, pointing. "That goes out into the garden, over there, behind the barn."

Turning to Hamish again, Isla then said "Now, the attic..."

He cottoned on immediately, grinning. They located the little hatch in the wall after moving the tiny bed away from its place.

Isla retrieved the marble and placed it within the replica

hatch space. She looked at her brother, and he nodded eagerly. "Watch where it goes," she said in a hushed voice, then pushed the marble away, out of sight. Away it rolled.

They listened to it as it moved through and down the house. The marble was out of sight much longer than it had been previously, Isla thought to herself. Then, it stopped.

"Where is it?" Hamish asked.

"I don't know... I thought I heard it... here, give me a hand." She motioned for him to get hold of one end of the dollhouse. She took hold of the other. "Now, lift. Careful!"

As they lifted the house up slowly from where it stood on the table, they watched as the marble rolled out from where it had been hiding.

"It goes under the house. It's a secret passageway!" Hamish chortled in glee.

Isla whispered, "Maybe *that's* how we get to the beach."

"Can we go explore?" Hamish asked, suddenly wide awake and raring to go.

Slowly, Isla shook her head, considering. "I don't think Aunty Marion will like us to say we're going around the island, especially after yesterday... not in the mist."

Hamish looked up and ran to the window. "It looks a bit brighter," he called back to her hopefully. Isla got up and joined him.

It did indeed look marginally less grey and misty outside, but she still wasn't convinced. "I don't know..."

Hamish was sure of himself, however. "Hob says this kind of mist always goes by the afternoon. The sun eats it."

Isla laughed at him. "The sun can't eat anything, silly."

He stuck his tongue out at her. "It can so, Hob said!"

They waited until mid-morning, and then it turned out that Hamish's prediction came true. As the sun peered out from beyond its 'eaten' mist, Marion appeared in the living room, where they'd been sitting with their mother.

"I'm just nipping out to the village," she called brightly. "We're out of milk. Glenn's still not been back, so I'm having to traipse out to get it myself! Who'd have thought a goat could be so tricky to keep!"

They waved their aunt off, and then Isla and Hamish quickly went into the kitchen, and approached Hob, who was just starting to rise.

Knocking gently on the chimney, Hamish called out, "Hello Hob. Morning! Are you awake?"

The brownie slowly opened his chimney to them. "The hoose been talking to ye, lass?" he squeaked. Hamish looked puzzled.

"Yes, thank you Hob. We... were hoping to go exploring..." Isla didn't know how to ask, but Hamish jumped straight in.

"Could you please look after Mother for us Hob? We won't be long. And Aunty Marion has just gone out. Mother won't be much trouble, I don't think. And Basil's here to protect you!"

Hob grinned, toothily. "It'd be me pleasure! Aye, yer mother is safe as hooses wit me. Don't ye fret. No need for the goat. Ye're in good hands with a broonie."

They thanked him profusely and then went back upstairs, well stocked by Hob with cakes which they both stuffed in their pockets.

"Ready?" Isla asked as she lifted the hatch door away from the wall.

Hamish nodded, anticipation shining from his eyes. Isla ducked inside and crawled forward. It was dark. She sneezed and switched on the torch that she was carrying with her. Flashing it around the room, she didn't see much of anything until a small light winked back at her. She moved towards the glimmer that she'd seen and, Hamish close at her heels, soon found herself at a metal grate. The light from the torch had bounced off a silvery corner of the grate. She called for Hamish to come and help her move it. Grunting at the weight of it, they persevered, and were rewarded with a dull thud as the grate fell forward.

Isla shone the torch to see what lay before them. To their excitement, the children saw that the grate had hidden a rickety set of stairs.

They crawled through the space where the grate had stood mere moments before, one by one. To Isla's great relief, she found they could stand upright once they manoeuvred into the stairwell.

As they crept down the stairs, stealthily avoiding the rogue creaks and grumbling of the ancient wooden floorboards, Hamish asked "Why do you think there's a secret staircase? Do you think Aunty Marion knows about it?"

Isla shrugged. "Maybe it was once used by bootleggers.... Or pirates!" Hamish's eyes widened in the half-light, like saucers as they reflected the torchlight.

"Pirates?!" He looked both anxious and excited. "Do you think Aunty Marion is a bootlegger?"

Isla laughed. "No! But I don't know if she knows about this. She has her own way in and out... so maybe she does. But she's never come into our room, so I guess, if she *does* know about it, then she doesn't use it."

Hamish nodded, wisely. "It's too small to get in there anyway. It's made for our size." Hamish's excitement over the possibility of there being pirates on the island (even if they were long gone) got Isla to thinking about what they might find at the other end of the rickety, windy staircase.

She whispered to Hamish, "Hamish, you know... yesterday?"

He nodded, focussed on his footing, the steps gradually becoming steeper as they sloped down.

"I... I didn't really get lost in the fog."

"But you told Aunty Marion..."

"I know, but... I did get lost, but I was on the sea. I took the boat out... a storm came."

"Isla! You should have told me! Why didn't you take me?! You *always* get the adventures. It's not fair!"

"I'm glad you weren't there Hamish. No, shush. A big storm nearly capsized the boat. You could have been... well, *I* could have been... well, I was really scared."

He gaped, "You *were?*"

She nodded. "Yes. It was the most scared I've ever been in my life. But listen. I got rescued."

He piped up, still looking slightly anxious. "By who? Mr. Mackenzie?"

"By *whom*," Isla corrected automatically. "No, it wasn't a person. Well, it might have been..."

Hamish stared at her, clearly confused.

"You know how you didn't think that anyone would believe you about Hob?" Isla started, trying to think how she could explain.

"You *didn't* believe me," he replied flatly.

"Yes, well, anyway. I know he's real now. But that's the point. You may not believe me."

"Yes, I will too!" Hamish's defiant voice echoed in the narrow stairwell, reverberating around the walls.

"Shhhhh!" she hissed quickly through her teeth.

"Sorry," he whispered, contritely.

"There was an animal in the water. It rescued me!" She hurried on, not letting her brother interrupt. "Do you remember the picture book we had at home about different animals? Well, I'm sure it was a seal. It pulled the boat away from the storm and saved me! It took me to a little island, and I was stuck there because I'd lost an oar in the storm. Then, later, I found both oars back in the boat. It must have found it again! And, and Patch was there, helping it I think, and, and... I think the seal can turn into a person." She finished breathless, having motored her way through her account.

"You mean..." he said, slowly struggling to unravel all that his sister had said, "you saw a mermaid?"

Isla frowned. "No, I don't think so... It was definitely a girl. And then a seal. And then a girl. I saw it in the book of folklore that's in the playroom... I think the seal is a selkie!"

Hamish whispered the word 'selkie' to himself. "What's...?"

"It's a seal, or like a seal, I'm not sure, that can turn into a human."

"But how?"

She shook her head. "I don't know. The book didn't say." She stopped. They'd reached the bottom of the stairs. She was sure that they were far below the cottage now, the number of stairs which they had climbed down was more than a single house could possibly merit. Looking ahead, Isla saw that they were standing in front of a simple wooden door.

Isla took a breath and turned to Hamish. "The girl from the sea... She told me to come and meet her today."

Hamish hopped from one foot to the other in excitement. "You mean, I might see a selkie too?!"

"I don't know what's on the other side of the door. If I'm right, we might be on a beach, down below the house.

But I don't know. And I don't know if she will know where we are, or if she'll even be here."

Hamish pushed the door in impatience. "Well, let's go look then!"

The door didn't move. He tried to rattle it, but the wood was so solid it barely budged. Isla stopped to think. Not all doors *pushed* open. Taking a chance, she put her hand to the door's surface and slowly slid it to the left. It obliged, and soundlessly and effortlessly glided into a cavity in the wall. Beyond the doorway lay the sea.

CHAPTER 10

THE OTHER ISLAND

They stood there for a moment before they turned to each other, cheering, exultant in their discovery.

A pebbly shore was the only thing which separated them from the waves of the sea. Hamish darted off, ready to explore their new discovery. Isla took her time in joining him. She wandered out, looking around cautiously. She saw that the doorway that they had come through was cleverly camouflaged to mimic the rockface in which it was hidden. A near-invisible seam around the doorframe was the only clue as to what was really on the other side of the rockface.

She piled a neat tower of pebbles to the side of the door as she slid it shut. Turning away, she looked back and was relieved to see that she could identify where the opening was straight away. She hoped it wasn't as obvious to anyone else who might chance by.

Running down the beach, she joined Hamish, who was busily trying to skim pebbles as their father had taught them.

Pip, pip, pip

"You did it!" Hamish turned and smiled back up at her. "There aren't many waves. It's easy!"

"Look!" Isla said, pointing.

In the distance, they could see a fin making its way through the water towards them. The sea creature jumped, and they cheered. "Patch!" they shouted and waved.

The porpoise drew closer. The children could hear the chattering it made as it neared; its unusual clicks and whistles sounding like it was trying to speak to them.

So absorbed were they in watching Patch as he swam towards them, they didn't notice their companion on the beach until a footstep crunched on the pebbles behind them.

The children wheeled around, startled.

There, stood the same girl that Isla had seen the previous day. She was taller than Isla, but she seemed to be not so much older. Her long, mahogany hair dripped damply down a strange, dappled grey shawl which she wore about her as a cloak, and down onto her bare feet.

Isla looked up at the girl's face. She was pretty, Isla decided, but wild. Sparkling grey eyes looked back at her.

The girl grinned; slightly jagged teeth brilliantly white against the tan of her skin.

"I've seen you both together. Once before." The girl had a soft accent, and spoke slowly, as if easing herself into an unfamiliar language.

"I'm Isla, and this is my brother, Hamish." Isla spoke up, sounding more confident than she felt. Hamish just stared at the girl, open-mouthed.

Isla stuttered. "Y-You... you rescued me, yesterday?"

The girl nodded, slowly.

"But why? And who are you? *What* are you?"

Smiling mischievously, the girl disappeared in front of

their very eyes. In her place, now much lower on the ground in front of them, lay the same seal which Isla had been rescued by the previous day. She recognised the dappled markings on its coat, and realised they were the same markings as had been on the shawl which the girl was wearing. The seal barked, making Hamish jump.

Isla pinched him. "See?!" she whispered. He nodded mutely; eyes huge in his small face.

The girl reappeared an instant later, laughing, which, Isla supposed, was the barking sound she had been making in her seal form also.

"You're a... selkie?" Isla whispered.

The girl cocked her head to one side. "Aye," she replied, as if it were obvious.

"But *who* are you? And what do you want?" The question sounded rude to Isla as soon as she had spoken the words, but they were already out there, irretrievable.

Hamish nudged her, already aware of what could happen if mythical creatures were angered.

But the girl didn't seem to notice any slight.

"I've been sent to fetch you," was all that she would say. She pointed, and they followed the direction of her gaze.

A large grouping of rocks, which they only now paid attention to, was sheltering a boat not dissimilar to the rowboat Isla had been caught and rescued in the previous day. Isla and Hamish stood there for a moment, looking back and forth between the selkie girl and the boat.

Finally, Isla asked, "But where are we going? And who sent you?"

The girl replied shortly, "If you want to find out, follow me." And with that, she resumed her seal form, beginning to swim out, away from shore.

Hamish scrambled into the boat. "Come on Isla! I want

to find out!"

Still, Isla hesitated. "But we don't know if she's friendly, or where she's taking us... or anything at all really!"

Hamish shouted impatiently, "She rescued you yesterday, didn't she? And Patch is there, so it *must* be alright!"

Sighing, Isla let her curiosity get the better of her. She dragged the boat (with Hamish firmly ensconced within) down to the water's edge and then scrambled in herself. She pushed off with the oars, calling out, "We're coming!" after the selkie's retreating figure.

The tide carried them out towards where the seal and porpoise were waiting. The seal took hold of the rope floating from the boat, and all the children could do was sit and watch as they were towed further and further from shore.

Isla kept a close eye on the direction that they were taking. It seemed to her that they were gradually moving closer to the rocky island which she had encountered the previous day. Despite the sun shining brightly down on them, she shivered. A cool mist suddenly appeared all around them. Then, as quickly as it had emerged, it disappeared, vaporising as the boat passed through it. Hamish pointed excitedly at the island, which was now visible to them.

"Look, Isla! Look!"

Isla nodded, wondering silently why they were now back at the stretch of rocks which had seemed so barren to her the previous day. The mist that they had just passed through puzzled her also. She whispered to Hamish, "Hey, did you notice the mist before we came through it?"

He shrugged, too interested in their impending shore landing.

The scrape of the hull of the boat against the gravel beach prompted both Isla and Hamish to jump out of the vessel, and automatically Isla pulled it further up onto the shore.

"You don't need to do that." The girl had rematerialised, human form now assumed. "It'll be safe here."

"Oh." Was all that Isla could think to say.

"It's no normal island," the girl continued. "You'll see. Follow me."

She turned and began to walk up, away from the boat, towards the rockface. Isla and Hamish both ran after her, Hamish turning and waving goodbye to Patch, who splashed seemingly a response back to them.

"Wait... where are you going?" Isla panted as she caught up to the girl. "And where did that mist come from, and go? And... what is your name?"

"You ask a lot of questions," the girl said, laughing at Isla.

Her laugh was a throaty, barky laugh, but not unpleasant, Isla thought. She rolled her eyes and repeated the question, "What's your name?"

The girl stopped, looked Isla in the eye, and sighed, tapping her foot, rather impatiently Isla thought.

"I am Dina. This island is hidden from those who we have not welcomed. The mist acts to guard us from harm, and we are going to see Rhodric."

The girl, Dina spun away and continued her quick trajectory away from the shore. Isla stamped her foot and protested angrily, "But who's Rhodric? And you still haven't said where we're going!"

Dina ignored her, and Hamish whispered to Isla, "I don't think she likes talking very much."

Isla whispered back, "I'm not sure she likes *me* very much!"

They'd reached the mouth of the cave that Isla had taken shelter in. Hamish hesitated, looking nervously at the dark interior which Dina was striding into.

He looked to his sister apprehensively. Isla herself had a sense of trepidation, but she gamely held out her hand to Hamish.

"Come on, let's not get left behind."

Together they walked cautiously into the cavern, following the sound of the selkie girl's footsteps. Further and further they walked, the darkness blinding them. They held onto each other, Isla taking care to right Hamish when he stumbled.

Then, the darkness slowly lessened. They could see a light beginning to appear in the distance. Dina's voice echoed back to them. "This way."

They quickened their pace as they saw her standing silhouetted against a bright entrance way.

They gawped. Through the cavern's previously concealed opening, a most unexpected sight greeted them. A great expanse of rock pools lay ahead of them. But they were no ordinary rock pools. Each was the size of a house, and in the rocks, dwellings were obvious. They were not houses as Isla and Hamish knew them to be... nor were they dark and gloomy caves. Instead, they were bright caverns, open to the front allowing the children to see inside. The front of each cavern sunk down to a pool of water and rich tapestries covered the floors of the caverns sloping upwards.

Other dwellings, Isla noticed, were built purely in the deeper pools which lay scattered about. In the centre of all the rock pools was an enormous rock, which had its own cavern clearly illuminated by the sun. A grand set of stairs stretched upwards, and what Isla thought to be a balcony was raised over the edge, allowing whoever was stood upon it to be fully visible to those below. She craned her head, peering to see whether anybody was there.

She noticed Hamish silently tugging at her arm.

"What?" she asked, still trying to examine the structure in front of them. Then, as her brother's pulls became more frantic, she looked down, and then around them.

A great number of selkies were slipping out of the different rock pools and caverns where they had been hiding. Some were in human form; others were in their seal form. All were looking at Isla and Hamish, but whether with fear, curiosity or anger, Isla couldn't tell.

Dina stepped forward, and a grizzled seal came shuffling towards them. Isla pushed Hamish behind her, and stood her ground, alarm coursing through her. The seal was large, and as it got closer, they saw that its pelt was marked not only by age but by many scars, crisscrossing it haphazardly.

Dina put a hand on her arm, her cool touch making Isla flinch. "It's alright." She said quietly. "That's Rhodric."

As she spoke, the seal changed its form. Now, standing before them was a scarred and greying man. He had the look of a warrior of times gone by, Isla thought. His frame was slightly stooped, scars running from his shoulder, across his chest and under his selkie skin garment worn almost as a toga, all the way to his other shoulder.

His deep green eyes scrutinised them both, and then he held out his arm. "Well met," he rumbled, breaking the silence which had fallen.

The selkies around them returned to whatever they had been doing prior to going into hiding. Hamish watched them in fascination. Young pups were playing in the pools outside the caverns, being carefully watched by their observant parents. Some, in human form, were binding nets, and yet others were pulling in fish from the deeper pools around them. It was, Isla thought in wonderment, most like a farm, as the different compartments of the underwater caverns appeared to host different types of fish, and only the biggest were being kept. The rest were thrown back if they did not meet whatever criteria it was that the selkies required. Others, in seal form, were leading a group of what looked to Isla to be adolescent pups. It appeared that some form of training was taking place, as the older selkie dived to the depths, and then one by one the youngsters followed suit.

She turned her attention back to the selkie whom Dina had called 'Rhodric'.

"We have been waiting for you," he said. "It has been a long time since we have had the sons and daughters of the Calder Sea in our midst."

Isla and Hamish looked at each other blankly. Hamish piped up, "Penny and Duncan are our parents."

Rhodric did not seem fazed, but just watched them, waiting, it seemed, for something.

Isla asked nervously, "Are you the leader of the selkies?"

Rhodric gestured for them to sit down on a rock close by. Dina remained standing, attentive to what was being said, but also watchful. She stood to be able to see the cavern door as well as the tribe of selkies. Isla and Hamish sat as directed, and Rhodric began.

"I am Rhodric. I have been the caretaker of the selkie folk of these parts for fourteen years. Our King has been stolen, and we are now all at risk."

Isla interrupted, "Risk of what? Stolen by whom?"

Dina looked over at Rhodric and muttered, "They ask a lot of questions."

He nodded, replying, "They have a lot to learn."

Hamish and Isla sat, waiting for him to continue, fascinated by all that they saw.

"There is a powerful being in these parts. It holds a power. For millennia, the selkies have ruled this sea, the Calder Sea, but now, with the King lost, our protection has weakened. There are ancient ties of power between the King or Queen of the selkies and the sea. The sea protects us when we have our rightful leader with us. But now... we do not know where he is. And our home is in danger. The power is growing. It wants to take over the sea territories. It wants to destroy us."

Hamish broke in, "I've never heard of the Calder Sea before," he said, still puzzled.

Rhodric replied gravely, "It is far past due. For the pair of you, you are the rightful children of the sea. Your father, Lord Duncan, is our King. You have selkie blood running through your veins."

CHAPTER 11

BEGINNINGS

Isla sat silent, astonished. Then, she sputtered, "I think you've got it wrong. Our father isn't a selkie. And neither is our mother. Besides, you said that you have been the 'caretaker' for fourteen years. Our father went... missing... a month ago. So, it can't possibly be true. And, also, if our father is a selkie... that would mean..."

"That your aunt Marion is also a selkie." Rhodric finished, calmly. "Aye, so it would."

Hamish frowned. "But Aunty Marion hates the sea. Well, she never lets us go near it."

Rhodric sighed, finally sitting. "It is a sad tale lad. Well, for the lady.

"Lord Duncan, he is a prince of these northern sea territories – what we call the Calder Sea. He saw your mother, one day, as she was visiting these parts - visiting on the island. Duncan was charmed. He went to talk to her and was swept away by her beauty and her wit. He had never met a selkie who could match her spirit, he said. And, so, he left. He renounced his kingship that very eve, and he left the charge of the selkie people to his sister.

"Marion was deeply troubled, for she soon realised that the sea did not share Duncan's same desire for shifting power. Duncan retained the power shared between him and the sea. Marion went after him, to try and change his mind and bring him back to his rule and his people."

Isla butted in angrily, "Well, she didn't. How *dare* she try and take our father away from our mother!" Hamish's brows were furrowed, but he didn't say anything.

Rhodric inclined his head. "Rightly or wrongly, Marion had made her choice. Her choice cost her dearly. As she left, she knew she must be quick, for once in human form, a selkie must not remain on land for longer than twelve hours, else may not return to that land for seven years once returned to the water. But a selkie may not revisit their seal-form without their selkie skin. Once Marion landed on the island, she tried to find Duncan, to bring him back. But she couldn't find him. He had already left with your mother. Frantic, she vowed to swim to the mainland to find him. But when she returned to the beach, where she'd hidden her selkie skin, it had vanished."

Isla gasped, "Somebody took it!"

Hamish shouted, "Who?!"

Rhodric shook his head. "She did not know. And we still do not know. But there she was, stranded on the island you now call your own, and she could not return to the sea. I was asked to be caretaker of this land, and our people, until the day that our lord or lady was restored to us, but the power still lay with your father."

Slowly, Hamish asked, "What changed? Has Father...?"

Rhodric opened his hands, palms lying flat. "We do not know. All we know is that his protection over us is diminishing. The seas grow angry. The storm yesterday, it had you in its sights, lass. That is no unkind act of the sea. That anger holds power behind it. As Marion has not been given the sea's power, as our leader, we do not know what has happened."

Isla asked, "But if all this is true, what does this mean for our mother? Did she know that Father and Aunty Marion were... are... selkies?"

Again, Rhodric shook his head. "Your father never told his new bride about his past, about who he had been. He truly gave up his life here, his people. He knew he would never return. But the sea afforded him its protection, in a way, over you both, and over your mother. Now he is gone, I fear that your mother is in grave peril."

Hamish whispered, "What do you mean?" Isla put her arm around her brother's shoulders.

"With your father's protection gone or weakened, your mother may be one of this being's targets. It is seeking to undermine what is left of the sea's connection to your father. It may be that your mother is at most risk."

Isla and Hamish exchanged worried glanced. "But Mother is sick already. She won't move, doesn't speak... she doesn't know who we are," Isla said, a sob stuck in her throat.

Rhodric's gaze darkened. "Then it has begun," he said solemnly.

"Isla," he said suddenly to her. "You have swum in the waters, have you not?"

Isla shook her head, "No..." Rhodric looked at her, waiting.

"Not the sea," she whispered. "The loch."

"You must swim in these waters to regain your protection," Rhodric said. "Come." Isla got up but didn't follow him.

"Wait. Why?"

Rhodric turned to her. "These waters are still safe. Still protected. As your father's protection over you has dimmed, you must restore it by regaining the sea's protection."

"But why not Hamish?"

Rhodric interrupted her, "You have given the waters of the land time to creep in and remove what was yours. I can see it. It is why you were so easy to target in the storm. Hamish has not been in the waters of the island. Is that not so, Hamish?"

Hamish nodded, suddenly embarrassed. "I can't swim," he whispered, red-faced.

Dina smiled at him, but not unkindly. "This is where you will learn. It is safe. We all learn to swim here, in these waters." She pointed to the pools where the pups were chasing each other, flopping in and out of the water with ease.

To Isla's surprise, Hamish nodded and smiled at the older selkie girl.

Her brother's acceptance helped Isla to make her decision. She stepped forward and down into the pool. The pups stopped, fascinated by her. The mothers inched protectively towards their pups.

Isla took a deep breath, keeping her eyes open, and dived into the heart of the pool. As the cool water met her skin, she realised immediately that it was completely different from swimming in the loch. The brightness of the water, and the light filtering through it, dazzled her. Sparkles reflected off a minnow's small form, as it darted in and out of the base of the pool. A warmth filled her; she felt the sun creep into her bones, and the water instantly soothed and dissolved the knots in her arms. The physical exhaustion of the previous day's ordeal slipped away. She was now alert; her skin tingled, and she felt the water move to her left. Zipping around, faster than she thought possible, she spotted a curious seal pup sidling its flipper into the edge of the water. A mischievous impulse seized her, and she kicked off, somersaulting in the water, and tickled the pup's flipper. It squealed and immediately jumped in after her.

They chased each other up and down the pool, until Isla finally let it catch up to her. Growing tired of the game once it had caught up to her, the pup climbed out of the water.

Isla followed it, reluctant now to leave the water. As she emerged, she saw that Rhodric stood smiling and Dina was staring, now with some interest. Isla thought she even looked slightly impressed. Hamish, meanwhile, appeared a trifle concerned.

"You see, you are your father's daughter," Rhodric said, giving her a helping hand out of the water. Isla remembered what her aunt had told her after the first time she had seen Isla swim. Suddenly, it made sense.

She wrung her hair out over Hamish when he tentatively asked, "Is it cold?" He squealed and hopped around.

Dina said to him, "Come on, your turn."

Isla didn't understand at first why Hamish seemed to trust this selkie when he had refused to allow her and Marion to teach him how to swim. Jealously, she watched as the girl helped Hamish into the water, and then it dawned on her. Dina had the same confidence and self-assurance that their father had. Her jealousy faded, and she marvelled at the sure way the girl had with the swimming lesson.

Isla whispered to Rhodric, "Is Dina your daughter?"

Rhodric shook his head. "Nay. Murdina is not my true-born child, but I raised her, so she is as good as."

Isla asked, "Murdina? Not... Dina?"

The grizzled selkie shrugged. "She prefers Dina. But, one day she will grow into her true name."

"What happened to her parents?"

Rhodric replied shortly, "They're gone. When she was a bairn. But that is her story, not mine, to tell."

Isla wondered about that. "But you told us about Father and Aunty Marion...?"

Rhodric turned to her, and sternly answered, "You had to know your story. Your true story. What you now know belongs to you because it is yours. Everybody, human or selkie, should know their own story, but not every story is everyone's to tell."

Isla stayed quiet a moment or two after that as she tried to work out what he meant. In silence, they watched as Dina was joined by the curious selkie pup Isla had played with. It splashed Hamish playfully, and Hamish, uncertainly at first, timidly splashed it back. Their game escalated, and soon Hamish was jumping around, trying to splash the pup before it wriggled away. Soon, he was jumping so far, he lost his footing. Seemingly without realising, he was swimming after the pup, diving and chasing it as Isla had.

Isla laughed, happy to see her brother finally at play. His head bobbed up out of the water, face registering surprise at how far he was in the pool. "I'm swimming!" he shouted, just before the seal pup splashed an enormous spray of water over Hamish's head. Spluttering, he ducked under the water, and the seal squealed as Hamish tweaked its flipper.

Rhodric said softly to Isla, "You see, you are both of the sea. You belong."

Pride, happiness and exhilaration filled her for a moment, but she sobered quickly as her thoughts took her away from the island which they had been brought to.

"But what about Father?" She whispered. "And Mother? And Aunty Marion? What will happen to them?"

Rhodric exhaled slowly, his eyes not leaving the pools where the swimmers were. "I cannae tell you that. We have been looking for sightings of your father ever since we felt the sea loosen our powers here. But it is like this island, not visible to those who aren't supposed to see it. That's what it feels like. As if he is being concealed.

"As for your mother. It is likely that she will be restored once your father is found..."

Isla frowned. "What do you mean, 'likely'?"

Rhodric didn't reply.

Finally, Isla asked, "And what about Aunty Marion? Who stole her selkie skin?"

Rhodric shook his head. "We have not found it, and neither has she. She searches for it still, I believe but less now that you have come to the island."

With a pang, Isla wondered, if her aunt did find the selkie skin, would she leave them? Then, they would truly not have anyone...

Rhodric repeated, gently, as if reading her mind, "She does not go so much in her searching now Isla."

She muttered, "But this is her home."

"As it is with you."

Dina wandered out of the water and came to join them, shaking off the water droplets which she had been unceremoniously splashed with just moments before.

"I do not think any more swimming lessons are

needed," she announced. "He and Alken are getting on just fine."

"Can I... can I look around?" Isla ventured. She was curious now, to find out more about where her father and aunt had come from. There was so much that she didn't know.

"Dina will show you," Rhodric gestured. The girls both hesitated, Isla looking towards Hamish, and Dina towards her guardian, with reproach or not Isla couldn't tell.

"Hamish will be fine. Go." He motioned again, and Dina sighed, almost imperceptibly, and began to walk away. Isla wasn't certain whether she ought to be following or not, until Dina turned, asking "Well, are you coming?"

Isla nodded, and jogged to catch up.

Dina began to talk as soon as Isla was level with her. "We came through the main entrance to the selkie colony through there," she pointed to the cavern.

Isla asked, "And it's hidden to anyone who comes to the island? Might I have been able to find it if I'd looked the first time? Yesterday?"

Dina shrugged, "But you were not brave enough to go through the cave."

"*You* just left me here. I didn't know!"

Dina shrugged again. "But you are here now."

Isla couldn't think what to say to that. She found the selkie girl to be very odd indeed. She tried again, "So... the island. It's only visible to people who are welcome here? But how do people know if they are welcome?"

"Those with selkie blood are welcome, and they are the only ones with eyes to see."

"What, you mean that nobody else can see the island? Even if they go through the fog?"

Dina replied, slightly impatiently, "Of course not."

Isla asked, persistent in finding out the answers to her questions, "But Rhodric seemed worried about whoever it is that's out there... whatever it is that is making my mother... not be right."

Dina spoke gravely after a moment's pause, "Great magic *could* discover us, it is true. But so far, nothing has breached our borders. So, it is safer for us here, with our remaining protection from the sea, is it not, than where you live on land."

They carried on walking, past the immense structure. Dina pointed. "That is our seat of power for the King or Queen."

Isla looked up, amazed. "My father lived there?"

Dina nodded, "And his sister, before she went to try and retrieve him."

Isla's face darkened, "She had no right!"

They advanced past the steps. They were even larger up close than they had appeared from the cavern entrance. Boulders formed the base of the steps and upon closer inspection Isla could see the intricate carvings which had been etched into each. It seemed, to Isla, as if each step told its own story. Dina beckoned to begin climbing. She pointed out to Isla as they climbed, "There you can find the history of our people. Selkies are proud of our storytelling, and of our ability to recall our own stories." She showed Isla the first step. It was a woman, unlike any type of etching or sculpture that Isla had seen before. "This is Nulla, the Sea Mother. She gave birth to selkie-kind." As Isla looked closer, she saw with fascination that the image showed a lady ornately carved, standing over the sea. Her hands were held over the waters, drops falling from them. The drops hitting the water were seal shaped.

"How..." Isla ventured, and Dina broke in, somewhat

proudly, "Her blood gave us life. With every drop of blood, a selkie was formed when her blood mingled with the sea. She gave the sea life, and balance."

Curious, Isla asked, "Where is she now?"

Dina frowned. "Nulla is no more. She came, and brought life to the oceans, and then she departed. No selkie knows where, or when. Stories say that she was a mortal human, and that she so longed for children that she was not able to have, that she made a pact with the sea. The sea gave her selkie children, and she then gave them back to the sea. She was able to see her children when they took human form, but the rest of the time, they belonged with the sea. She loved the sea, and the selkies say that this love made our existence possible."

Isla listened intently. She had never heard such stories before. She wasn't sure whether to believe what Dina was saying, but there she stood, listening to a selkie girl. She'd seen the impossible be made possible. If *that* were real, then surely anything was possible.

"But, if she couldn't see her children unless they were human...and selkies can only be on land for a small time before they cannot return... then, how...?"

"The sea gave the selkies this land, to be on as they chose, human form or seal form. Nulla was given her home here, to be with her children. And for many years she was happy. But her children had more of the sea in them than she had expected, and eventually she saw that her children loved the sea more than they loved her. She drifted, and found love with a fisherman, from the land. She left the island. Once she had left, she was not able to return. She had no selkie blood, and she could not find her way back in."

Isla whispered softly, "That is so sad."

Dina shrugged, "'Tis but a story, no more. It is not known whether it is truth, or whether it is a mere story seal folk tell to their children, warning them of the fickleness of humans."

Isla flushed, "But my mother..."

"Took our King and protector away from us." Dina retorted angrily. She walked up further steps, bypassing many carvings in her anger. Each seemed to show a different king or queen, and the story of their reign – at least, that was what Isla saw very quickly as she struggled to keep pace with her guide.

"Wait!" Isla puffed as she skipped to keep up the pace, finding the incline that they were racing up difficult to manage. Dina stopped at a step; it was not the last in the ascension, but it was the last step which was carved. The rest were blank.

Dina pointed. "You see? These are for future kings and queens," she said, confirming Isla's theory. "This one, this is your father's reign."

Isla stopped and examined the carvings intently. There, she saw a good likeness of her father, in both human and, she supposed, seal form. A crown was on his head. He was looking away from the island, to the shore. Then she looked at another frieze. She froze in horror at what it depicted; many selkies, in their seal form, were shown dead or dying. Although there was no colour in the carvings, she sensed the violence, and that the pool emanating from the bodies was not water.

"What happened?" Isla asked, quietly. She held no anger in her now.

"Once your father left the selkie folk," Dina replied softly, her voice tinged with sadness, "the protection which lay over our land was weakened. Your aunt did not know that she did not bear the protection bestowed upon your father, for, they both did not realise that he was still rightfully King. There was an attack. Our borders were not breached, but our sentinels and warriors were caught unawares as they investigated rumours of a threat out beyond our borders. All perished. Your aunt was able to stave off the worst and strengthen the bonds of protection around this very island, but it was too late for those who had not been within these waters. That was when she realised that the sea had not recognised the passing of power. If the King had been here, still, our people would not have been slaughtered." A tear rolled down Dina's face, although her voice remained steady. Something clicked in Isla's mind.

"Rhodric said your parents were lost," she said softly.

Dina nodded, brushing her face clear. "My parents were amongst those out beyond our borders. They had named me 'Murdina'; it means 'sea warrior'. I would have followed them to be one of our people's guardians. But we do not have a warrior-kind anymore. They were... the best," she whispered. "There is no-one left to fight. And our enemies grow stronger. We are all left here, to be contained within our own borders for as long as the protection holds. But now, it grows weaker every day."

Isla looked down to where her brother was still playing with the seal pups. She felt a pang, as she realised that the selkies down below could be the same as those which she saw carved in stone before her.

"I'm sorry." Isla didn't know what to say. She was suddenly conflicted. She and Hamish were here, and there were so many of the selkie-folk who weren't. And Dina's parents. All because her father had turned his back on his people to follow her mother. Guilt flooded her.

The older selkie girl touched Isla's arm gently. "'Tis not your fault."

Isla nodded, mutely. Then said, "But if my father had..."

Dina shook her head. "He did not know. How could he? And then, it was too late. And with Lady Marion... she did not know that she would not be able to return. The fault lies with the one who attacked us."

Suddenly, Isla could see the girl's warrior heritage clearly visible in her ferocity.

"I *will* find who is behind this threat to us!" Dina promised. So fierce did she look and sound, that Isla was extremely glad that the selkie's fury was not directed at her. She felt sure that anyone in the path of that anger would be immensely unfortunate.

CHAPTER 12

THE PROMISE

As Isla watched the activity below, peaceful and playful combined, she wondered if this was the life that her father had known before he left. She knew how much her parents loved each other, and she couldn't help but wonder whether it had been worth it. Whether she and Hamish had been worth it. But, she reflected, her father must have thought so. He had done everything he could to protect them, and she remembered the passion and conviction in his voice when he announced his decision to go and join the fight that was mounting. Her mother had not understood, and had stood there, motionless and tears forming in her eyes. But her father had remained resolute. Isla wondered whether he had been so adamant to join because of what had happened to his own people once he had left. If his part in the war would help to protect those whom he had left his people for. In that moment, she knew, that to her father, they had been worth it.

She turned and caught Dina looking at her. The older girl was watching her, and she was, for the first time, looking at her with genuine warmth. No longer the mischievous smile, indifference or guarded expression. She said slowly, "We've both lost people. I... I don't have... There are not others my age here... I don't know how to..."

Isla smiled. "I'd like to be your friend." She hesitated. "If that's alright?"

Dina nodded, smiling back. "I would like that."

"Good," Isla replied. "There's nobody on the island my age either."

Awkwardly at first, they smiled at each other, and then genuine smiles appeared on each girl's face. A solid friendship was born in that moment.

Dina led Isla back down the steps. As they wandered, the selkie girl pointed out the areas for agriculture, of the fish pools, where the selkies cultivated different schools of fish for food and for introduction to the wider ocean waters once they were fully grown. The fact that the selkie folk were working at all astonished Isla.

"Well, who else is going to look after the sea, if we do not?" Dina asked with a laugh. "Humans?"

They walked through the rock pools, swimming where it got deeper, and they dived into the depths. Dina transformed into her seal form and began a series of flips and circles in the pool. It was hypnotic, and almost dance-like, Isla thought, as she watched. But there was form and purpose in it. She pictured a horde of seals imitating the movements which her new friend was making, and she was immediately reminded of the drills and manoeuvres which she had witnessed taking place through the streets of London when the soldiers marched through, on their way to embark to the front. Battle drills.

Resurfacing, Isla asked the question hesitantly, as, she thought, it could mean something entirely different in this new world that she and Hamish had stumbled into.

Dina nodded, bashful but proud. "I learnt it from Rhodric. The training drills that all warrior selkies learn. But I am the only one who trains. The others are... farmers... mothers."

"But how will you fight? If you need to?" Isla asked.

A determined expression settled on Dina's face. "We must find Lady Marion's selkie skin. If she is returned to us, we will have better protection now that the King has..." she paused, suddenly remembering who she was talking to. "...Disappeared. For, surely once she is restored to us, we will be able to finally root out this creature and its fiendish power and be done with it for good. And it *will* answer to us for what it has done," she continued fiercely.

Isla turned to her, and knew that she had to do something, anything, to help protect this island. For, it was partly hers too, she realised.

"I'll help," she said, sounding braver than she felt. "Hamish and I will be able to look on the island, on Arraway, better than you can, I think. We've explored it so much, now that we know what we're looking for, we'll *have* to be able to find it! Besides," she added, with vigour of her own, "if it helps our mother get better, then we'll do whatever we need to do!"

Dina nodded, and said firmly, "Agreed."

Their pact made, they continued exploring. A family of seals was playing in front of one of the caverns, with the barked consent of the matriarch who was watching over her pup's excited play with Hamish and the other pups. Proudly, she waved a flipper, inviting the girls into the cave. Out from the rock pool, the cavern floor sloped upwards, leading to a raised sleeping area. Dina pointed out the tapestries which Isla had noted on their arrival.

"It is a tradition, passed down from mother to daughter, or father to son," she said, showing Isla the detailed patterns, which ran across each. "Legend has it that this was Nulla's earth gift to her children. Selkies may not need things like this in the sea, but on land, we like to be comfortable. And selkies like beautiful objects, so we learned to make them. Each family has their own pattern, the weave of which is passed down to future generations."

At Isla's questioning look, she added, "I do not know what my family pattern is. I was not old enough to be taught."

Isla stood, admiring the selkie's handiwork, and the loom standing in the corner of the sleeping space. She guessed that the weaving must be undertaken whilst the selkies were in their human form. She asked, trying to tactfully change the subject. "Is there not a kitchen in a selkie home?"

Dina looked at her blankly. "What is a kitchen?" She asked, puzzled.

"Oh. Well, it's a room where you make meals. You have an oven, a cooker top..." Isla saw that the selkie was still confused. She thought hard; she'd never had to explain what a kitchen was before!

"When you have food that needs to be cooked, like meat, or fish or... vegetables. And you need to make them better to eat!"

Dina looked at Isla as if that were the silliest thing that she'd ever heard.

"Why would you need to make a fish better to eat?" She asked, laughing. "You catch it, and then, you eat it! And that is the best way to eat a fish."

Isla looked at her, horrified. "You eat it... raw?" She made a face, and Dina suddenly looked equally shocked, and replied, "You mean, you *don't?*"

Isla shook her head. "We just never have. Humans don't really eat raw food. Maybe vegetables... sometimes."

"What are 'vegetables'?"

Bewildered at having to explain the everyday things which she took for granted, Isla searched for an explanation. "They're out of the ground. Plants that you can eat. They're green sometimes, and people say they're good for you. But not a lot of people actually like eating them!"

"Ah," Dina nodded, understanding brightening her face. "Like seaweed."

Isla raised her eyebrows but nodded slowly. "I suppose so." The selkie way of life was strange indeed she thought.

"But where do you eat? We have dining areas in our houses, where we all eat together." Isla asked, trying to find a parallel to the way of life she knew.

"We fish, and we do sometimes eat together, especially the pups. But mostly, we eat as we catch when we're out at sea, in the open waters. But, the older ones, we hunt together, so, I suppose we eat together also," came the reply.

Isla's curiosity was piqued. "How old are you? I can't tell." She'd guessed that the girl must be older than her, but she couldn't tell by how much.

"I will see fifteen turns of the tide when the sun grows cold."

Isla was confused. "But the tide turns each day. No, twice a day."

Dina shook her head. "The tide changes. Each year, it sees a slightly different pattern. Each passing year we call a 'turn of the tide'. So, I will be fifteen years old, in human terms... in the twelfth month as you count it."

"Oh, I didn't know... I'm going to be fourteen turns of the tide in two months."

Dina laughed, but not unkindly. "You will *see* fourteen turns of the tide."

"Oh, yes." Isla blushed, feeling a little embarrassed. "What do you mean, 'when the sun turns cold'? Do you have different months to us?"

Dina nodded. "We have four seasons, as I believe do you, but we measure them by the strength of the sun. First comes the birth of the sun, then the peak of the sun, then the wane, and finally the coldness of the sun."

"Oh," Isla said again. "I was born in September... the ninth month... the wane of the sun?" Dina nodded, "A time betwixt the peak and the wane of the sun." It was appropriate, Isla thought, as she now found herself caught between worlds, why not between two seasons of the sun?

They walked back out of the selkie cavern and through the settlement to rejoin Hamish and Rhodric. As they walked, the sheen of Dina's selkie skin stirred a thought in Isla's mind. Shyly, she asked, "If Hamish and I are half selkie... do we... do we have selkie skin too?"

She waited, hopefully, before Dina shook her head sympathetically. "Your father, Lord Duncan, is a selkie, yes. But your mother is not. As you were born to a human mother, you were not born with a selkie skin. 'Tis not how it works. Only true born selkies, those with two selkie parents, are born with their selkie skins. I'm sorry. It is a gift we do not take lightly. It gifts us the whole realm of the sea, if we were to choose to, or be able to," she added darkly, "go beyond our borders."

Isla sighed. She had guessed as much, but secretly had hoped that there may be hidden selkie skins for her and Hamish, somewhere, that she might be able to use to change form as the selkies before them did.

"What happens if I were to swim with you, with the selkies, in the sea? I can swim – we both can," she said, pointing to Hamish.

Dina shook her head, uncertainly. "I do not know the extent to which you can keep up with us if we were to go on a full hunt. We always go in seal form, and I have not seen humans swim as we do. You can swim, well for a human. Your selkie blood helps you in the water. But I do not know. It is unusual. I do not remember stories of humans coming to the island before or joining with us in a hunt."

"But there have been others?" Isla ventured. "Like me and Hamish?"

Dina nodded slowly. "So we are told. But not for many, many turnings of the tide. Before even Rhodric's memory goes back. But, there, the selkies always came back. The call of the sea was too great. They could not stand to be away from it."

Isla frowned, not able to believe what she was being told. "You mean, they left their children behind?"

Dina shrugged. "That is how it has always been. They did not wish to, I think, but their nature did not allow them to remain landbound for many years. It is hard for a selkie to bear, being apart from the sea for any great length of time."

"But our father..."

"Does not follow the normal selkie way," Dina said simply. "It was not understood. Not by many. Especially not his father. The old King. Murdoch was his name. He raged and raged for days, weeks, months. He became mad, and went to fight the invasive force by himself, so enraged and battle-blind was he. He did not survive. Your aunt was truly left alone, and that is, perhaps, why she was so determined for Lord Duncan to return. Why she took it upon herself to fetch him back."

They had reached the rock pools where Hamish was still splashing his way back and forth, grinning from ear to ear. He got out of the water, dripping wet, and cried out, "Look, Isla! I've been swimming! I'm *good!*"

Isla nodded, smiling back at him. She called out, "We need to head back soon Hamish. We don't want to let Aunty Marion worry. Again," she added guiltily.

Hamish nodded and waved a goodbye to his newfound friends.

Isla turned to Rhodric. "We will look for Marion's selkie skin on our island," she promised. "We'll try to help." Rhodric inclined his head, acknowledging the promise made.

"You are always welcome, children of the Calder Sea. May the waves be always at your back."

Isla nodded, uncertain as to how to respond to what she thought was a formal selkie farewell. She heard Dina murmur behind her, and she spoke aloud the words which she had heard her say.

"And may the sea keep you and guard you."

Rhodric smiled, and bowed as they left, following Dina back through the cavern which they had come through.

Isla and Hamish pushed the boat off the shore and hopped in. Dina transformed, and, in seal form, she swam out, leading the boat back towards where Patch was still waiting for them.

Hamish turned to his sister, eyes shining. "Isla, can you believe it? Father's a King! Wait until we tell Mother! And he'll be happy I can swim now, right Isla?"

She nodded, smiling. Then, slowly said, "But, Hamish,

Mother doesn't know about Father. And we need to help Aunty Marion find her selkie skin to help the selkies. If she does, then Mother will get better."

Hamish nodded, determination and then doubt crossing his face. "We'll find it Isla... but will Aunty Marion leave us if she gets her selkie skin back?"

Isla didn't know what to say. Thinking, she said, "I don't know. I think she has to help the island. Her people. And Mother will be herself again. I don't know Hamish. But is it fair for us to keep her?"

Hamish's eyes filled with tears. "But I don't *want* her to go!"

Isla smiled sadly, and said, "Well, we need to find it first, don't we? Besides, what about your friends on the island? They need her too."

He thought about it for a few moments and wiped away the tears which had formed in his eyes. "We'll help Aunty Marion find her selkie skin," he announced in a shaky voice. "But Isla. How do we tell her that we went exploring... won't we get in trouble?"

Isla shook her head. She hadn't thought about that. "Well," she said brightly, hiding the uncertainty that she felt. "It's about time Aunty Marion told us the truth, don't you think? We've had enough secrets."

CHAPTER 13

MARION'S STORY

Back on the shores of Arraway, Dina waited until Isla and Hamish had hidden the boat back where they had found it. They waved as she swam back out, leaving them to make their way back to the cottage.

Finding the little tower of pebbles which marked the entrance to the secret passageway, Isla slid open the door, and they made their way up the long, winding staircase, following the torchlight which Isla was shining up the stairs ahead of them.

They were very conscious of each creak and groan of the floorboards under their feet and winced each time they reached a particularly noisy step. By the time they reached the entrance to the loft space, they were exhausted both from the climb and from trying to keep quiet.

Isla was tense, and crept into the attic space gingerly, hoping that they would not be discovered.

The attic remained as dark and dusty as they had left it. Isla shone the torch around, and Hamish scouted around to see if there were any other footsteps on the floor. He shook his head. "I think it's just us," he whispered, grinning, white teeth clearly showing in the dim lighting.

"Ok," Isla whispered. "You go first. If anyone is out there, Aunty Marion won't think it's suspicious if you come out of strange places. She's probably used it by now!"

Hamish stuck his tongue out at his sister but went softly up to the hatch and pressed his ear against the door. He listened, intently, for a few moments, then, very carefully, he pressed the hatch door open. Isla hung back, having switched the torchlight off. She waited, as Hamish darted through the opening. Mere seconds later, he poked his head back through, blocking the light.

"Come on," he hissed. "The coast is clear."

Isla grinned. They'd done it! She crept through the hatch door where her brother had gone, and once through, gently closed the hatch back up. Hamish pushed his bed back into place.

"There," he said, not without some satisfaction. "And nobody knows where it is now.... Apart from us," he added as an afterthought.

"And Hob. Maybe. Probably," Isla murmured, thoughtfully.

"What do you mean?" Hamish piped up at once. "Why do you think Hob knows? Why did he never tell us about the secret passageway?"

Isla dusted her face off, saying as she did so, "He gave me the clue which made me look at the dollhouse. I think Hob knows a lot about what goes on here, on the island. And I bet he knows about Aunty Marion too. But he said that he's not allowed to talk about some things."

"What do you mean? Who said he can't talk about anything? Aunty Marion?" Hamish peppered his sister with questions, one by one, not waiting for a response. "And do you think he knows how we can help Mother?" was his final question.

Isla shrugged and held her hands up. "Woah, one at a time! I think it's some kind of brownie code," she said, remembering what Hob had told her in the kitchen. "It didn't make much sense to me at the time, but I get the impression that there are some kind of rules in place that the brownies have to follow, and I don't know whether they're only allowed to talk about brownies, not the rest of the island or sea. Maybe, especially, the sea."

"Oh." Hamish looked puzzled. "But Hob tells me everything."

Isla raised a questioning eyebrow at him.

"Well, maybe not, I don't know," Hamish muttered. "But I reckon he *would*. We're friends! And surely, he wouldn't keep anything from us that could make Mother better, right Isla?"

Isla was struck by one of the questions which Hamish had asked. "Hmmm," she said absently. "What's that Hamish?"

He threw his hands up in the air, making a loud sound of exasperation as he did so.

"Oh, sorry. What?" Isla asked, focusing her attention back on him. "No, wait, you asked whether Hob can talk about Aunty Marion or not. I don't know. But maybe he might know something about her selkie skin," Isla mused.

Hamish looked horrified. "Hob wouldn't have taken it! He's my friend!"

Isla put a placatory hand on her brother's arm. "No, I meant, he might be able to help us find it. Maybe."

Suddenly, the sound of the front door opening and closing startled them. "Quick!" Hamish whispered. "Aunty Marion's back!"

Isla shushed him, and then said. "Alright, quick. Wipe your face and go down to where Mother is. Or the kitchen. You know, where you always are!"

They could hear Marion singing to herself in the hallway. Wiping his face frantically, Hamish rushed down the stairs as stealthily as he could. For once without his tell-tale crashes and bangs, Isla gratefully thought to herself.

Her aunt's humming didn't falter, but Isla heard it quieten a little as she poked her head into the living room where Penny lay. Isla opened the door carefully. Peeking out, she looked for any sign of her aunt. Seeing none, she tiptoed down the stairs as fast as she could, as quietly as she could.

Once at the bottom of the staircase, Isla ran into the playroom and collapsed onto a chair, adrenaline coursing through her veins. Gaining her breath back, she brought a book out of the bookcase and sat, waiting.

Sure enough, soon the door opened, and Marion cheerfully called out, "Had a good day Isla? I've just seen Mrs. MacGregor. She was asking after you and Hamish, and your mother of course. She's sent along some goodies."

She held aloft a small white paper bag, out of the top of which Isla could just about make out the shape of a sugar mouse.

Isla tried to smile, but her stomach was doing somersaults, and all she could manage was a slight grimace. She cleared her throat, nervously. "That was nice of her."

Marion smiled, nodding, and looked over to her. "What have you found to read? Anything interesting?"

She came in and looked closer at the title. She blinked. "Where did you find that?" she asked; her cheerful tone had dimmed slightly, Isla thought.

"It was on the bookshelf. Didn't you put it there, Aunty

Marion?"

Marion slowly shook her head, not taking her eyes from the front cover of the book. *"Scottish Myths and Legends.* No. I did not."

Isla plucked up the courage and looked her aunt square in the eye. "We've been finding out a lot about all sorts... brownies... selkies..."

Marion sat down in a chair, opposite Isla.

"I see," she said slowly. "And what have you learnt?"

Isla took a deep breath and blurted out "We know. We know that Father is a selkie. And that you're a selkie. And that you tried to get Father to stay with the selkies and not go onto land and marry Mother, and that you got stuck here, and can't go back. And... and we met Rhodric. And we saw the island. I'm sorry that we went out on the sea, Aunty Marion, but now we know." Isla finished lamely, unsure of what she had just said in her haste to confess and see what her aunt had to say.

She was met with silence for a few moments, and then, Marion said quietly again, "I see." And then, "I suppose Hamish found the brownie."

Isla nodded, confused. Why wasn't her aunt talking about what she had just discovered. She couldn't tell whether Marion was angry or what emotions were being hinted at by her words.

"Meddling brownies," Marion muttered.

Isla spoke up immediately, "Hob didn't tell us."

Marion raised her eyebrows. "Hob is it?" Isla bit her lip, uncertain whether she should have said that.

"I can take a guess or two as to where that book that you are reading has come from," Marion continued. "So, you know. I suppose you think badly of me, if you think that I went to try and stop Duncan from going with Penny."

Isla didn't answer. She couldn't disagree with any honesty, so she just waited for Marion to continue.

"Let me begin at the beginning, perhaps that would be best. Then you can decide what you think of me. So, selkies. We are a peaceful folk by nature, and we hold dominion in these waters. The island which I presume you visited has been the home of the selkies for time beyond memory. It may be hard to understand, as you have known nothing but the human world, but the selkies, the water, the sea, it is all-encompassing. It is our life. And whilst we have the land to settle on if we so choose, no selkie, well almost no selkie, can abide to be far from the water. It is truly all we know, and all we wish to. And that is the way it has always been. The sea has given us much – it offers us protection and, together, we work with the sea to protect it in turn. We cultivate where we can, and prune where it is needed. And so, the balance is maintained in the Calder Sea. The seat of power has long lain with our family. And Duncan, he received the kingship. I believe, with human rulers, it is due to age, or to the first-born male, is it not?"

Isla nodded, enthralled by her aunt's story. She had learnt some from Dina and Rhodric about her father, but she realised gradually, there was much more to learn.

"Well, it is not so amongst our selkie tribe. Power and authority are passed from generation to generation, but not upon the death of the leader, but at the direction of the sea. It is the sea's choice, in the end, who it chooses to lead."

"How does it choose?" Isla asked, despite herself, too curious to wait for her aunt to finish the story.

"Well, my father, your grandfather..."

"Murdoch" Isla remembered. Marion nodded. "Yes, Murdoch. He was King of the selkies for a great number of years. And as the years passed, he grew increasingly proud, and eventually saw himself as the reason for our people's success and power in the sea. For we were a tribe well-renowned for our craftmanship, of our skill as warriors, and our ability as farmers. We were respected, even admired, and feared. For peace was our nature, but we were well able to defend ourselves and our territory.

"And we did well. We looked after what we had, and our territory was teeming with life; our resources were rich, and we were the envy of the seas. And therein lay the problem. For Murdoch wanted more. He wanted us to expand our territories. Conquer expanses of sea which were not ours. And he began to use his gifted power to do so. He stirred up the sea, against its will, and sent hunting parties out, and he accompanied them, stirring the waters, unsteadying the balance which we had so long protected and maintained. And the sea retaliated. It took Murdoch's power as leader away from him. He accompanied his raiding party, and they were not successful. They fled back to our waters, and he retreated into himself, slowly becoming bitter. Madness eventually took over. Duncan and I, we had always resisted what our father was trying to do. Duncan understood that the sea was not ours to control, but we are its custodians. He tried, time and again, to change our father's way of thinking. But each time he was met with Murdoch's unshaken belief in his own supremacy. It was as if he had forgotten that it was the sea which had bestowed upon him his position and power.

"The way that it had always been with our people is that leadership is passed down whilst the former leader is still alive. And then, the next leader is raised up to be the king or queen of the selkies, with the guidance and support of the former leader to settle them into the new era of power. But it was not so with Duncan and Murdoch. As has always been the tradition as heirs of the former leader, Duncan and I were brought by the sea to the waters where leadership is chosen and transferred. Murdoch did not accompany us. His power had already been taken back by the sea. He was angry and had no joy in our future, either of us, as the new leader of the tribe. The sea tested us both."

"How?" Isla asked, eagerly.

"The sea is a living power, it is always moving, always present; it supports all life within it, and it is part of us, part of our blood. Our connection to the sea, as selkies, allows the sea to understand, to... not communicate as you would see it, but rather to determine our characters. It was close, or so we have been told by those who have seen many whom the sea has chosen. I believe that the sea recognised Duncan's regard for it, and indeed the sea had borne witness to the times when Duncan had tried to stand in Murdoch's way, even though he was thwarted in his aims and deeds. Both of us were content to lead, or to be led, as we had all been taught and brought to expect as we had grown. For, it is ultimately the sea to form the choice and to raise up the leader. Our family, our bloodline, has traditionally held the seat of leadership, as I believe we have mostly recognised the balance required. And, so, Duncan was chosen. I was glad for him. I set myself to living in the colony as a subject rather than monarch. I met another selkie, from a different tribe who ultimately decided to join our tribe, and we began to live within the selkie colony. A new family. We had a child."

Isla gaped, uncertain as to how to respond. Marion's eyes held the clue. Tears began to form, and Marion paused a moment before continuing.

"We were happy. Besides the fact that Murdoch remained cantankerous and mad, he stayed out of the way, not giving Duncan the advice he may have needed had Murdoch been a different sort of leader. And then, one day, Duncan was patrolling in the waters close to our boundaries. He came close to shore, and there it was that he spied the most beautiful creature he had ever seen."

"Mother," Isla whispered. Marion nodded.

"Tuppence was, is, one of the most beautiful human women I have ever met. Her very spirit was so joy-filled, vibrant and full of life, Duncan was lost. Not only drawn to her by her beauty, but her very nature spoke to him. In human form, he spoke to her, and learnt that she was a stranger, visiting the isles. He decided to follow her. You see, Duncan's love for your mother was so strong, he was even able to leave behind all his ties, to his people, to these lands and to the Calder Sea. The sea had seen the arrogance of Murdoch, and the selflessness of Duncan, and had weighed that in the balance. It chose the leader it believed would put the sea above all else. But it had not taken into consideration Duncan's love for your mother, which, in the end, outweighed his sense of duty to his people. And so, he left. I was happy for him. Truly, I was. And I was ready to take on the leadership which Duncan left to me.

"But, as it turned out, it was not his to give. The sea did not consider Duncan to be truly gone, so his power as leader never truly transferred. Once he had left, something stirred in the waters around our own. It sensed weakness.

We were on high alert and knew that our borders were not the peaceful place that they once had been. Fearing a threat from those whom we had antagonised under Murdoch's leadership, I sent a party out. Our finest warriors, many of whom had been the heroes of our tribe. My own love was amongst those who I sent.

"We waited for their return. But no selkie came back to us. I tested my powers as leader for the first time, but the sea did not respond. Instead, news of a sea boiled with death came back to us. We never again saw those whom we had sent."

Isla whispered, horrified, "I'm sorry."

Marion inclined her head. "As was I. And enraged. I sent a follow-up party, which I accompanied, to the tribe we thought responsible. We were met with denial of any knowledge, save for a foreshadowing which they had received. A selkie female met us, she was long in tooth, advanced in years, and her eyes were no longer able to see what lay around us. However, she was able to see much deeper. A darkness was rising, she said. And it had not finished. All my rage disappeared, and panic set in. I was so afraid, Isla. You see, I knew deep in my heart that our island, even as protected as it was, was vulnerable to further attack. I did not think that we would win. My child was all that was left to me. And I would not risk that life.

"I informed the council of my decision to retrieve Duncan. I did not care about his happiness, I am sorry to say, Isla. For, my love of our people washed away the joy I had once wished him. I remained nearly the last of our bloodline still with our people. I entrusted my child to the care of the selkies on the island and I gave what blessing I could, powerless as I was, and passed over what charge I had to the council until my return, which, at the time, I believed to be imminent.

"But, as you see, it was not to be. I took on my human form and hid my selkie skin as I came ashore. I searched for Duncan, but I could not find him. I looked all over, and eventually discovered that he and Penny had crossed over to the mainland. I could not think of anywhere I would wish to be less, but I was determined to find him. I knew that the only way that I could catch up to him in time to ask him to return would be if I were to swim to the mainland, in selkie form of course. I returned to the beach, to the place where I had hidden my selkie skin, and it was not there."

Isla broke in, unable to contain herself. "Who took it?" Marion shook her head. "I do not know. I was not able to discover it. Desperate, I watched the sun setting, and calculated how much time I had left before I would not be able to return, in my human form. It was not a great issue for me, for I had no desire to be landbound again. And yet, I had no means of returning to my home. Even if I were to locate a boat to row to the island, a selkie without its skin is not permitted to enter." She replied to Isla's unanswered question. "It is considered by the sea to be a rejection of the gifts which it has bestowed, and so, a selkie without its skin is not permitted to find its way back."

"That's not fair!" Isla burst out angrily! "Why should the sea get to decide? And how can it decide that anyway? Also, it's not fair! Your skin was stolen!"

"Have you ever seen the sea in a midst of a storm, Isla? When the waves crash, and the waters roil, and the wind whips through the current and still cannot change the direction of the tide?"

Isla nodded, vividly remembering the storm she had

been caught in so recently.

"The sea has many phases, many faces. It is wild, savage, unpredictable, peaceful, tranquil, turbulent, terrible, beautiful. It does not obey the human laws of what is right and wrong. It simply is. And so, it gives us life, or takes it when it chooses. It is not cruel. It is only what it is. And that is something that Duncan never fully appreciated, I think," Marion said, considering as she did so.

"The sea is capricious. It does not serve the purpose of others and does not obey. But the duality of right and wrong, that is the humanity of the selkie. And that is the balance that we may bring. A self-serving selkie, or a selkie which accommodates the whims of the sea too greatly – both are evils in their own way. One is of a selkie's own design, and the other is not through a deliberate act of will, but rather a deed of inaction which may lead to a great many unintended consequences."

"Like my father," Isla ventured, questioning. "He left the sea to act as it chose to do, rather than stay with it."

Marion nodded. "Although he did not realise he did so. The foothold of power which he left was taken advantage of. I still do not know by whom.

"As I was searching for my selkie skin, lost in a strange land, among the humans whom I now care for greatly, but at that time could understand nothing of, my father Murdoch and the remainder of those loyal to him took it upon themselves, guided by the madness of the former king, to seek out the darkness which had already taken my love from me."

"What happened?" Isla hardly dared to ask

"They too disappeared. And the power grew deeper, it seemed. With every selkie that disappeared, the threat crept closer. I did not find this out until much time had passed.

166

But the island stood safe. The strongholds held, and the barriers, our last line of defence, they held still. I was unable to return, and it turned out that Duncan, well, he was soon to be a father. I found out once I managed to communicate with him in the strange ways, as I found them, that were available to me at the time." Marion sighed, and Isla saw that her aunt carried great sadness in her.

"I had word that my child was lost to this world," she whispered. "My beautiful baby. Taken sick with the protection weakened. And did not recover."

Isla reached out to give her aunt a hug, which Marion tentatively accepted before continuing, "After that, I accepted my fate here. I learnt the ways of the island. It seemed as if the land heard my sorrow and lament, for it provided me with the cottage that we are in today. And Basil and Billie," she said with a shaky laugh. "They were sent to protect me. From what, I did not, and still do not, know. But they seem to have done their duty thus far, do you not think, lass?

"I learnt to dull the grief that I held, the longing for my home, learning the human ways, of cooking, of food – so different from our own ways within the selkie colony. The plants which grow in abundance here, I learnt to cultivate and grow to suit my own purposes. 'Garden' – we do not have that term; did you know that?"

Isla shook her head. "What did Father say, or do, when he found out?" she asked.

"What was there for him to do?" Marion shrugged. "Any other selkie... I do not know. Stories have told us that they returned to their waters, to the sea and to their people. But Duncan is not like other selkies. He would not abandon you." Marion said firmly, looking directly at her niece.

"He loves you so much, each of you. There was no way that Duncan would ever choose to leave you, even for the sake of his people. After all, if he returned, he would not have been able to return to you. Not for a great deal of time. He would have missed you growing up, Isla. And Hamish. Hamish would not have been born."

Isla gulped. She hadn't thought of it like that. It suddenly all became a lot less black and white in her mind.

"I'm glad Father didn't go back," she eventually whispered, feeling incredibly guilty and selfish as she thought about the consequences which her father had unleashed through his decision. To her surprise, her aunt smiled at her, understanding clear in her grey eyes.

"I know Isla. And it is not wrong. I learnt that, eventually." She squeezed Isla's hand. "And I am glad that you and Hamish are both here and have found the secrets which I have been unable to tell you. And you see, it is not so bad as I had feared. The borders have held. My people are safe. Their way of life has changed, but they are safe where they remain. And, I have gotten to know my beautiful niece and my very charming nephew. How could I wish differently?"

The warmth with which she spoke made Isla certain that she genuinely cared for them. Isla nodded, but inwardly she was in turmoil. Marion noticed.

"What is it?"

Isla swallowed; her mouth suddenly had gone dry. "Well, we were on the island today. The selkie island..."

Marion nodded, encouraging her to continue.

"And Rhodric... he said that ever since Father has gone missing... you know, now... that the protection is fading around the island." Seeing Marion's face pale at her words, she forged ahead. "And, Aunty Marion, Rhodric said that Mother being, well, not Mother – that's because Father's protection over her has gone."

Isla recounted what Rhodric had said, and that she had swum in the selkie pool to restore her own protection. Marion frowned. "I suppose I should stop swimming in the island lochs myself. I have felt a darkness. When the fog rolls in..."

She tailed off, and then reached over to Isla. "Isla, please forgive me. I think I have not been fighting when I should have been. It may be that my own protection here has weakened. I promise you; I will be on my guard. You shall not lose me as you have your mother... for now. She *will* be restored to us."

Isla nodded, out of habit rather than any true belief.

"Do you still look for your selkie skin?" Isla asked, guessing the answer. Marion nodded, slowly.

"That's when you disappear, isn't it?" Isla asked. Again, she received a silent nod of confirmation.

"Hamish and I are going to help." Isla announced. Marion shook her head. "Isla. I have looked everywhere. And besides, I can't leave you and Hamish."

Isla shrugged. "When we find your selkie skin, we'll find the person who's stolen my mother.... And my father." The last was a guess, but she thought it to be true. "And then, we'll make sure that they *stop* doing everything, to us, to you, to the selkies." Determination steeled her voice, and Marion was clearly surprised by the passion which she now saw in her niece.

"Whoever is responsible, lass, is extremely dangerous. And not to be trifled with. I will not put you and Hamish in danger. Promise me that you won't go looking for it, Isla."

Isla opened her mouth, ready to refuse, but at that moment, Hamish burst through the door.

"I can swim, Aunty Marion!" he said excitedly, beaming as he did so. As he distracted their aunt with his animated stories of his newfound ability, he turned and winked at Isla behind their aunt's back.

CHAPTER 14

HOB HELPS

Saved from having to lie directly to Marion, Isla slipped out of the room in relief. She guessed Hamish had managed to get some information from Hob, and she crept into the kitchen to find out what the brownie may have revealed.

Hob was nowhere to be seen, so Isla knocked quietly on the chimney.

"Psst, it's me. Are you in there?"

She stood back as the brick swung outwards towards her. Hob poked his head out cautiously.

"Hi Hob, sorry to disturb you." Hob smiled widely, each of the gaps clearly visible between his teeth. "Aye, nay bother. It's no a disturbance. Was speaking with the wee laddie just noo."

Isla nodded eagerly. "Yes, that's what I wanted to ask you – did Hamish tell you what we found?"

Hob inclined his head. "I ken the hoose told ye where ye must look. And ye foond it?"

Isla replied, "Yes, thank you Hob. But we found out about Aunty Marion... and Father, and that Aunty Marion is stuck here, and the island is at threat Hob! All because Father went missing. And now, Mother is in danger too!" She realised that she had forgotten to ask her question. She added hastily, "And, Hob, you seem to know a lot about what happens on the island. Do you know about Aunty Marion's..." she lowered her voice to a whisper, although she wasn't sure why, "... selkie skin?"

Hob spread his hands. "Ah told the wee laddie, I do not ken aboot the location of hidden objects that are ootside the hoose. But there may be someone who can help."

"Yes?" Isla asked hurriedly, impatient to know more. "Let's go!"

Hob shook his head. "Not noo, lass. We must go at night. 'Tis the way."

"Oh, alright. But who is it? Are they on the island?"

But Hob would not reveal his secrets. He merely whispered conspiratorially, "Tonight. Hamish and ye, meet me ootside. Two o'clock. Don't wake the goats."

And with that, he put a finger to his lips and quickly closed the brick in again and disappeared.

Isla skipped out of the kitchen in her excitement although, she thought, Hob was being unnecessarily mysterious. She slipped into the room where her mother was, finding her sitting, blankly staring at a plate of sandwiches which Hamish must have brought in from the kitchen before he had found her and Marion. She guessed that he would be back in shortly, and waited, sitting next to her mother. Isla took her mother's hand gently, surprised at how roughened her palm had become. It used to be so soft; yet another effect of the hospital work and foraging that she had undertaken in recent months. Isla looked at her own hands. They too were no longer the hands of a city girl. Instead, they were calloused and brown from the weeks, no, months, which she had been outside, learning about the island and how to row. She smiled and held her mother's hand a little tighter. "See," she whispered. "We're the same."

She held onto her mother's unresponsive arm a little longer, and added softly, "We'll get you back Mother. We're going to find a way to get you back. I promise." She leant forward and gave her mother a gentle hug. "I love you Mother," she whispered. She lingered a moment, and then drew back. She couldn't tell whether the tears on her mother's face were Penny's, or whether she herself had left them there. She wiped the tears away and sat, silent, with her. That was how Hamish found them when he entered the room a few moments later.

"Isla! Did you know, Aunty Marion was just like me!" he paused. "Well," he qualified. "Kind of. Aunty Marion didn't know how to cook until she got onto the island either!"

Isla smiled at her brother's infectious enthusiasm. "So I heard! So, Aunty Marion told you a bit about when she came to the island?"

Hamish nodded his head sagely. "Yep. I know all about the house, and the island, how it helped her. She told me!"

"What do you mean the island helped her? She told me that Basil and Billie were sent to protect her, but I forgot to ask by whom!"

Hamish took a seat importantly. "Aunty Marion said that when she set foot on the island, and found out that she couldn't leave, she was really upset and didn't know where she would live, or what she would do, because she hadn't really met humans before, not properly. She said that she wandered around, and then she heard the sea talking to her."

"The sea talking?" Isla interjected. "What do you mean? How can the sea talk?"

Hamish shrugged. "I don't know. She just said that she followed the sound of the sea, but it was going inland. Up the hill. And that's when she found the cottage. Calder Cottage. That's what it was called. And that's how she knew it must be for her. She went in, and nobody was inside, and..."

"And I found my way into the most beautiful house, and I knew that even though I was far from my home, I could never be *too* far from it. Not in this house." Marion finished, standing in the open doorway.

Isla turned to her aunt. "But how did you know that somebody else wasn't living in it?"

Marion smiled. "It was empty. Not dirty or dusty, just empty. And once I started to get used to my strange new way of life here, I began to venture out a bit. And the people that I spoke to - they had never seen the cottage before. It was, as if to them, I had secretly appeared on the island and built myself a house. I wondered at the time, and this is how I believe it to be even today, whether it was like the island."

Isla's eyes widened in understanding. "Only selkies can see it," she breathed.

Marion nodded her head. "Or at least until it was occupied, I think. You likely heard tell of Nulla?" she asked. Isla nodded, but Hamish had not heard Rhodric tell this part of the story. Marion explained, "The mortal who, out of her longing for children, made a pact with the sea, and created the first selkies. When she was no longer able to make her way to where her children were, she, I think, must have retreated here. And I believe that the sea took pity on her and provided what she had lost - her home.

And, as her soul longed for the sea, so she kept the cottage and named it Calder Cottage. For, I did not. The name stood with the house."

Isla thought back to when they had first arrived. "Aunty Marion, you said, when we came to Calder Cottage, the day we arrived... you said it was an old family name."

Marion nodded. "The tribe of the Calder Sea. For our protection, for your protection, we changed our name to Gelder. For, whilst there are many who do not know the name of our tribe, of our home, there may be those that would wish the bearers of that name ill will."

Hamish grinned. "So, I'm really Hamish Calder?" he asked. Isla didn't understand why he was so happy until Marion nodded, and he began to hop around the room crowing, "We really belong up here Isla! It's really our home! Our name says so!"

Marion laughed at her nephew's antics, but gradually calmed him down, saying, "But, promise me that you will not use that name. Not now. It may not be safe."

Hamish sighed; his high spirits dampened. "Will we ever get to call ourselves 'Calder'?" he asked hopefully.

Marion considered. "Perhaps sometime. I hope with all my heart that one day, it may be safe to do so. Truly."

That evening, after they had had supper, Isla and Hamish bade Marion goodnight and set off to bed. Isla waited until the door was firmly shut behind them, then whispered, "We're going tonight." Hamish nodded; eyes bright with anticipation. "Hob said we need to leave in the middle of the night!"

"What else did Hob say, Hamish?" Isla asked, curious again at the secretiveness of the brownie. Hamish shook his head. "He just said that he knew somebody who might be able to help. But he didn't know anything himself."

"Oh well, that's pretty much what he told me too. But he was being very mysterious!"

Hamish frowned, thinking. "I don't think that brownies are really supposed to talk too much about their secrets. That's what I was thinking when I've been talking to Hob."

"But he tells us all the brownie stories!" Isla said, surprised.

"Yes.... But they're all stories which have already happened. And they're funny. Hob never tells us about where he came from, or about how brownies know where they're supposed to go - which brownie house they should choose to live in, or anything like that."

"Oh!" Isla was taken aback at how insightful her brother had become. "He did say that he couldn't tell me about the other folk like him... I thought he meant selkies. He gave me a puzzle to work out instead, So, he has to show us instead of telling us. I wonder why. And who do you think makes the rules?"

Hamish shrugged and yawned. "Don't know. But it's only four hours before we need to go."

"Why on earth do we need to go at two o'clock in the morning, anyway?" Isla muttered as she threw herself into bed, fully dressed.

"That's easy," Hamish yawned again. "Brownies are awake at night. That's when they do all of their work." He yawned again and crawled into his bed, pulling the covers over his head. "Wake me up at two, Isla?" he mumbled.

Isla thought she was too excited to sleep, so she kept an eye on the watch she'd borrowed from Hamish. She watched the minutes tick by. Slowly, her head bowed, and she fell into a restless slumber.

With a start, she woke. Panicking, she clutched the watch and peered at the hands, straining her eyes in the dark. She gasped. Two minutes to two! She shot out of bed, pulling on a knitted jumper.

"Hamish wake up!" she hissed, shaking him awake.

"What's the time?" he mumbled, blearily.

"Nearly two! Come on! Let's go!"

Grumbling, Hamish got himself out of bed, moving sluggishly until Isla hit him with a jumper she'd picked up for him to wear. "Here, come on. Put that on. It'll be colder at night. Come *on*, Hamish!"

She bundled her brother out the door, and together, they crept down the stairs and out of the front door, wincing at every slight noise they made on the way.

They met Hob by the front gate; the brownie was already outside, sprightly jumping from one foot to another. Isla had never seen him so animated.

"Come on then! On yer bikes! It's time to get pedalling!"

Isla blinked. She hadn't expected to have to cycle anywhere, not at this time in the morning. She and Hamish both stared stupidly at their bicycles, already leaning against the gate. Hob clapped his hands impatiently.

"What did ye expect? A magic carpet?! Hurry oop!" he squeaked and jumped into the basket on the handlebars of Isla's bicycle.

With a sigh, Isla climbed onto her bike, and began to pedal. Hamish followed behind her, still half-asleep by the looks of it, she thought.

The chill of the night air spurred them both on, and they increased their momentum, legs pedalling furiously, accompanied by the questionable musical talents of their brownie guide and occasional loose directions. "Oop, oop, go further. Ye're taking the whoole night! Aye, quick, right, aye, no, left. And oop, oop we go!"

Isla realised that they were heading to 'The Mountain' as Marion had affectionately named it. Warm now from their exertion, she peered out into the gloom. Their way was lit only by the stars, which, thankfully, were out in force.

"Are we nearly there, Hob?" Hamish whispered loudly.

"Aye! Stop!" The brownie commanded loudly. The cool air did not seem to bother him in the least, and he hopped off the bicycle and began to scramble up the steep slope of the hill - where they had finally reached the base.

"Come on Isla, let's go!" Hamish called, as he scurried after the disappearing brownie.

Puffing, Isla followed, biting back angry exclamations each time a gorse bush jabbed her, or her foot was caught by a hidden rabbit hole.

"Oh, drat it all!" She muttered as a particularly vicious thorn scratched her arm. She caught up to Hamish, whispering furiously, "Are you sure he knows where he's going?"

They stopped and looked all around them. Hob had vanished. Straining their eyes, they peered around, calling softly, "Hob?"

His head popped up suddenly from beneath their feet.

"What are ye waiting for? Follow me!" Isla stared, bewildered. Was the brownie *in* a rabbit hole? She got down on her hands and knees to gain a closer look.

"Hob, we can't fit down there..." she began, then stopped. "Ohhh." Understanding dawned. For, she had just seen that a large rock had partially obscured the entrance to a small cavern in the hillside. She beckoned Hamish over and pointed. Eagerly, he tried to barrel through, but Isla held him back. "I'll go first," she whispered. He pouted but let her take the lead.

She took a breath, then followed Hob's retreating voice. Crawling forward, she braced herself for rocks to stab her hands and legs, but she was pleasantly surprised to find that the ground was soft. The air grew warmer as the light grew darker in her gradual descent into the ground.

For what felt like forever, they crawled, delving deeper and deeper into the earth. Hob stayed ahead of them, calling out directions as they could no longer see. The brownie, it appeared, had no difficulty making his way in the muffled blackness their route had drawn them into.

Suddenly, Hob's voice sounded a great deal closer, and Isla realised the musty smell of the earth had given way to the fresh scent of the early morning air, and she detected the familiar tang of the sea as she smelled the air around her.

She blinked in the brighter light that they now found themselves in. Slowly, her eyes adjusted. She could make out Hob's silhouette outlined against the starlit sky. Hamish bumped into her with a grunt as he caught up.

"Oof," he muttered. "Where are we? Where's Hob?"

Hob's voice filtered back to them. "We have almost made it. Follow me." His shadowy form hopped out of sight, and Isla crawled forward quickly enough to see that he had landed, catlike, on a ledge that stood below the tunnel entrance. Somewhat less gracefully, she tumbled forward and landed with a small thud.

"Ow!" she groaned. The ledge had been further down than she had expected. She looked up and sidled to the side quickly as Hamish's legs draped over the tunnel exit, and the rest of him followed soon after. As Hamish picked himself up, Isla looked around at where Hob had brought them. They were standing on the edge of a deep hollow. The slate stone they were standing on led downwards into the middle of the glen, where a semi-circle of boulders circled a large boulder which was raised above the others. A small fire was burning behind the central boulder.

Again, Isla smelled the air around her. The salt in the air niggled at her. Surely, they were not so close to the island's edge as to be by the sea? But there was no denying what she felt; she sensed the sea from where she stood. Isla couldn't explain it, but it felt almost as if it were calling to her. She shook the thought away and turned to look at Hob.

The brownie bowed, and proudly waved to the hollow in front of them. "Welcome to the Broonie Glen," he squeaked. "This has been ma home fer ninety years, and the home of the broonies on this island fer more time than any broonie can count."

Hamish asked eagerly, "Will the brownies help us, Hob?"

Hob put a finger to his lips. "We cannae make much noise. 'Tis a sacred space fer us broonies. Look, that is the Broonie Hearth. That fire burns at all times. It reminds broonies that a hearth is the home fer our people, and the chief broonie tends to the Broonie Hearth. 'Tis the chieftain we are going to see."

"Where is the chief, Hob? And where are all the other brownies?" Isla asked curiously.

"Chieftain Pealle. He is here - somewhere. He will come oot when he is ready." Hobe dropped to a whisper. "The chief is rather auld. We cannae tell how auld he be. Some broonies say over seven hunnerd years!"

His voice regained its normal volume. "Chieftain Pealle will greet us when he is awake. But the other broonies, they are all in their hooses now, I ken. We have no broonies here under the age of one hunnerd years."

Hamish gaped, "Does that make you the youngest brownie, Hob?"

Hob flushed and shuffled his feet in embarrassment. "Ah'm not the auldest broonie, and ah was the last to leave the Broonie Glen, aye, but ah'm auld enough to manage a hoose, wee Hamish!"

"I didn't mean it was bad," Hamish whispered quickly.

"Just, where are the young brownies?" Isla broke in.

Hob frowned. "We have had nay young broonie fer as long as ah ken. Ah was always the only broonie – ma friends were aulder, and once ah lived here, there was no more broonie born on the island. But there will be, one day."

Hob continued, as they reached the centre of the brownie circle, "Broonies are different to humans. We do not groo oop and have wee bairns. We leave, go to our hooses that we choose, and after we have lived and helped in the hooses and are ready to come back to the Glen, then we have our broonie bairns."

Isla said, shocked, "But, they must be *really* old when they have children then!"

Hob shrugged. "Aboot six hunnerd years, or so. Mebbe more. We pass on what we ken, and then we watch our bairns groo, and then, we go. 'Tis the way of the broonie."

Isla whispered softly, "That sounds really sad."

"'Tis the way it has always been," came Hob's reply.

Hamish asked eagerly, "So, where is Pealle?" Isla wasn't sure whether her brother had heard any of Hob's explanation, he was too busy looking around.

"It wed be "Chief Pealle" to a hooman as yerself, ye wee whippersnapper." A croaky voice grumbled behind them. The children looked around for the source of the voice, and then adjusted their gaze a foot lower.

There, stood a hunched and ancient brownie. He had long tufts of white hair, and crinkled, wrinkled skin which looked to Isla to be so thin that it would tear at the slightest touch.

His murky eyes were clouded slightly, but his gaze did not waver as he shook a knotted stick in their direction.

"Hoomans to the Broonie Glen, Hob?" he rasped. "Never has a broonie done such a thing!"

Despite his size, his anger was so palpable that they each took a step back. Hob gulped, audibly.

"I didnae tell them anything, yer Chieftaincy."

"Ye were discovered?!" Pealle rattled angrily.

"I found Hob!" Hamish defiantly stepped forward again. "Hob is my friend. Our friend. He didn't tell us any brownie secrets. But he said that you might be able to help us!"

Isla walked to her brother, astounded. She had never seen such fire in him. Emboldened, she too took a step closer to the ancient Chieftain.

"Your Honourable... Chieftainship. We would not have dreamt to intrude in your sacred glen. But you are our only hope. Hob said he knew that if anyone would be able to help us, it would be you. Well, he didn't say, you exactly, or where we were going, but he said he could take us to someone who could. Anyway, here we are... and you are who he brought us to!"

She stopped, unsure of how the brownie was reacting. Hob stood, head bowed, chewing his lip nervously.

The brownie chief finally gave a cursory nod, appearing

pleased.

"So, what be yer business with auld Pealle? What is the help only *ah* can give?"

Hob spoke up, "Ye Chieftaincy. Only so wise a broonie could mebbe help the hoomen bairns. They are looking fer something long stolen. A selkie skin."

"Oh?" The brownie elder raised his bushy eyebrows. "Oh, aye? A selkie skin. But not yer oon?"

Isla shook her head, "It belongs to someone we care about very much. And she's been trapped here for a long time. It's time for her to go home."

Pealle sighed. "I do not ken of a selkie skin on this isle," he said, yawning. Isla's head sank, and she saw the crestfallen look appear on Hamish's small face. "Please?" she said urgently. "Anything you know... or might have known... anything! It really is important!"

The thought of her mother's listless face drove a note of desperation into her plea.

Turning his head, the brownie chief fixed her with his cloudy gaze. "I didnae say I know of one on *this* isle lass. But time was, ye might find what ye'd be looking fer across the water."

Isla resisted the urge to hug the cantankerous chief.

"Thank you! You mean on the mainland? Do you know who took it? And why?"

Yawning again, Pealle shook his head. "Ma auld brain can only recall so much. But 'tis wise to be careful over the water. Not all good lies yonder."

Hamish stuttered, "Is it dangerous?"

The brownie considered. "Something is stirring. The broonies do no ken what it is. But we fear 'tis no welcome. Dangerous? Fer some, mebbe. Fer some as have sea blood in them. The tide... it is changing"

He yawned again, and then turned and went back to the large boulder he had appeared from. He placed a hand against it, and a doorway appeared. He looked back and rasped. "Good fortune to ye."

CHAPTER 15

MARION DECIDES

Hob led the way back up to the tunnel entrance once Pealle had disappeared. Hamish whispered to Isla. "Did you see the brownie door, Isla? It was like...magic!"

Isla shrugged. "It's just a door Hamish. In a rock. But still. Just a door. But why must all brownies speak in riddles?!" She muttered. "Obviously that's where the thing is that's hurting Mother. Over there, across on the mainland. But why couldn't he just *say* so?" She huffed and rolled her eyes as she considered their encounter with the wizened brownie."

Hamish shook his head. "I think it just sounds normal to them," he replied. "Hob talks like that all the time."

"Well, it's annoying!" She quietened as they reached the tunnel entrance and followed Hob back up the claustrophobic underground trail.

When they emerged, grimy but exhilarated from the climb, they saw that the sky was slowly growing lighter.

"Come on, quick!" Isla called to Hamish. Hob was

already by the bicycle. "We need to get back before Marion wakes up!"

They cycled in haste, allowing the natural descent of the road to rush them towards the cottage, racing the dawn. The sky was tinged pink by the time they reached the gate. "Phew." Hamish whistled. "I think we made it! Thanks Hob!"

Isla heartily agreed. "Thank you so much Hob. Now, we know where to look next. We couldn't have done it without you!"

The brownie didn't smile or respond as he normally would. Instead, he turned his ear towards the cottage, listening intently. "Get doon!" he hissed suddenly. They ducked on command, just before the front door of the cottage opened.

They crawled nimbly around the wall and hid in the shadows the morning light had created. They had had just enough time to stow the bicycles in the bushes by the gate. Isla hoped fervently that they were well out of sight. Footsteps crunched softly along the pebbled path leading to the gate, which soon swung open. With a click, the latch closed back in place and the footsteps resumed, growing louder as their owner grew closer. They each held their breath, and Isla put a hand to Hamish's head, pushing it down as he began to peer up to see who it was. She looked up, and saw their aunt walking past them, not towards them as she had feared. She had a look of concentration on her face.

When she had walked out of earshot, Isla whispered to Hamish and Hob, "Go move the bicycles. Back to where they're normally kept. Then, Hamish, get washed. You look like you've been tunnelling! Hob, can you please check on Mother?" The brownie nodded, but Hamish squawked indignantly, "What about you?"

Isla stood, cautiously. "I'm going to see where Aunty Marion is going." She whispered, "Don't worry, I won't get caught!" Hamish still looked confused, as she explained.

"Aunty Marion might be in danger. Especially if she's out alone. I'm just going to make sure she's alright."

Hamish nodded. Isla heard a whispered "be careful" as she left, and she waved as she set off at a fast walk, taking care to stay on the grass to avoid her own footsteps giving her away.

Like a shadow, she flitted across the bracken and grass, taking care to keep enough distance between herself and her aunt to avoid detection. However, she kept her in her sights. Isla was grateful for all the exploring she had done on the island, for she was not at all tired as she kept to the same steady pace her aunt was setting.

She wondered where Marion was going. She didn't understand why her aunt was out so early in the morning – although, she supposed, she did have a habit of walking at strange times. But as they continued, Isla wondered at the direction they were taking. It was not quite the way that she, Hamish and Hob had just returned from, but it was not dissimilar. They sloped inland, criss-crossing the moorland terrain. She closed her eyes for a moment, and listened intently, trying to focus on the sound which she could just faintly make out. The birdsong had distracted her for a time, but she could now make out... Marion speaking?

Isla crept a little closer to her aunt, closing the gap between them as much as she dared; it sounded like her aunt was talking to herself. Intrigued, Isla strained her ears, hopping from shadow to shadow to remain unnoticed.

"All this time," Marion was softly murmuring. "All of

this time, I did not listen. Why did I not let it guide me? And now, it may be too late!"

She increased her pace and Isla, now more intrigued than ever, hurried to match it.

"Oh Marion, you foolish selkie. If you'd listened to the sea... oh, I could have been home again..."

Marion stopped so suddenly that Isla, unprepared, had to dive into the heather to avoid being seen. She peered up through the plants which sheltered her and could just make out that her aunt had frozen. Her eyes appeared to be closed. She was taking deep breaths, not as if she were... scenting, or inhaling, but as if she were... deeply concentrating, Isla thought.

Then, she opened her eyes and nodded to herself, changing angle slightly and walking a trajectory that was barely noticeably different to the approach which she had previously been taking.

Isla suddenly realised what her aunt was doing. She herself had felt the call of the sea. And, she thought, that must be what Marion was doing. She was following the guidance of the sea. Isla was as certain of it as knowing the difference between night and day. She knew then that Marion was following an internal compass that only she could follow.

Quietly, Isla picked herself up and followed. They were heading back inland; Isla could see the mountain taking form, now enrobed in the early morning's golden light.

The haze gently lifting off the purple heather gave the morning a mystical glow. Reverently, Isla watched as her aunt glided through the mist, her hair shimmering as it caught the emerging light, a beacon which Isla continued to follow.

Hardly daring to breathe, she navigated boulders and

roots as stealthily as if she had been tracking for years. The shadows were receding, allowing Isla to see her path more clearly, but as the darkness faded away, she felt exposed. Should Marion turn at any point, she would be discovered in a moment. Darting silently between bracken and heather, she shadowed her aunt as closely as she dared.

Marion stopped short. Isla froze. She could just about make out that her aunt's eyes were closed again. She dropped flat to her stomach as Marion wheeled around to the left. Her heart in her mouth, Isla watched in surprise as Marion put a hand out in front of her, almost as if she were searching for something. As Isla crept up closer, she saw Marion kneeling next to where a hillock was rising from the moorland. Sidling forward, camouflaging herself in a patch of gorse, Isla peered through the undergrowth. The sweet, nutty scent of the yellow flowers filled her nostrils, and she hurriedly stifled a sneeze.

Cautiously, she looked to where her aunt knelt. Marion hadn't appeared to have heard anything untoward, her attention solely focused on whatever lay in front of her. Isla strained her ears once again and was rewarded with the soft tones of Marion's voice faintly carrying back to her on the breeze.

Isla couldn't see what had captured Marion's attention, but she caught her aunt's exultant cry, and she turned towards the sound.

"Here! Oh! I have you at last! All this time... and it was here!" Marion's excited voice rang clear. Isla could hear her laughter, and then what sounded like faint sobs.

She was close enough to see her aunt's shoulder shaking, as she pressed her face into her hands. No, into what she was holding. Isla saw a flash of silver and knew that Marion had finally found her selkie skin.

Her heart sank.

As much as she had wanted to find the stolen skin, at the same time, she knew she wasn't ready to lose her aunt back to the sea. Dully, Isla closed her eyes.

Her ears, hearing now sharpened, tuned into the murmurings she could now hear Marion making. Although initially hardly paying attention, her ears pricked up when she heard Marion whisper, "But, the bairns, why now... after so long. 'Tis cruel. Cruel indeed. To abandon Isla and Hamish... and so uncertain that I could have any power if I were to return... And Duncan... if Duncan... if he lives still, I would be lost to them and Penny, and useless, powerless to do anything. I would see my people... and watch them perish."

Isla hardly dared to believe her ears. After all, Marion could leave. She was finally free. In wonder, she watched as her aunt pressed her selkie skin to herself tightly. And saw as she slowly placed it back within its hiding place.

"To not return for seven years, and Penny... Penny unable to look after them... I could not forgive myself."

Isla listened as Marion slowly stood and looked down at the place which had concealed her true identity for so long. She shook herself, and head held high, turned and walked away. Towards Isla.

Again, Isla flattened herself as much as she possibly could, and willed herself to not move a muscle. Marion walked straight past her, lost in thought. Isla caught a glimpse of her face as she passed. Surprised, she saw no trace of regret on her aunt's face, only an oddly peaceful expression. She inched her head slightly to watch as Marion picked her way lightly through the bracken, back the way they had come.

Confused, Isla waited until her aunt was fully out of

sight, and then crept forward to where she had seen her aunt crouch down. She frowned. She couldn't see anything other than the gentle slope of the hill. She closed her eyes, remembered that Marion had let her other senses draw her to the selkie skin.

She reached out, in her mind's eye, and saw the sea, the waves racing onto shore. The crashing of the waves seemed so real. She opened her eyes again, and was almost surprised to see that there was, in fact, no water lapping at her feet. Again, Isla closed her eyes, and took herself back to the scene of the sea.

This time, she let the sound of the water envelop her. She concentrated. When she moved slightly back a step, the sound dimmed, ever so slightly. She stepped forward again, and the noise grew louder once more. Slowly, she lowered herself to where she had seen Marion crouch, and was rewarded by the sound of the sea growing in intensity. She reached out, towards where she thought the sound was clearest, and almost jumped when her fingers grazed a smooth surface.

Isla opened her eyes and saw that she was touching a well-camouflaged stone. She nudged it, and it rolled easily, revealing a small fissure in the hillside. Tentatively, Isla felt inside, and drew back sharply when she touched something soft. She drew a deep breath and quickly plunged her hand inside, this time clutching at whatever it was that she had just felt. She exhaled in relief when the object she drew out didn't turn out to be an angry biting creature. Instead, the morning light caused the selkie skin she was holding to shimmer; the silver-grey coat dazzling her with its beauty. With the same awestruck sensation she had witnessed in her aunt, Isla slowly placed the silky fur back into its hiding place.

She could scarcely believe that Marion had chosen to leave it hidden. But then, thoughts of her father popped into her head. If he was still alive... no, she mustn't think like that. Her father, alive, but missing, meant that Marion might not have the power she needed from the sea to break the hold over her mother.

Isla gulped. Seven years without her mother, father or Marion... she couldn't imagine it.

Suddenly angry, Isla covered the selkie skin's hiding place once again, this time leaving a marker for herself; a broken twig stuck into the ground beside it. She wanted some answers. Whoever had stolen the skin, they were the one responsible. She burned at the injustice of it. She thought of Pealle's veiled caution of the land over the water – the mainland... the fishing village. If even the brownie chieftain had not had knowledge of the selkie skin on the island, they were facing a dangerous threat indeed.

Aching with anger, Isla resolved that she would find the person responsible. She would make them give her parents back... somehow.

But first, she needed to find out who it was that she was searching for. As she made her way back to the cottage, a plan gradually formed in her mind.

CHAPTER 16

ACROSS THE WATER

Isla flitted into the cottage, silently scurried up the stairs and was met by a bleary-eyed Hamish when she opened the door to their room.

"Where did you go?" Hamish blurted. "Where did Aunty Marion go? Did she know that we were out?"

"Shh!" Isla hissed back. "She didn't know that we were out, or where we were – she didn't see me." She paused for a moment. "I followed her the whole way – I guess she was just awake and wanted to go for a very early walk."

"Oh." Hamish sounded a bit disappointed. "But isn't it a bit strange that Aunty Marion went out so early on the day that Hob took us to the brownie hollow?"

Isla shrugged, the lie coming more easily to her than she thought possible. "I don't know Hamish. She just went out and came back. It was pretty boring really. The sunrise was pretty though."

She yawned, not having to pretend how tired she was.

"Get some sleep. We'll have to be up soon so that

Aunty Marion doesn't wonder why we're not up."

Hamish nodded and fell asleep almost as soon as he had tucked himself under the covers. Isla waited until his breathing shallowed and she was sure that he really was asleep.

She crept out of the room and out of the cottage as quietly as she had entered. Down the track and along the burn she ran, breath puffing in clouds ahead of her in the cool morning air, until she reached the loch. She slowed as she watched the morning mist rise slowly in a haze over the water, where it partially obscured the rowboat. She jumped into the boat, untying the thick rope from the jetty as she went.

Determination fuelling her, she picked up the oars and threw herself into the motion. Across the water and down the hidden inlet she rowed, out onto the open sea. Instead of following the waves out towards the selkie island, Isla turned and headed out, across the sea, away from the island and towards the mainland.

The crisp air waking her, she rowed quickly, buoyed by the tumbling waves around her. From the corner of her eye, she thought she saw a familiar shape leaping out of the water. She turned her head. Patch. She resumed her rowing, her mind as busy as her arms. She had no doubt that her voyage across the sea would soon be reported back to the seal folk. But she was still not ready to tell of Marion's discovery.

She turned her head back to the sea in front of her, watching the island shrink away. She had to find out what was on the mainland.

The closer she drew to the fishing village, the more she thought about what she would find. Not sure where to start looking once she got to the bay, she pulled the rowing boat up just beyond the point, and docked behind a tree, whose branches were reaching out to the water. As she tied the boat up and scrambled onto shore, she stepped back to assess her handiwork. She pulled a few loose branches over the boat. There, it was mostly hidden from view, she thought.

Unless somebody specifically came to look for the boat, she didn't think it would be spotted. Certainly not from land. With a last glance back at the sea, and Patch's receding dorsal fin, she set her shoulders and started to make her way around the point to where the fishing village lay.

Isla followed the sounds of the village waking up. She guessed it must be close to five in the morning. The people in the village were stirring. Chimney smoke unfurled in the air, and she caught snippets of conversation from the emerging fishermen. She veered away from what soon promised to be a bustling harbour, although her stomach rumbled as she smelled the unmistakeable aroma of smoking fish. She wished she'd thought to bring some breakfast along with her.

She wasn't sure why she wasn't immediately drawn to the centre of the village – she had been brought up in a busy metropolis after all. Instead, she found that she preferred to keep to the narrow path that wound its way along the top of the cliff edge, overlooking the harbour. As she got higher up the path, Isla realised that she could see around the point to where the ferry was stationed which they had taken on their very first day. Pausing, she wondered, surely they hadn't been guided over to the mainland to find that Mr. Mackenzie was the one behind it all?

She shook the thought away firmly. It was unthinkable.

And yet, if she wasn't drawn to the fishing village, why be led to this side of the sea?

A furry bundle jumped out onto the path at that point, landing inches away from her. As it closed the distance and jumped up pawing at her and whining happily, tail wagging furiously, Isla recognised the pup. "Tarn!" she whispered. "What are you doing here?"

Isla looked around, expecting to see Mr. Mackenzie appear around the corner next. When he didn't, she looked closer out towards the ferry point, and saw that a small cottage was standing at the far end of the point. She guessed that was where the pup came from.

"Come on, you're not where you're supposed to be." She clicked her fingers and started to walk in the direction of the cottage. She'd gotten a few metres when she looked back to see a quizzical Tarn staring after her, still where she'd jumped out at her.

When Isla turned to go back to her, Tarn yipped, wagging her tail once more, and turned and trotted off in the opposite direction. Isla called after her, but the pup continued to run along. Closing her eyes, Isla thought she heard the faint sound of the sea coming from the direction in which Tarn was rapidly disappearing. She quickly broke into a jog to try to keep up with her four-legged guide. As they ran along, Isla took stock of where they were now heading. They were back now along the track which Isla had just come from, dipping down close to where she'd tied up her boat, and then further, along the coast in the opposite direction.

Panting slightly in her pursuit of the dog ahead of her, Isla raised her hand to brush her hair out of her yes. As she did so, she lost sight of Tarn. She looked around to see where the pup had gotten to, but was interrupted in her search by a gruff, "Oy there."

Isla jumped, unaware that she had almost stumbled into a garden; the owner of which was now looking at her rather furiously across a well-manicured hedge. She thought she recognised the man, and it took her a second to place the strong brogue of his accent.

"Where de ye think ye're scurrying off to? Off to cause mischief are ye? Well, not on ma watch!"

He shaded his hand around the bright sun which was streaming behind her. As he did, he blinked uncertainly, and pulled out a pair of spectacles from his pocket and perched them on the bridge of his nose. When he did, Isla finally placed him. The white-haired, bristly moustached and bespectacled gentleman in front of her was the conductor whom she and Hamish had encountered when they first arrived on the train. His voice lost its accusatory tone as soon as he had put his glasses on.

"Ah, don't mind me. Sorry about that lassie. Ye're not one of the wee tykes from the village doon yonder. They like to play tricks and play havoc with the garden, so they do. But ye were one of the wee ones who were going to the island? I remember."

Isla nodded, uncertain as to how to respond.

"I do apologise. Not introducin' meself. I'm Angus Begbie."

"I know, you're the conductor," Isla said, sure she had it right.

"Aye," he said, nodding, still looking at her rather warily. "Station Master if ye please. But, if ye're over the island, how'd ye get across here? At this time of the morn? The ferry'd not be running yet I wouldn't have thought. Surely ye didn't swim?"

A strange look crossed over his face as he spoke,

197

vanishing in an instant when Isla shook her head.

"I rowed."

He nodded curtly, seeming unexpectedly disappointed at her response. "Aye, that would be the way. I just... ye reminded me of someone..." His words faded as he looked out to sea, beyond where Isla was stood.

She waited awkwardly for a moment, looking around for any sign of Tarn. The Station Master shook his head sharply as if waving away a memory, and brusquely said, "Well, I'm to the station. Train's due in soon."

Isla nodded politely, and stood aside to let him pass, watching him walk away down the path, towards where the station must be located. She frowned. Something niggled at her. There was something that didn't seem quite right about Angus Begbie, something about the way that he'd stared out towards sea with that far-off, covetous look in his eye. She closed her eyes again and felt the sea tug at her.

"Maybe *he's* what Pealle was trying to tell me about," she whispered to herself. She looked down the path, in the direction which the station master had disappeared, and then back at the house. It was non-descript in many ways; its plainness the sole remarkable feature about it. Grey pebble-dash walls closed over chipped and flaking grey paint on the doors and window frames. She suspected that at one point they may have been white. The more she examined the house, the more she felt it was quite a neglected dwelling. The surprise was the beautiful lawn laid out in front of it, such a drastic contrast to the house behind; she wouldn't have guessed it to belong to the same owner.

The grass was well-kept and a vibrant green, and dozens of rose bushes dotted the edges of it, providing a floral perfume that almost distracted from the sad dwelling behind it. Almost.

She placed a hand on the gate, but immediately let go as she heard a whistle in the distance.

"Tarn?" Mr. Mackenzie's voice called. "Where are ye, ye wee scamp?"

The dog in question chose to reappear at that precise moment, tail wagging, eyes glinting and alert. The pup gave Isla's hand a quick lick as it rushed past to answer its master's call, and Isla heard the ferry master's voice recede back into the distance when it appeared the pup had re-joined him.

Isla waited a moment or two before retracing her steps to where she'd left the boat. She was sure that there was more to Angus Begbie than met the eye, as she couldn't shake the uneasy feeling she'd had when she first noticed his interest on how she'd gotten to the mainland. She had to explore further.

"There's something in that house," she muttered to herself. But there were too many people around. She hadn't counted on that. Thoughts whirling, she determined that she would come back and try again at night. Now that she knew where she was going, she was able to plan ahead.

Sighing a breath of relief when she reached the boat safe where she'd left it, she noticed two bubbles of air rise to the surface of the water right next to the boat. Then, a familiar grey head popped up out of the water. The seal changed shape before her. Dina's hopeful eyes gleamed back at Isla as she quickly asked, "You found something?"

Isla laughed and splashed the selkie as she climbed into the boat. "I see Patch has been telling tales."

Dina put on an innocent expression, "Why have a messenger porpoise if you cannae use him?" she smiled, revealing the slightly wicked curve of her teeth as she barked a laugh from the water, which Isla couldn't help but echo.

"I wouldn't have expected anything less. But, yes, I've found something. Well, Hamish and I both did. But it's both of our discovery. I need to wait to tell him, too."

Dina snorted. "Little laddie's back at the beach. He's waiting for us."

Isla rolled her eyes. "Trust him to pretend to be asleep. Alright, I'll tell you when we're at the beach. The three of us."

Dina nodded, but eagerly asked. "Just tell me. Did you find it? Is Lady Marion coming back to us?"

The lie came to Isla more quickly than it had before. "Not yet," she said unwaveringly. "But we've found clues. I think I know where the answer lies to who might be behind all of this."

Her words appeared to ignite a fire in her selkie friend. Dina's teeth snapped shut, a deadly expression in her eyes. "Aye, and when I find them, they'll rue the day."

Isla gulped quietly. She did not want to be the one to anger Dina, and yet she'd already lied to her. She hoped that she hadn't made the wrong decision.

She nodded her agreement. "We'll catch them. I promise." Taking up her oars again, she pushed off from the shore and, with Dina's help back in selkie form, navigated the rowing boat to the hidden beach below Calder Cottage where Hamish could be seen sitting on a large rock.

Isla brought the boat onto shore, and older sister voice at the ready, accusatorily said, "You were supposed to be asleep!"

"So were you!" her brother quickly shot back.

Behind them, Dina laughed. "So, nobody's asleep. But you have found something?"

Hamish nodded importantly, an accomplishment, Isla thought, considered he was mid-yawn. "Yes, I went to ask Hob if he knew anything..."

"Who is Hob?" Dina broke in, looking confused.

"Hob's our brownie." Hamish explained. The puzzled look cleared from Dina's face and she nodded her understanding. "Brownies have a habit of knowing everything they can. But they can be riddlers at times."

"So we've noticed," Isla said drily.

"Anyway, Hob said he didn't know anything about Aunty Marion's selkie skin," Hamish continued, throwing Isla a dirty look. "So last night he took us to the brownie chief. And Pealle said that he didn't know of a selkie skin on the island, but..."

"But he said we might find what we're looking for across the water," Isla interrupted. "So, I took the boat and went over this morning."

Hamish's eyes gleamed with curiosity. "What did you find Isla?"

She shook her head. "Nothing specific. I didn't find any monsters or water goblins, I don't *think*. Well, maybe..."

Isla proceeded to describe her encounter with the station master and explained her suspicions about the man. As she recounted her morning's meeting, she suddenly remembered the feeling that she'd had when they'd arrived at the train station that first day.

"Remember when we got off the train, Hamish? When we were waiting for Aunty Marion? I was sure that there was something there at the station – something watching us."

Hamish gaped. "And *he* was there then, too. Isla, it *must* be him!"

She nodded. "I think so. We'll need to go back when it's quieter. And dark. We'll need to find out when there's a train due in late, so the house will be empty."

Dina spoke up, "I'll get Patch on it. He can find out."

Hamish blinked at her. "Patch can find out information even from the mainland?" Dina nodded. "The gulls talk a lot. *Too* much," she added darkly. "But they're useful sometimes."

"Alright, we'll come back down here this evening. Do you think Patch will know by then?" Isla asked.

Dina nodded. "Yes, we'll meet you here tonight."

Having made their plans, the trio departed, each on their separate ways. Hamish took the secret passageway through the cliff back to the cottage, Isla went to take the boat back to the loch, and Dina to liaise with Patch.

For the rest of the day, the children got on with their normal routines; Isla sat with their mother in the garden, keeping a watchful eye on Basil and Billie. Hamish and Marion chatted and joked together in the kitchen as they set about baking and cooking for the day ahead. Listening to Marion's peals of laughter coming from the kitchen, Isla thought that somehow a weight seemed to have lifted from her aunt's shoulders. The tinge of sadness that had clung to her since they had met had nearly vanished. Nearly. Isla thought back to the early morning, and Marion's decision to leave her selkie skin behind. Maybe it was because *she* had been the one to choose, Isla thought.

Whatever the reason, she sat back and smiled as she took stock of the happy sounds around her. Had both her father and mother been there, *fully* been there, it would be a perfect day. But with the shadow of her mother and missing father present in her thoughts, Isla watched and waited, whiling the time away until the evening appeared.

Hamish and Marion served up dinner, and Marion smiled at them as they cleared their plates ravenously. "You know what? I fancy a bit of a cycle to the village. Either of you care to join me?"

Isla and Hamish shook their heads, Hamish saying he would stay with Penny, and Isla suddenly remembering that she was at a pivotal point in the book she was currently reading.

"Alright then, I'll see you both soon, if you're not in bed by the time I'm back. Going to do a little visiting with Mrs. MacGregor. She was kind enough to bring round some homemade tonic for Tuppence. So, I will go and return the bottle. Have fun!"

She brightly bid them farewell, and they watched her as she rode down the track. Hamish rushed to ask Hob to stay with their mother, and they then quickly made their way out through the secret door, and down the hidden staircase down to the beach where Dina was waiting for them.

As they slipped through the doorway onto the beach, Hamish checked his watch. "Nearly nine o'clock," he said. He looked anxiously over to his sister. "That'll still give us time, right Isla?"

Isla nodded, but she wasn't sure. It did seem late for a train to be running. She shrugged and said, "I guess we'll see!"

Dina must have been looking out for them as they saw her transform into girl form as they approached. In the distance, Isla could see Patch's fin slice through the water. A second later, the porpoise jumped in the air. As he did, Isla could hear an excited chatter coming from the porpoise's direction.

Dina smiled, translating. "Patch says we need to hurry."

They raced to drag the boat from its hiding place to the sea. Puffing, Isla asked Dina, "How long do we have until the train comes in?"

Dina called over her shoulder. "At about ten, I think. Perhaps just before."

Getting into the boat, Isla calculated in her head. Twenty minutes to the island – maybe less if Dina helped pull the boat, and then ten minutes to the station master's house. That would leave about fifteen minutes to search the house. Not a lot of time, she reflected, but it was all they had.

Rowing hard, Isla looked over to Hamish. "You'll need to come help me look in the house Hamish. We won't have much time."

He nodded and asked, "Can Dina help too?"

Isla considered. "No... Somebody needs to stay with the boat. You never know, we might need to make a quick getaway!" She meant it as a joke, but Hamish stared at her wide-eyed.

"Really?" he breathed, looking a bit scared but equally impressed. Isla was about to say that she had only been joking, but before she could, Hamish squared his shoulders bravely, sitting up straighter, saying, "We'll do it. We'll find whatever that man is hiding. Even if he *does* turn out to be a water goblin. We're on a mission. Just like Father."

Isla nodded, smiling at the confidence her brother now had. She couldn't wait for her mother to see what a change had happened in the timid little boy she had known.

The wind picked up, sending Isla's fiery hair streaming in the wind. As she rowed, faster and faster, Isla figure-headed the boat; a beacon of justice personified, racing across the sea, intent on setting her family free, once and for all.

The rest of the voyage was quiet. Neither Isla nor Hamish spoke; Isla concentrating on the task at hand. As they crossed the waves, their way guided by the emerging stars in the dusky evening light, Hamish kept Patch in sight, smiling each time the porpoise jumped close to the boat.

"I think he's telling us to get a move on," Hamish said to Isla.

"I'm trying!"

Hamish very wisely kept silent after he heard the bite in his sister's voice.

Silently pulling up to the spot on the point where she had moored the boat earlier that day, Isla quickly tied up and helped Hamish out of the vessel. Dina emerged from the water, changing to her human form as she did so. She pulled herself into the boat.

"I'll wait here, I heard your plan."

Isla nodded, and looked at the form Dina had chosen to assume. "But what if you're seen?"

Dina shrugged. "I'd wager a girl on a boat would look less odd than a seal waiting by a boat, especially one by itself."

Isla nodded. "Just be careful. Try to keep out of sight."

The selkie girl grinned, teeth glittering wickedly. "Just let anyone try anything. They won't know what's hit them."

"Just..." "Be careful. I know. I will. The two of ye both best be the ones to be careful."

Dina's words followed them as they climbed the hill away from the boat, Isla leading the way. Their footsteps sounded loud to her in the silence of the evening. She turned to Hamish and put a finger to her lips as he stepped on a twig which made a particularly loud 'crack'. He nodded, impatiently, but did begin to take more care in looking down at where he was walking.

Soon enough, they found themselves at the station master's cottage. In the dark, it looked even more ominous than it had in the light.

Hamish gulped audibly as he looked at the dilapidated building, shadows looming threateningly over its many cracks and broken windows.

"Come on Hamish. It's empty. He's out. Look, it's dark inside." Isla strode forward, more bravely than she felt. She hadn't yet planned how exactly they would get inside the house.

As she approached the doorway, she saw that the wood was battered and warped by the elements. What looked like a gap in one of the panels moved slightly in the breeze that had followed them up from the sea.

"Look, Hamish," Isla whispered excitedly. "It's open. He mustn't have locked up before he went to the station."

Tentatively placing his hand on the door, Hamish looked up at Isla, grimacing as the door swung open with an almighty creak. They both froze, listening for any signs that the house was not occupied. But nobody came charging out. No further sound at all was made, in fact.

Isla let out a breath that she'd been holding. Looking to Hamish, she placed a finger on her lips, and walked into the hallway. Her eyes took a moment to adjust to the gloom of the interior. Hamish, having followed her in, walked straight into the back of her.

"Ow!" she hissed. "You have to stop doing that!"

"Sorry, Isla," came his muffled response.

"I didn't think to bring a torch. I can't believe it!" Isla clapped a hand to her head as she berated herself for her lack of forethought. She was interrupted by Hamish's persistent tapping on her arm.

"What?!"

"I brought a torch. I left it in the secret staircase in case we ever needed it. And I, well, brought it along. Here you go."

He meekly offered the torch to her, and Isla swung around and gave her brother a bear hug.

"Hamish Gelder... Hamish *Calder*, you are a genius!" She caught Hamish's grin as she switched the torch on. A watery stream of light wavered over the room.

The hall itself appeared empty. A pair of slippers lay abandoned by the side of the door. The tattered footwear was sprawled amongst sizeable piles of dust.

Crinkling her nose in disgust as they stepped forward further into the house, Isla picked her way gingerly around the grimy cups and plates which were scattered indiscriminately on the floor.

Hamish squeaked as something scuttled over his foot.

"Shush! It was probably just a beetle!" Isla said in response to her brother's claims he'd seen a rat. She fervently hoped it *was* just a beetle, although she half-suspected he was right.

"Come on, it's lighter in here. I'll stay here with the beetle and go through that cupboard and those drawers. You take the torch and see if there's anything upstairs that will help Mother."

She handed the torch back to Hamish with more confidence than she felt. The dingy living room they were standing in, along with the rest of the wretched house they were in made her feel sure that they were in the right place. A sense of urgency gripped her. They had to leave before the station master returned.

"Quick! Go!" She whispered to Hamish, who nodded and scampered through the door at the end of the room. His footsteps clunking up the stairs proved her theory of the layout of the house.

Approaching the desk that was leaning lopsided in front of the window, Isla could make out in the moonlight that this, too, had not seen the touch of a duster for quite some time. The desk was covered in what looked to be old train timetables. There were four drawers within the desk. Isla heaved them open one by one, wincing at the groans they made from years of disuse. She peered into each one, not finding anything other than a few scrap pieces of paper, a letter opener, and a rather dirty handkerchief.

Exasperated, she turned and began to rifle through the cabinet hiding by the door. The dusty glass in the door rattled as she examined and replaced the weathered maps held within. She glanced at them before losing interest. They appeared to be maps of the local area, the islands around the mainland. She fumbled as she went to put one of the maps back on the cabinet shelf. It fell, skittering under the cabinet. Isla sighed and bent down to retrieve it. Peering into the shadows under the cabinet case, she could see nothing. She gritted her teeth and slowly put her hand into the void, trying not to think about the scuttling creature they had already seen in the room. She felt around, sighing in relief as her fingers hit upon the escaped papers. As she drew them back towards her, she noticed that there was a floorboard which jutted up at an odd angle. She wondered...

Putting the map to one side, she put both hands on the floorboard and gently pulled it. It moved effortlessly, one side lifting as if on a spring, revealing a hidey-hole within.

Silvery moonlight filtering in through the window

illuminated the room. There, under the floorboard lay a single lock of hair, and a tuft of silky grey fur which Isla instantly recognised. Selkie fur.

"So. Ye're back."

Isla jumped and turned. Angus Begbie was standing right behind her.

CHAPTER 17

THE STATION MASTER'S TALE

"I... I..." Isla stuttered.

"Ye thought ye'd come and break into ma hoose? Oot to steal what ye can get yer grubby hands on?" The station master's bushy eyebrows furrowed, and his voice shook in anger.

Isla would have been intimidated in most circumstances, but his accusations made her blood boil. She took a step forward, fists clenched in tight balls by her side.

"I am *not* a thief."

"Oh, a hot-headed thief are ye?"

"I said. I'm NOT a thief. I've never stolen anything in my life! But you... *You're* the thief," Isla sputtered.

The station master's face turned red. "Ye dare stand in ma hoose, not invited mind ye, and dare to accuse *me* of being a thief?" he bellowed.

"*You* stole a selkie skin."

As soon as Isla had spoken the words, the colour

drained from the station master's face. "What did ye say?" he said quietly.

Emboldened, Isla said again. "I saw the fur. Right here. That's from a selkie's skin. Who's is it? And how dare you steal a selkie's skin! You trapped her! And, whatever you're doing to the selkies and the island, you need to stop it now!"

His eyes narrowed. "I dinnae ken what ye're talkin' aboot. But it may well be there's a doctor roondaboot to tend to whatever condition it is that ye're sufferin' from. Fairy tales and nonsense. Selkies and such, pah! Child's stuff and auld wives' tales!"

Isla had clenched her jaws tight and white spots appeared on her cheeks in her fury. The station master took one look at her ferocity and hastily took a step back from the intensity of her anger. At that moment, Hamish came hurtling into the room.

Isla grabbed the closest implement she could find – which happened to be a poker. She held it aloft, brandishing it towards the station master and motioned Hamish to stand behind her.

Hamish gave a frightened look at the old man standing across from his sister and hurried over to her. Isla noticed as he did so that his arms were laden with books and papers. She couldn't work out what expression Angus Begbie was currently wearing. He seemed perplexed as well as angry.

Hamish whispered loudly "I thought he was supposed to be at the station – the train is coming in."

The station master scoffed. "Thought ye'd get away with breaking and entering ye wee hooligan! Too bad fer ye, the late train has been cancelled. No services running late now, with the blackout, aye, and Edinburgh trying to keep its tracks safe from the skies."

Isla brandished the poker once more. "Hush water goblin! Hamish what did you find?"

He showed her some of the volumes he was holding. "Look! It's all about selkies. And the islands. And here, "*Encounters with the sea-folk*". It's got bits underlined, and look at these!" Hamish brought out heavy sheets of paper. Isla recognised the artist's paper her mother used to paint on before the war. On each page were drawings, delicately sketched in ink and charcoal, each beautifully detailed. The artist had quite some skill, Isla thought. Each drawing was that of a seal, or a selkie woman. Pages and pages of the soft, downy fur of the selkie, dappled in the same intricate pattern on each page. The artist had captured both the playful and soulful gaze of the selkie, and Isla could see that the eyes of the seal and the woman held the same expression. As she turned the pages, she gasped. The artist had managed to capture the change from seal to woman almost faultlessly. There, on the same page, the graceful transformation of the seal to human form of the selkie change was unmistakeable. A sweep of charcoal dashed from one to the other, cloaking them both in the magical transformation.

Isla turned the page to face the station master. "You see!" she cried triumphantly. "You do know what I'm talking about. And you have a lot of answering to do, water goblin. Starting with, where is my father?"

As Hamish and Isla both glared at him from behind the poker, the man who called himself Angus Begbie gave a weary sigh and sat down on the shabby armchair behind him.

"I cannae say I ken what ye mean aboot a water goblin," he sighed in his thick accent. "But, aye, ye're right that I do ken what a selkie is."

"Aha!" Hamish cried. "So, you admit it!"

The man shook his head, still looking confused, but his anger had disappeared. Instead, a deep sadness was now etched into the lines criss-crossing his face.

"Her name was Emelda," he croaked. "I was a younger man, used to walkin' along the sea front. I used to love the sea. But I've learnt it can be cruel as well as beautiful. One mornin', I was doon by the shore, waiting fer the sun to rise. And I saw her. I couldnae believe ma eyes. The most beautiful creature I'd ever seen. She was changin' form. The light was so low, I didnae believe it at first. Thought ma eyes were playing tricks on me. I kept quiet and watched. She was just oot the sea; her selkie skin aroond her. Just turned her face up to the sky, and she waited for the sun to come up. I'd gone doon to the shore, to find the sunrise, aye, but I foond the love of me life.

"I didnae make a peep. 'Angus,' I said to meself. 'Ye'd look a great fool if ye're wrong.' So, I waited, and watched, and with me own eyes, I watched as she turned back to her seal self after the sun had come up. She didnae see me but dived into the waves. I rushed home and looked fer all of me mammie's and grandmammie's books and fairy tales of the islands. There, I foond all the stories that I'd laughed at all of ma days. One of the stories that I read that day, havin' now decided it was all true, was that selkies like music; that they're drawn to it oot the water. So, every day after that, fer two weeks, I went doon to that same spot, and I took ma fiddle. I played every mornin' before the sun rose – fer hours on end. Ma fingers were blistered and bleedin' but I still carried on. Then, one day, when I was aboot to give up, she appeared oot of the water, in her human form. And she came up to me. She said she'd been

213

watchin' me, every day that I'd come doon to the shore to play."

Isla and Hamish were transfixed by his words, and he gave a dry chuckle as he recounted his tale, a far-off look in his eyes.

"She said she didnae ken what all the racket was and had come to investigate if there was a caterwauling gull that had been caught in a trap. But then she said she'd stayed to see what the loon with the wooden box was doin' fer hours on end. I figured then that not everythin' I'd read aboot selkies was true; and I was determined to get her to leave the sea fer me. I wooed ma Emelda fer nigh a year, each passin' month she'd promise that she'd come live with me and live on the land. I worked hard, to prove that I could make her happy. I bought this hoose. And one day, she appeared at the door. I could have been knocked doon by a gust of air. But I was happy, and she was too, ma bonnie beauty from the sea. She never strayed too far from the shore, but that was fine with me. I knew she'd chosen me over the water, and I loved her fer that.

"Then, a big storm blew in, and ye could hear the waves crashin' – fer miles and miles! Emelda got restless, never in, but always doon by the waves. She came up to me one day, and she gave me her selkie skin. She held ma hand and told me to keep it safe, somewhere she'd not find it on a stormy day. I laughed and thought her words to be in jest. But I did what she asked of me. I hid it where ye've just seen. I thought I'd been clever in choosin' that very spot, in plain sight but oot of mind. At least, so it was fer me. Every time the weather was fair, we'd laugh and joke and we... we were simply happy. Even she. But on those days when the wind would change, and the storms would rage... on those days she would wander. Up and doon the coast. Even

214

inland. She roamed, and I couldnae stop her. And then, one day, she'd gone. I thought nothin' of it fer a day or two – as that was how it got to be, but somethin' made me check the hidey hole that I'd thought meself so clever at choosin'.

"Her selkie skin was gone, and all she'd left behind was a curl of her hair, and a small snip of her selkie pelt. I never foond her again. I looked, and I played; over the coast, doon by the shore, over yonder on the island. Fer ten years I searched. But she never came back. I knew that she couldnae step human foot on land fer seven years, and at eight I still had hope. At nine, I was still searchin', but at ten... I knew I'd never see her again. That was thirty years ago."

The man blinked and brushed a hand against his face. He looked roundly at the children standing before him.

"But I'll tell ye one thing fer certain. I have *never* stolen from the sea. But it has stolen from me."

Isla slowly put the poker down. Hamish pulled her arm frantically, whispering "water goblin" so that only Isla could hear, but she ignored him. In her heart, she knew that Angus Begbie, as cantankerous and untidy as he might be, was not the sinister creature that they had come prepared to do battle with. Instead, she realised, he was nothing more than a broken-hearted old man. Sadness had weighed him down, and he wore it around him like an anchor. But he was nothing wicked.

"I'm so sorry Mr. Begbie. And... I'm sorry we broke into your house."

The station master grunted. "Quite a pretty apology seein' how handy ye seem to be with a poker!"

Isla flushed and quickly slid the object back to where she had picked it up from. "I truly am sorry. We, this is

Hamish, my brother – we... we've lost our father. Well, *we* didn't lose him, but he is missing. We... we thought we'd find some answers here."

Hamish piped up, "*Someone* took him away from us."

The station master frowned and rumbled. "These are dark and tryin' times, I'll not dispute that. 'Tis a terrible thing to lose a parent, aye, at any age, your'n especially. I am sorry I cannae help ye with ye father." He frowned again, and asked suspiciously, "But ye didnae come in here accusin' me of stealing yer father... well, not only that. Ye said 'selk*ies*'... and the island. And sommat aboot a goblin?"

Her heart sinking, Isla realised that he wasn't as slow-witted as she had first thought him to be. Mind racing, she replied quickly before Hamish could interject.

"We were playing make-believe. Hamish came up with the idea of a water goblin." She winced as she felt Hamish's angry fingers jab her square in the small of her back.

"But we read stories about selkies, and that they haven't been seen in these parts for many years... you see," she continued, opening her eyes innocently, "we needed to distract ourselves somehow, with... with our father... and, well, our play-acting seemed to become real. At least, to us. And then, I met you, and you seemed to be very interested in whether I'd come from the sea, so I joined the dots..."

Angus Begbie huffed and appeared appeased, if no more amicable.

"Aye, well, I can understand ye tryin' to take yer mind off... well, there we are. And ye managed to find out somat that not a lot of folk know. But yer game-playin', it's dangerous. Ye're lucky I don't try and press charges. But, aye, ye'll keep quiet aboot what ye foond. And I'll not tell the police... or yer aunt," he finished, with a knowing nod.

Isla and Hamish looked at each other in horror. Police!

They hadn't even considered that they might get in trouble with the police, so confident were they that they had found the monster they'd been looking for.

"Sorry, Mr. Begbie." "Thank you Mr. Begbie." They said simultaneously.

The station master coughed gruffly.

"We... we should be going, Mr. Begbie." Isla said nervously. She felt it was high time they met Dina back at the boat.

He nodded, standing. Hamish crept a little closer to Isla as he did so.

"I'll nay bite ye laddie." Angus Begbie's growl was not angry, but it made Hamish jump all the same.

"I'll walk the pair of ye back doon to wherever ye came from." It wasn't a question. All Isla could think to do was nod meekly, as she saw the station master's attempt at a smile. He was just lonely, she concluded.

"Hamish, why don't you go put Mr. Bebgie's papers and drawings back where you found them?" Isla prompted. Needing no further encouragement, Hamish darted out of the room and Isla could hear the footsteps trot up the stairs.

"Those drawings were beautiful, Mr. Begbie," Isla said, awkwardly trying to fill the silence which followed. "The selkie... she was beautiful. Do all selkies look the same?"

"Och no, they're all different. Emelda was a beauty, seal or human."

"Is it just the one selkie you've seen then?" Isla asked innocently.

The station master had shaken his head before he realised what he had done.

"Which other selkies have you seen?" She asked sweetly, but Isla knew that she had uncovered something.

Something Angus Begbie had not wanted to disclose.

He coughed, nervously, and shuffled his feet, looking down at the ground. "I didnae meet another selkie, so to speak."

"How do you know they don't all look the same then? Is it another selkie *pelt* that you've seen?" Isla pounced.

He looked trapped. His face rapidly took on the appearance of a moustached beetroot. "Aye, so, ye've foond me oot. A clever one, that ye are, lass. I will tell ye... but I'm ashamed of meself. It is not the act that I would ever do. No, 'tis not. It was in the years after ma Emelda had left me. I'd gone to the island, yonder. Where ye came from this evening. I'd felt a pull, somethin' tellin' me to go. And, I went, and I foond this selkie skin, hidden away so 'twas. I knew it was not the selkie pelt that I knew and loved, but a different selkie. And, I thought to meself, 'Angus, ye've a chance here to let some poor fella keep the love that he no doubt will lose one day, same as ye.' So, I took it." He whispered.

Isla stared. Did that mean, he was the one who had taken Marion's selkie skin?

"Aye, lass. Ye've a right to stare so. A wicked deed. Aye, I realised it later. I hid it back here, on the mainland with me, but a guilt crept in and began to eat away at me. As time passed, and as I got aulder, I knew that beyond all things, I wanted me own love to be happy. If she was happier in the sea than on the land with me, well, it was a bitter pill to swallow, but I foond that I wished her well. She'd given me more time than I had a right to. And that got me to thinkin'. It was no ma place to steal another selkie's skin - I'd taken the very choice away from that selkie that Emelda had been able to make. Keepin' a prisoner on land, that was wrong, I ken. Ma guilt ate away at me, and I've put the selkie pelt back on the island. Back where I think it had been hidden. I hope that the selkie whose pelt it is has foond it noo. If'n they want it."

He looked shamefacedly at the girl who had broken into his cottage. One guilty party to another, Isla thought. She nodded. "Mr. Begbie, I think you did the right thing, putting it back. You've given that selkie its life back."

He nodded, at a loss for what else to say. The rumble of footsteps hurtling back down the stairs broke the silence, and Hamish rattled through the door, out of breath and eager to get going.

They trudged out the door and down the path; Mr. Begbie leading the way with a torch that was far superior to Hamish's. Hamish's little quavering light brought up the rear. As they walked down to the boat's moored location, Isla wondered for the first time how they would explain Dina. She hoped that the selkie girl would stay out of sight.

Isla didn't have long to wait. The strong light of the station master's torch soon led them to the boat. Hamish crept up to Isla, "What about Dina?" he hissed. Isla shook her head, thinking quickly on her feet.

"Thank you very much for showing us the way back Mr. Begbie!" she called out loudly, causing a bird to swoop out of the branches of the tree sheltering the boat, cawing angrily.

When it had gone, silence reigned. Isla paused, then turned to the station master with a cheery smile. "This is us, Mr. Begbie... we'll see you around the island if you're ever over that way!"

Hamish scrambled down to the boat and began to untie the vessel from its moorings. The station master nodded uncertainly. "Aye. Mayhap. I dinnae cross the water much noo. Just the once... recently..."

As the old Scotsman shone his torch down across the water and onto the boat which Hamish had now liberated, he suddenly froze. Isla turned just in time to see where his attention had been drawn to. The light from the torch was reflected in Dina's deep eyes. She was peering over the side of the boat, looking up from the water. She must have jumped overboard as they approached, Isla thought.

Dina blinked and ducked down, out of sight, but it was too late.

"A selkie!" Angus Begbie shouted. His old age seemed to evade him for a moment as he jumped around, casting his torchlight wildly about. Isla ran past him and joined Hamish in the boat, grabbing the oars which he held out for her. They could clearly gear the gruff tones of the station master as they started to cast off from the shore.

"Aye! A selkie! Watch yerself! The mark. Look to the mark on her face. A selkie mark!"

He lumbered down to where they were slowly distancing themselves from the land, still looking around for Dina. But the girl had no desire to be further discovered. As she rowed, Isla cast a glance backwards. There, in the moonlight, she could just make out the ripple Dina's seal-form was casting on the sea's still surface.

"Come back!" the plaintive cry followed them. "I just want to see if ye have word of ma Emelda... Come back!" His heartfelt call faded as they finally lost sight of the spot they had moored the rowboat in. Isla rowed steadily and they watched the station master's crumpled figure grow smaller and smaller in the distance.

CHAPTER 18

THE MARK

When they had rounded the point, the boat rocked slightly, and a dripping wet Dina slid in besides them. "What happened?" she asked fiercely. "Why did you let the water goblin go? It nearly got me!"

Isla kept rowing, but calmed the selkie girl as best she could, explaining what they had found.

"I cannae believe a human discovered me so," Dina muttered angrily to herself. "But, I suppose, less harm than a water goblin's discovery of me."

Hamish interrupted her muttering as he said, "Have you ever met Mr. Begbie's Emelda? Is she one of the selkies on your island?"

Dina shook her head uncertainly, "'Tis not a name from these parts. There are other selkie clans, not close, but they do exist."

"Like the ones your clan was at your war with?"

Dina nodded, "Yes, but I had not heard of this name. To me, it sounds like a name from warmer waters. We selkies here do not travel to the warmer seas so very often. The Calder Sea is our home. I do not know if the warm water clans would fare well in our waters... I have heard that there are clans, far, far beyond our sea, but I cannot fathom there is such a need to leave the clan as happened in this selkie's case. 'Tis not natural."

Isla was curious. "So you will stay here, with your clan, forever?"

Dina shrugged, her face inscrutable in the darkness. "I cannot say for certain, but I will be with my clan. I do not think that I will leave the Calder Sea. These waters are all I know. Selkies should not leave their home and clan."

Again, Dina spoke fiercely, and Isla felt a ripple of shame drifting through her own mind. Her father was guilty of leaving his clan. As was his sister. All because of their family. She cleared her throat awkwardly, and the selkie girl looked at her.

"Of course, if some selkies did not leave, we would never have become friends."

Isla, looking up, caught the white teeth of Dina's apologetic smile.

Hamish, oblivious to the entire exchange asked suddenly, "Dina, what did Mr. Begbie mean about the 'Selkie mark'?"

Dina's hand went to her face. "The selkie mark - all selkies have one such, from birth. It forms a mark on our skin, which is the same as a marking on our pelts. Humans don't often look for them, or notice them... He must miss the selkie very much if he was able to see it so quickly."

In the dark, Isla could just make out Hamish's frown. "But I can't see it and I'm sitting right here!" he sounded perplexed.

"Here. Shine your light on my face." Dina was sitting

opposite both of them, and as Hamish directed his torch beam to Dina's face, both children leant forward to see for themselves. The flickering light showed up what was significantly less visible in the moonlight. On Dina's cheek there was a small change in pigmentation which was shaped in a swirling pattern, reminiscent of the waves in the sea.

Hamish and Isla were fascinated with Dina's mark once they saw it in the light.

"But I don't understand how I didn't... how *we* didn't see it before," Isla wondered.

"It's because you weren't looking for it." Dina answered, shrugging. "Those that know, see. I don't know why it is, but it has always been so." Self-consciously, she touched a finger her face again. "In our human forms, we can recognise one another by our selkie marks also."

The rest of the voyage back to Arraway was quiet. Dina sat in silence, looking out to sea. Hamish's eyelids drooped lower and lower, until at last his little snores gave him away. Isla rowed, studiously taking her mind away from the growing ache in her arms and shoulders. She thought about how the evening had unfolded. She didn't know where they would look now – she had been *so* certain that they were going to find the answer to getting their mother back.

When they got back to shore, Isla shook Hamish awake, and Dina bade them goodnight. Before she went, she promised to keep looking. "Keep your eyes open on land, and I'll be doing the same in the water."

She vanished into the sea, leaving Isla and Hamish to make their way back to the cottage. As they neared the stairs, Hamish sleepily yawned, "I don't know that Dina was right about only being able to see the selkie mark if you're looking for it. I saw the same mark on Aunty Marion's arm once, but I wasn't looking for it. I just thought it was a burn or something."

He let out a huge yawn once more, "But, I don't know I've really noticed Dina's before, so I don't know. Maybe she is right."

They'd reached the entrance to their room, and Hamish all but rolled into bed and resumed his snoring almost immediately. It took Isla longer to get to sleep; something in the back of her mind was nagging at her, keeping her awake. She couldn't work it out, but something that Hamish had said bothered her.

A restless night gave way to an early start for Isla. She threw her clothes on and crept downstairs and into her mother's room. She sat by her mother's side, placing her hand gently on her mother's cool forehead. As she smoothed a wisp of hair from her mother's brow, Penny's eyes opened. For a split second, Isla's heart jumped. But, in a moment the all-too familiar vacant expression returned to her mother's face.

"Come on, Mother, let's go outside. We'll see the sunrise."

Compliantly, Penny rose to her feet and stood placidly as Isla wrapped a blanket around her shoulders. She led her silent mother through the hallway to the bench outside in the garden. It was still dark, but flecks of pink were beginning to tinge the skyline, heralding the beginning of the day.

They sat, quiet; Isla snuggling herself up against her mother's shoulder. She remembered the mornings in London, when her mother would be the one to wake her up and lead her to the window with a cup of tea to watch the sunrise together. She could almost imagine they were back there now, sitting in companionable silence as they waited for the new day to appear.

A soft bleat drew her back to the present. Basil's face nudged at her mother's hands and she let the goat stay as it was, keeping them both company. As the sky bloomed with gradually layered shades of orange, yellow and red until it was aflame in colour, Marion joined them. She waited until Isla gave her a welcoming nod, and then sat beside Penny, putting an arm around her sister-in-law's shoulder. Aunt and niece sat on either side of Tuppence Gelder; a flame-haired guard, protecting their charge. When the sky had fully transitioned from the blaze of dawn to the cool morning light, Isla turned and looked at her aunt and mother. Her attention was drawn to Marion's arm, still around Penny's shoulders. Her sleeve had pushed back up her forearm, revealing the mark that Hamish had remembered a mere few hours earlier.

"What's that on your arm, Aunty?" she asked, breaking the silence.

Marion looked down to see what Isla was referring to and pulled her arm back in towards herself.

"It's a mark, given by the sea to selkies. A sign that we are given the sea's protection. But it also tells our story; the clan we come from, and our family."

"What do you mean?" Isla asked curiously.

Marion smiled shyly at her niece's inquisitiveness. "I'm not used to speaking freely of our selkie life and ways. I'm sorry, of course you would want to know."

She placed her arm back where it had been and pulled her sleeve back up.

"You see, each selkie, every true-born selkie, I'm afraid to say Isla - much like our selkie pelts you won't have one - but each selkie will have some form of identifying protective mark. These, here, they are symbols of the sea," she pointed to a swirl in the centre of her mark, "and these, these are the marks that my mother gave me, passed to her by her mother before that."

"Oh, so they're not all the same?" Isla asked, frowning.

"No, the mark is passed down from mother to daughter. Much like the mark is passed from father to son. We each bear the mark our parent has given us - female to female and male to male."

Isla went quiet, her mind trying to process what she had heard. Surely not...

"But surely some selkies will have very similar marks to each other?" she fumbled over her words.

Marion shook her head, puzzled. "Clans will have similar symbols for the sea's protection, but the shape will vary clan to clan. The identifying family mark, however, is only the same between direct descendants. It enables us to trace our ancestry very easily!"

Isla was silent once again. The mark which she saw before her on her aunt's arm was identical to the mark that she and Hamish had seen for the first time on Dina's face.

But that would mean...

Dina was Marion's daughter.

And Marion, she didn't know. Her daughter was still alive!

Isla's conscience battled with her mind; her internal thoughts were in turmoil. If she told Marion, she would go and retrieve her selkie skin and leave Isla and Hamish behind. Forever. If she didn't tell her aunt... Marion would never find her daughter. Dina would not know that her mother was still alive, that she hadn't been abandoned.

Marion's gentle voice broke into Isla's thoughts, making her jump with a guilty start.

"Why do you ask, Isla? You look as if you've seen a ghost."

Isla blinked, and her selfish desire to keep her family together won out. "Oh, I was just thinking – Hamish said he saw a mark on one of the selkies on the island, but I was trying to work out why he could see it but I didn't."

"Oh," Marion paused, thinking. "I don't know. You're right. Generally, it's not visible if it's not known about. But perhaps... perhaps it is because Duncan was... *is* a true born selkie. Mayhap it has something to do with the lineage of the male line."

"Because Father is a selkie, Hamish might get more selkie-sight? And Mother isn't a selkie - so I don't get it? Not from the start, anyway?" Isla asked.

Marion gave a sad smile. "I don't know for sure, but that would be my guess. I know it's not fair, but..."

"But that makes sense." Isla finished. She didn't mind. It would make Hamish happy to know that he was closely linked to their father in that way. Isla sighed. She knew she had to tell her aunt the truth. She opened her mouth, steeling herself...

CRASH!

She jumped again, turning at the cacophonous noise that had just sounded from the direction of the kitchen. She rose quickly before Marion could react. She didn't want Marion to catch Hob unawares in the kitchen.

"It's probably Hamish. Sleepwalking. He does that sometimes. I'll go check on him," she babbled as she walked quickly towards the back door to let herself into the kitchen.

Isla wasn't fully certain why she so anxious to not let Hob get caught - she guessed he might not take kindly to being surprised, and she didn't want him to leave Calder

Cottage. She wondered what on earth Hob was up to. He was never usually noisy. Maybe it *was* Hamish sleepwalking!

She stopped in shock as she neared the kitchen. The back door was open, and there in the kitchen, Billie was stamping her hooved feet angrily, head lowered, making ready to charge at a countertop. There, trying to hide behind a cookbook, was Pealle. Hob was watching the scene unfold in scared fascination, peeking out from his hidey-hole in the chimney.

The crash that Isla had heard had not been Hamish sleepwalking, but Billie bulldozing her way into the kitchen.

"Billie!" she shouted. "*What* is wrong with you? Get *out!*"

She heaved the maddened goat out by the horns and deposited her outside the kitchen door in an angry, bleating pile.

"I'm so sorry, Mr. Pealle, your chieftainship." Isla cried, rushing forward when she was satisfied that the door was goat-proof once more.

The elderly brownie glared up at her, his bushy eyebrows drawn together in fury over the cookbook he was still sheltering behind.

"Ah cannae ken what ye must be doin' to greet yer visitors this way! Ah come doon to this *hoose* to see if ye've got yerself any news or if ye've had any luck, and ask if'n ah can help ye oot, and a barmy bleatin' *goat* tries to attack me!"

He pushed the book towards Isla, who caught it, staggering slightly at the force with which it had been propelled towards her.

"Chief Pealle was here askin' aboot yer expedition," Hob squeaked. He'd clearly never seen the brownie chieftain so angry and was more than a little terrified at the older brownie's rage.

"Ah'll tell ye somat fer nothin'," the brownie chief hoarsely rasped. "Ye won't see me agin. Yer on yer oon!"

With a speed Isla would never have credited to the brownie's vast age, he hopped to the window furthest from the door that Billie was audibly guarding – her head butting against the wood every few moments. He slid the window open and climbed out, quickly blending into the undergrowth and away from the cottage, disappearing from sight in a matter of moments.

"That was... odd." Isla said to a shaky Hob.

"Aye. A grave offence. His great chieftainship doesnae come doon from the mountain. Nay. Not ever. It was a great honour fer the broonie chieftain to visit a broonie hoose. Ah'll be cast oot, fer sure!"

Hob's misery was evident in his voice, and crumpled face. He wrung his hands, looking so crest-fallen that Isla felt a great wave of pity for him.

"I'm sorry, Hob. I'll try to make it right with him later. I don't know why Billie's acting so strangely! They don't seem to like visitors, those goats..."

She trailed off, the events of the past few moments distracting her. She cast her mind about, to think of something to tell Hob to cheer him up.

"You'll not believe it Hob! We didn't find anything on the mainland. It was a dead end. But... And don't tell Hamish yet, but we have a cousin!" She said, in her aim of cheering the brownie up. However, Hob didn't seem to hear; his pointy ears were folded down over themselves as he rocked back and forth morosely.

"What ma granddaddy would say to me. 'Hob. Disgrace of a broonie! Offendin' the great high chieftain himself!'"

Hob's plaintive voice quickly turning to a wail prompted Isla to close the window, with a slam so forceful the bush shook outside the window. However, the noise did have the effect of seeming to calm the distraught brownie, or at least quiet him, which she was grateful for.

Not long after, Marion's voice drifted through the hallway.

"Everything alright in there, Isla?"

"Yes thanks Auntie. Billie got into the kitchen somehow. Made a bit of a mess."

Isla just about made out her aunt muttering, "bleeding goat", and footsteps walking back down the hall towards the garden again. She looked around for Hob, but all she saw was the door to the brownie hole swinging shut.

She didn't see Hob for the rest of the day.

Hamish couldn't entice the brownie out either, and he stared at her with a puzzled frown when Isla tried to explain what had happened.

"Oh. But surely he'll understand. Basil and Billie are just a bit... strange. Especially Basil," Hamish muttered darkly.

Isla refrained from telling Hamish about *everything* she'd found out from their aunt. As she shook her head in response to her brother, equally puzzled about the goats' behaviour and the brownie chieftain's reaction, guilt gnawed at her.

CHAPTER 19

DISAPPEARANCE

Isla's guilt at keeping her secret from both Hamish and Marion drove her out of the house the following morning. Tossing and turning in the night, she'd resolved to make her way over to the selkie island. She had to tell Dina.

Isla found her way to the secret beach below the cottage, slipping away from Hamish and Marion as they played cards in the garden. She had half-hoped to find Dina there already, waiting for her. However, when she walked amongst the rocks harbouring the rowboat; all she found was the boat, just where they had left it the previous night.

She perched on the edge of the boat, and absently kicked her heels against its bow. The noise must have travelled across the beach and into the sea, for not long after, a familiar head popped up on the surface of the water.

Patch's pointy face jabbed up towards the sky, and from where she was sitting, Isla could make out the excited chattering coming from Patch's beak. He leapt out of the water, landing facing away from her. Patch repeated this performance several times; each time facing Isla chattering once again.

Until now, Isla had never really wished that she could speak porpoise, but she fervently did so now. She crinkled her nose in concentration. He was behaving very oddly, she thought, even more than usual.

On Patch's fifth landing, he smacked the water hard with his tail, and the sound reverberated straight through her.

"He wants me to follow him!" she thought, kicking herself for not having realised sooner.

Patch's erratic antics calmed as soon as Isla began to push the boat out from its hiding place on the beach, out down to the water. "Maybe Hamish would have understood," she muttered to herself as she got the boat out onto the water and picked up the oars, to follow the porpoise wherever he was trying to get her attention to go to.

It rankled slightly that Hamish had selkie sight, and that she did not. All because it passed from their father to the male line. She snorted. Ridiculous selkie logic. She wondered if there was anything else that she would miss out on which Hamish would discover, anything he could do by simple virtue of the way selkie genetics seemed to work.

However, before her thoughts took her too far down that path, she reflected as she rowed, that whatever Hamish could or would (or wouldn't) be able to do, she wouldn't change it. After all, she was her mother's daughter, a fact that she was incredibly proud of. She wouldn't swap her mother for any number of selkie abilities.

Thinking of her mother drew Isla's thoughts back to the

present. Maybe Dina had found out something about how they could get their mother well again. Or maybe she'd discovered some new information about their father's disappearance. "That's probably why sent she Patch!" Isla exclaimed to herself as she thought about it.

Isla's growing excitement about these possibilities dimmed when she remembered the reason she'd been looking for Dina to begin with. She still didn't know how she was going to tell her that her mother was still alive, and that her mother had chosen not to return to the water. Isla winced as the thought flitted through her mind. It wasn't *strictly* true. The lie resounded in her mind. Marion hadn't known about her daughter when she'd made her choice. Sighing, she felt her head begin to hurt. It was all getting quite complicated.

Momentarily, she forgot about her conundrum when she saw that Patch had been leading her to the selkie island. She rolled her eyes. Surely Dina wasn't *that* busy to not be able to come over to the beach herself? Isla looked over to Patch for an explanation, but all she found in return was some incomprehensible porpoise chatter.

"Well, thanks Patch. As always, it's been informative."

Perhaps Patch understood what she was saying, or perhaps it was just that sarcasm translated into porpoise, but either way, Isla was treated to a shower of seawater unceremoniously being splashed over her courtesy of Patch's tail fin. She gasped as the cold water hit her. She turned sharply back to see Patch rolling on his back, for all the world appearing to be laughing at her as he clicked his beak.

Isla shook her head. "Porpoises." She grumbled and trudged up towards the cave.

She thought Dina would at least be waiting for her *here*,

by the cave entrance, but again, there was no sign of her. Through the cave entrance she went. Isla didn't know what she'd been expecting to find but, if she was honest with herself, it would have been a little more than the quiet normality of the selkie community that she was faced with. But there they were; the selkie farmers tending to their pools, and the young pups sliding and splashing about under the watchful eyes of their mothers.

Isla waved as she passed a group of craftspeople in human form, busy shaping and moulding pots from clay. Now used to her presence among them, some of the selkies looked up and waved back, but the group made no particular effort to attract her attention or lose focus from what they were doing. Isla smiled politely and walked by. She was confused. Surely Dina had sent Patch to find her – so, where was she?

Isla spotted Rhodric talking to a group of selkies who were all gathered around him as he addressed them seriously. Hesitantly, she approached. Those who were still in seal form assumed their human forms. The unblinking and unsmiling faces looking back at her gave her pause.

Rhodric moved away from the group slightly, and she joined him, puzzled by the solemnity that surrounded him. She had never seen the selkie folk so serious.

"What's wrong?" She asked.

"Trouble in the border waters." Rhodric replied shortly. "Nothing we can't handle, but our borders are weakening every day."

Isla frowned. It appeared to her that age suddenly weighed upon him. They stood in silence for a moment, unsure of what to say; Rhodric seemingly lost in thought. Eventually, he shook his head, clearing his thoughts, and appeared to remember that Isla was there.

"Have you any tidings?" he asked hopefully.

Isla shook her head. "No... I thought we found something, but I was wrong. It turned out to be nothing. But I thought Dina might have found something. Patch led me here – I thought she sent him."

"Patch?" Rhodric looked at Isla uncertainly.

"The porpoise," Isla clarified, and immediately Rhodric's confusion cleared.

"Ah, porpoises. Chattery, excitable creatures. I wouldn't put too much stock in a porpoise. But if Dina sent it..." he tailed off as he looked over to the group of selkies who were waiting for him patiently.

Isla sensed that she wouldn't have his attention for much longer.

"So, have you seen Dina?" she asked, hoping that she would finally find out what the urgency was which Patch had conveyed.

Absently, Rhodric replied, "Nay. She's likely to be found out there," he said, pointing vaguely out to the water. "She's been away from the island much of the past few days. I have not seen her since last sundown."

Seeing Isla's frown of confusion, he added. "Don't fret. 'Tis not unusual."

Isla nodded, and Rhodric returned to the group and the discussion resumed in low, earnest whispers. Isla turned and made her way back to the boat, declining an invitation from Hamish's young selkie friends to join them in their sport in the pools.

"I'll come back with Hamish so you can play with him next time," she called to the disappointed youngsters.

Isla was in no mood to join in with their games – she was utterly perplexed. She had been certain that Dina had found something of great importance. Why else would

Patch be acting so strangely?

Back in the boat, she looked for the porpoise, but could not see him. "Hmph," she muttered. "Maybe he was pulling a prank..."

She rowed back to Arraway, keeping her eyes open for any sign of either the porpoise or selkie. But none appeared.

Over the next few days, Isla rowed Hamish over to the selkie island. Each time, Patch appeared, jumping and splashing frantically, but each time he disappeared from sight before they reached land.

Once on the selkie island, Hamish was absorbed in his play and adventures with his young friends, and left Isla to her own exploration and investigations. On the second day, Isla approached Rhodric once more after he re-emerged from his sentry duty on the selkie border.

"Hello, Rhodric. How is it today?" She nodded towards the outer expanses of the sea line. He looked exhausted, she thought, and even older than he had the previous day. His weary form was stooped, and he straightened with obvious effort.

"We are safe enough for today. The border holds."

"Was... Is Dina on the border?" Isla asked cautiously. She was met with a fatigued grimace.

"Nay. The lass will be here, or hereaboot. Taking herself off, she's on the scent of something, I've no doubt. She'll be here to report back at sundown. 'Tis our way. Scout and then report."

A flicker of disquiet began to stir in Isla's mind, but she pushed it aside. Dina was more than capable of scouting, exploring and looking after herself. After all, she'd been doing so her whole life!

On the third day, Hamish looked around, frowning as they approached the selkie island. "Where did Patch go?" He wondered aloud. Isla shook her head, pulling them up onto the shore.

"I don't know. He disappeared yesterday too. Your guess is as good as mine. Here, come on, hop out, will you? I can't push the boat up with your weight on it!"

"Hey! I'm not heavy!" he grumbled, but he obliged her, nonetheless. Isla laughed and ruffled his sandy hair as he did. "You've grown! You're bigger and heavier than when we got here. And now you've learnt to swim... I swear you'll eat us out of house and home!"

Hamish stuck his tongue out at her but grinned proudly. "Aunty Marion said that I'll need longer trousers soon, and new shoes!"

Isla laughed again at his excitement. It was true, Hamish had grown almost beyond recognition, not only in stature and appearance, but his confidence and independence had also grown. He was not her fragile younger brother anymore, she thought.

They jostled and laughed as they ran up to the cave entrance but stopped short when Rhodric appeared at the mouth of the cave. Hamish waved a cheery hello as he squeezed past to go find his friends, but Isla waited as she noted the sombre expression on the old selkie's face.

"What is it?" she whispered. "Did the border fall? Is anyone hurt?"

Rhodric shook his head, no.

"Dina did not report in last night. It is not like her. We have eyes out in the water, but nobody has seen anything. I've sent sentries out, but they have come back with no news."

The stern, authoritative demeanour of the selkie fell

away, and Isla suddenly saw the fear and exhaustion in Rhodric's face.

"I'm sure she'll reappear, you know Dina... she does what she wants!" Even as she spoke the words lightly, Isla did not believe them. Nor, she could tell, did Rhodric. Dina had disappeared.

"We will continue to search," Rhodric rumbled. "But I fear it is not safe approaching these waters any longer."

Isla opened her mouth to protest, but Rhodric held up his hand, stopping her. "Nay, stay to the land, to your own shoreline. I cannae say what is out there, but it bears us no good will. You must take care of your brother and stay away until it is safe. Until we stop this."

Isla swallowed. She did not know if she could keep her word – and she could tell that Rhodric would not take kindly to a broken promise. "We'll stay away from your island until it is safe," Isla worded carefully.

After all, she couldn't promise to remain land-bound! She vowed to herself to look for Dina – for her cousin.

Later that afternoon, once they were back on Arraway, Isla found her aunt tending to the vegetable patch in the garden of Calder Cottage. She knelt beside her, and wordlessly began to pull up some of the weeds which were creeping though the stalks and stems.

Marion looked up, and sensed Isla's mood. "What is it lass?" she asked softly.

"Why do bad things keep happening, Aunty Marion?"

Marion sat back on her heels and drew a deep breath. "Well, now, that's a big question. What are we talking about?"

Isla fiddled absently with one of the plants which she had just drawn absently from the soil. "I don't know. All of it, I guess. Mother, Father, the selkies having problems with

238

their border, more than before... it's getting bad now. And... D... one of my friends has gone missing."

"That is a lot, yes." Marion paused. "Well, some things are out of our control. Others... well, sometimes things happen because we are not paying attention. See these weeds for instance, we don't want them in our vegetable patch, but they've managed to creep through because we weren't paying attention. Sometimes they creep in because we haven't stopped them, sometimes because the seeds get blown in on the wind, and sometimes because other creatures bring them in. But now, it's our job to step in and look after the plants that we *do* want here."

"So... the problems on the selkie border might have happened because they weren't looking after the border?" Isla said slowly. "Or maybe... because you and Father weren't there..."

"It could well be," Marion answered sadly. Isla immediately regretted bringing the news to her aunt, feeling guilty about causing the distress that was now evident on Marion's face.

"But, sometimes, we can do something about what has gone wrong, and stop other bad things from happening?"

Marion nodded. "Sometimes it just takes courage to do the right thing. Sometimes it only takes one person to make a difference. Sometimes it takes a whole clan."

Isla thought about that for a moment. "What if you know what the right thing to do is, but you don't know what will happen if you do it?" she asked, thinking of the secret she held.

Marion smiled. "None of us can predict what the future may bring. All we can do is trust what our heart says. Why do you ask, Isla? Is there something on your mind?"

Isla slowly shook her head. "I was just thinking. Thank

you, Aunty Marion, I have to go do something."

Her aunt gave her hand a quick squeeze before she left.

"Whatever it may be lass, know that you have the courage and strength of a selkie warrior within you. You can do whatever it is that you have a mind to. Never forget that, and never let anyone tell you otherwise. The Calder Sea runs through your veins. Always remember who you are."

As she walked to the house to find her mother, Isla mulled over what her aunt had said. Suddenly, it came to her as she considered her aunt's words. "Of course," she breathed.

"The answer is the sea..." she whispered, so low that she wasn't sure if she merely thought the words or whether she spoke them aloud, but she looked at her mother as she did so.

To her amazement, she thought she saw the shadow of a smile flicker across her mother's lips, and a feather light squeeze of her mother's hand on hers. The next moment, Tuppence's demeanour was as blank as it had been previously. But Isla was jubilant. She kissed her mother's forehead.

"I know you're in there, Mother," she whispered. "And maybe... maybe I can bring you back. And I'll tell Aunty Marion... but I need to find Dina first."

Isla swiped off a renegade tear from her cheek. "You have a niece Mother, and Hamish and I... we have a cousin. But I need to find her so I can tell Aunty Marion. It's just you and me Mother, we're the only ones who know."

She kissed her mother goodnight, and went to bed, visions of the sea and the selkie island running though her mind. She hardly heard Hamish's soft snores, her thoughts occupying her well into the night.

Isla woke early, and tiptoed out of the room, leaving Hamish alone with the dawn chorus of the gulls.

She snuck out of the cottage, and made her way to the loch, to the boat.

Her plan had formulated as she had lain in bed, prompted by her aunt's words the previous day. The sea *was* in her blood. And also, in Dina's. Marion had followed the sea as she had found her selkie skin, and Isla was determined to do the same to find Dina. She looked up at the threatening clouds which were closing in fast. Gulping, Isla remembered the last time that she'd been caught in a storm on the sea. And Dina wasn't here to help her now. She frowned and shook the thought away. Dina had saved her; now it was her turn to save Dina.

The rumble of thunder sped Isla through the motions of navigating the boat through the inlet and out onto the open sea. She'd decided to go from the loch as she had a hunch that Patch's disappearance from the selkie island wasn't a coincidence. Patch, she guessed, knew where Dina was, and had tried to lead them to her, but she had ignored him. Now, Isla was fairly certain that Patch had disappeared to go up past the loch, and up the coast where she had not yet explored.

The heavy onslaught of driving rain met Isla as she rounded the point, turning left for the first time. She gritted her teeth as the ferocity of the elements increased. It felt to Isla as if the sky were possessed, unleashing all that it held over her, and she and her boat were its sole target. She had faced such an assault of the air and the deep before, but this time it felt different. Yes, there was a violent rage in the flaying water, which was scouring her arms and face, but Isla had grown in strength. Both her limbs and her mind battled against the fierce display of power against her.

Throwing herself against the rearing waves, she recalled how she had followed the inner call she had previously felt, the call of the sea. She drew upon that now, even as the waves roared and flung her little boat about. Amidst the howling of the wind and the peals of thunder threatening to overwhelm both girl and boat, Isla closed her eyes and stilled her mind, searching for the connection to the sea that was in her blood. For she felt, with deep certainty, that the storm that had arisen as she neared the open sea was no happenstance. Nor was it the work of the sea. Something, *someone*, with a great and dreadful power had harnessed the sea against its will and was now throwing the full force of the depths against her.

In Isla's moment of stillness, suddenly, she found what she was looking for. There, in the very heart of the storm, the distinct but familiar low crooning of the waves. If she concentrated on that note, low and faint as if being transmitted by one of the shells that she might pick up on the beach, Isla sensed the real struggle that was taking place below the water's roiling surface. Eyes closed, hands tightly gripping the oars that were inching her forward, Isla concentrated intently and felt an insistent gentle undercurrent nudging her boat along in the direction she was aiming for; the direction, she was sure, Patch had disappeared in.

The moment that Isla opened her eyes once more, it was as if her ears had been unplugged. Screeching gales buffeted her senses, and stinging salt spray seared her eyes. Worst, her connection to that one ripple of the sea that she had had, it was gone.

Close to despair, Isla tried once more. Shutting her eyes tight, forcing her mind to quiet, the noise around her seemed to dull, and she regained the barely perceptible connection that she had fleetingly found before. Determined not to lose her lifeline a second time, Isla drew a deep breath, and committed her movements with the oars to follow the signals and promptings of the current she was following. Disbelievingly, she found that the motion was easier, faster, and fluid as she let the single current guide her. She followed the subtle steering, eyes still tightly shut, and navigated the rising swells and pitching of the boat as if gliding on the surface of the loch. Isla imagined the sea's finger, beckoning her in the direction she was seeking. Still sightless, she hoped and prayed that she was being led to the destination she sought.

After what seemed an age, Isla finally felt a lull in the storm's seething. The rain ebbed, the waves gentled, and the wind softened. The sea, she felt, had gained the advantage in the battle it was engaged in. Cautiously, she opened her eyes, peeking from under her eyelids, curious to where she had arrived.

Amazed, she stared up at the now near-cloudless sky. To her left reared high, heather-topped cliffs, and to her right, a familiar head jutted out above the surface of the waves, and an excited chattering soon followed.

"Patch!" she cried, laughing in relief. "Where are we? Is Dina here?"

At her words, the porpoise rolled on his back, smacked his tail on the water, and resurfaced, still chattering excitedly. Isla sensed the current she had followed almost imperceptibly change tack, and her boat shifted ever so slightly to directly face the cliffs which she had just spotted.

"Alright, then... I suppose that means we're going that

way." Isla picked up her oars once more and urged her aching muscles to again do her bidding. Patch, too, seemed to sense the change in the sea, and leapt through the air as he swam up towards the cliff face.

It was only when she had neared the base of the cliffs that Isla understood why she had been nudged in that direction. What previously looked to be impenetrable rock now revealed itself to have a cleverly disguised series of passageways from the sea into the depths of the island. She followed the quickening of the current as she rowed alongside it, matching the tempo with her own oar strokes. Together, she and Patch entered a thin crevice in the rock edge. The gap was only just wide enough for the boat, and narrowed as it went up, blocking out the light.

The main source of light came from the sea itself. Isla raised her arm and found she could brush the wall of the grotto with her hand. A blue, shimmering light played on the walls and ceiling of the cavern in which she and Patch now found themselves, and the lapping of the water reverberated around the chamber. Isla felt as if she'd entered a different world.

Patch swam close to the boat; Isla wasn't sure whether it was because the porpoise was seeking or offering protection, but he remained close until they reached what looked like a narrow platform on the far side of the chasm. Isla threw the boat's rope around a rock and looked over to where Patch was watching her from.

"I don't know if you can understand me. You probably can, I think... But just stay here for a bit? Alright? I'm going to look for Dina." As Isla finished speaking, Patch clicked his beak in quick succession, which Isla took as agreement.

Steeling herself for whatever she would find, she took the first step up a jagged staircase that wound upwards away from the boat. Higher and higher she circled, deeper into the heart of the island. As she climbed, her feet growing heavier with every step, something in the back of her mind niggled at her. There was something familiar and yet alien about where she was. She closed her eyes. The familiar, comforting sound of the sea played in her mind. Opening her eyes once again, she focused on the sound. To her surprise, the sound of the sea was not coming from behind her, from the sea itself, but rather onwards, from inside the hill that she was climbing.

Onwards and upwards she went, her breath catching at times from the climb, all the while following the note of the sea. As she climbed, the sound grew. In the silence, it seemed almost deafening to her, but she was certain that she was the only one who could hear it.

One last turn upwards finally brought Isla to a peculiar chamber. It was narrow, and dark; seeming to house only the steps by which she had ascended. She could stand, but barely. Rough stone walls appeared to have been hewn from the rock hollow in which she was stood. Blinking, Isla noticed that a small glimmer of flickering light could just be seen coming from a sliver of the base of the rock.

"Well, nothing else for it," she whispered to herself. Gingerly, she pushed against the wall. Sure enough, the wall swung soundlessly forward. Thinking quickly, Isla grabbed a stone by her foot, and wedged it in the doorway.

With the door now open, she looked around. To her astonishment, Isla saw that she was now stood in the centre of the Brownie Glen.

CHAPTER 20

LOST AND FOUND

Blinking, Isla stood still, trying to gather her thoughts. The sound of the sea rang loudly in her ears, and yet, her eyes told her that this was impossible. In the centre of the hollow, the fire burned bright; cheerfully crackling as embers burned and sparked. A flat rock stood next to the fire. Seeing nothing and nobody around, Isla sat dejectedly on the rock, waiting for the ornery brownie chieftain to appear. She closed her eyes, and the powerful roar of the sea now rushed through her mind, no longer the gentle whisper she had had previously heard.

And then her mind pieced it together. "The answer is the sea," Isla repeated. Keeping her eyes shut, she focused intently on where the sound was coming from. Scarcely daring to breathe, she turned her head from side to side, trying to pinpoint the exact source of what she was hearing. It seemed to surround her. Tentatively, she put out her hand, and her fingers brushed along the rock that she was sitting on.

Not expecting to find anything, Isla let out a whispered shriek when her skin brushed against something soft and cool to the touch. Her fingers closed around it, and, heart racing, she tentatively brushed her thumb over the object which she held. It felt like... a bag?

Isla opened her eyes and looked at what she held. Previously invisible, it was now revealed to her gaze. It was indeed a small, velveteen bag which fit into the palm of her hand. It was drawn shut with string, and, fumbling over the ties, she soon opened it. To her disappointment, the bag appeared to be empty.

It was feather-light, and there was no discernible shape or object within. Suddenly, Isla was reminded of her brother's favourite trick when opening presents, and the idea came to her to follow Hamish's example. She shook the bag out upside down, over the rock. Drifting out, and landing silently on the rock table, came a single lock of hair. Her mother's.

At first, Isla didn't understand what she was seeing. "Why is Mother's hair here? In this place? Why couldn't I see it...? It's like a spell... now you see it, now you don't. But now, I do... Wait. A spell. Oh no you don't!"

Isla's fury rose in an instant as she realised the significance of what lay before her. The very answer to her mother's absence, there, in a lock of hair that she held in her hand. Whoever stole the power of the sea surely had the power and black heartedness to lock her mother's mind away.

Isla let out a cry of pain, and in a fit of rage, hurled the lock of hair along with the velveteen bag straight into the fire. As she watched it burn, a lightness entered the chamber and it felt to Isla as if blinkers had been removed from her sight.

She looked around once more. No longer did the brownie hollow appear enclosed and empty, now she could see bright lights, tunnels and sparkling gemstones lighting the way along different passageways. Heather and mountainside flora carpeted the floor of the cavern around the merrily crackling fire.

Amongst all these riches and visual wonders, Isla's eye was drawn to two seemingly dull objects. Yet, as she approached the base of the rock that she had been sitting on, Isla saw that what she had first taken to be rocks were much softer in appearance. Silky, grey, even dappled, she touched one and drew back instantly. Selkie skins. Two of them.

Isla recognised one immediately to be Dina's, but the other... she cast her gaze around wildly, for the first time truly taking stock of her newly revealed surroundings, looking for any sign of Marion.

Her aunt was nowhere to be seen. Clutching the selkie skins close to her, Isla closed her eyes, and heard, once more, the now gentled song of the sea, calling once more to her. It was coming from one of the paths that led from the centre of the brownie hollow. Isla gulped. She knew that she was not alone. Taking trembling steps forward, Isla followed the sea's call. Down the path she walked, hardly glancing at the rich rubies, vibrant emeralds and sparkling sapphires which lined the way. For there, she could see, just ahead of her, a chamber with bars.

From behind the bars, Dina flashed a jagged grin back at her.

"You took your time!"

Isla smiled back weakly, flinging herself at the bars. "How did you end up here?! Who did this?... Is Aunty Marion...?"

Isla felt Dina's hands prise her fingers away from where she had been pulling fruitlessly at the lock. She looked up to see her friend pointedly looking beyond her. "What?" Isla began, turning to see what Dina was directing her to. Then she stopped. In her haste, she had not seen the second barred chamber, slightly hidden as if it had been lost in shadow.

Behind the bars, a figure moved out into the light. There, standing smiling and crying with joy was a tall, weather-beaten man with a head of fiery red hair.

"Father!" Isla cried, leaping towards him.

Duncan stretched out his arms through the bars towards his daughter. "There lass, I'm right here. You're a sight for sore eyes! Isla, I've missed you! There, there sweetheart, it's alright."

Isla embraced him through the bars as far as she could, noticing as she did so that her father's bones were distinguishable through his threadbare Navy uniform. His beard was unkempt, and his hair long and beginning to matt. She looked up at him through watery eyes and saw that her father's face bore more lines than it had the last time that she had seen him.

She squeezed him tight to her, inhaling the familiar smell of the sea personified.

"How did you find me, lass?" Duncan croaked, his voice hoarse as if unused for some time. "And your mother, and Hamish? Where are they? How are they?"

Isla looked up again at her father, still unable to believe that she had found him, that he was here. Her mind brimmed with questions of her own.

"They're here, on the island," she replied quickly. "But... you? How did you get here? Have you been here all this time? We got a telegram saying you were lost at sea...

and I knew you weren't really gone Father. I just knew it! But who took you? What... What happened?"

Duncan placed a comforting arm on her shoulders. "Shh, Isla. Slow down! One question at a time!"

He laughed softly, the noise of which took Isla straight back to her childhood, a mere few years ago; a time when she had heard that very laugh every day. She pinched herself. She hadn't thought to hear her father's laughter for some time, and yet, here he was, and the sound of his laughter was music to her ears.

"I am so sorry that I left you and Hamish, aye, and your mother, for so long," he said earnestly. "And I'm even more sorry that you received word of my death." He smiled briefly. "I am, however, pleased to announce that reports of my death, as you can see, have been highly exaggerated... But, Isla, we need to get out of here. Is there a key outside?"

Isla shook her head as she looked around. "I don't think so, but I'll look." Isla looked over to Dina, to see whether she had any knowledge of a key or source of escape. All she received was a quick shake of the head in return.

Seeing no way of opening the doors to the cages, Isla tried rattling the doors. They did not budge. Suddenly, a wave of inspiration hit her. Patch! He could help!

"Wait here!" Isla called as she ran, heading straight back to the hidden staircase and then halfway back down the stairs, calling to the porpoise, "They're here! Go, get help!" A splash answered her. Taking that as a 'yes', she turned and ran back up the steps. Breathless, she found herself at the top of the stairs once more. Returning to the cells, she took a deep breath.

"Tell me, Father, what happened?" Isla implored.

Duncan sighed. "Very well, lass. But I warn you. There is something that I have not yet told you... It is a long tale..."

Isla interrupted, impatient to hear the elements of her father's story that she did not already know. "I know, you're a selkie, actually Prince...no, King of the selkie clan of the Calder Sea... but you chose to marry Mother, and so you gave up the kingdom to Aunty Marion. Oh, and Aunty Marion got trapped on the island when she was looking for you, so the clan have been left leaderless, but there's something out there... something that's threatening the selkies as they have no leader. Oh, and this is Dina. She's my friend. And a selkie. And... Hamish and I are half-selkie."

Duncan stood in inscrutable silence for a moment. He then cleared his throat. "It seems that all secrets are washed away when faced with the island and the Calder Sea," he said with a wry smile. "Isla, my love, I am sorry. I should have been the one to tell you. You've learnt a lot whilst you've been here!"

He paused and then said slowly. "Forgive me, but I do not know how long I have been... away. Time feels different in this prison. I do not know if I have been here for days, weeks, months... years?" he asked questioningly.

Isla shook her head. "We received the telegram some months back."

"Aha, that helps." Duncan nodded. He spoke quickly before Isla could form her questions again.

"I am afraid I do not know who our captor is," he said. "No, not truly. I have seen a glimpse here, and a glimpse there, but all the while, there has been a shroud over my vision. Perhaps, child," Duncan said, looking to Dina, "You have seen what I did not?"

But Dina again shook her head, answering fiercely. "I did not see what it was or who it was that took me. If I had, they would not be walking free at this time. It was not long after I left you, Isla, you and Hamish, on our return from the mainland. I was swimming. And then... I remember something grasped hold of me. And then, I awoke, and I was here. My selkie skin... gone. And I have been held, unseeing. Lord Duncan," she bowed gracefully, "has helped me to retain my sanity. I am sure if I had been locked away by myself, I would soon have lost my mind. When I find who our captor is... they will rue the day." Dina's bared teeth reflected the threat, and Isla shuddered, thankful again that she had not been the one to cross the angry selkie... well, not in this way.

"But how did you end up here, Father? The ship? What..."

"All in good time, Isla." Duncan settled on the floor, taking a seat. "Let me begin, before the ship, I think.

"So, you know that I left my place as King, and followed your mother to London. That was a shock, entering the world on land. I found it to be... different, and at first, I did not like it. I was unaccustomed to the ways of the land, and the people... humans have very different interests and ways of being. Especially in the big city. But I had chosen Tuppence, and through her, I came to see that the world of the land was not so very far removed from my own. The ways of people – they grew on me. And then, when you were born, Isla. Aye, and then Hamish, you three were the ones that mattered the most to me."

"Does... Mother know?" Isla butted in, curiously. Duncan shook his head. "Nay. Once I'd made the decision to leave, in my mind, that was my break from who I had been. I was no longer selkie. I was Duncan. She thought me very odd, of course, a true country bumpkin from the North, with no knowledge of how the rest of the world worked. And, she liked me, I knew that. She was patient in teaching me all about the city and she laughed at me... a lot." He smiled; eyes lost in the memories.

He looked at Isla with a wink. "Your mother also taught me how to laugh at myself. She informs me, quite often, that I took myself entirely too seriously before I met her."

"I love Mother's laugh," Isla said softly.

"But the most important thing that Tuppence ever gave me was her love, and you two. You became my world, and I hardly thought about my old life, who I had been... Even when I learnt that Marion had become trapped on the island, I did nothing. I could not leave you and Tuppence. All I could do was try to forget about it."

A thought suddenly occurred to Isla, and she couldn't believe she hadn't thought of it before.

"If you didn't want to go back, why didn't you give Aunty Marion your selkie skin, so she could go back?" Isla asked. Surely, her father didn't *want* his sister to have had the choice made for her?

Duncan smiled sadly, "Aye lass, and the thought of that was partly what drew Marion all the way from the sea and down to the city. Aye, your birth, that too. But I think the question of my selkie skin was the clincher. We had never heard of selkies swapping skins, it is just not done. But I offered her mine willingly, after all what need did I have of it? As soon as she draped my selkie skin around her shoulders, we knew why we had never heard it done before. It did nothing. It turns out a selkie's skin is unique – and is not a gift to be shared."

Dina snorted. "Every selkie pup knows that. That's what we are taught as soon as we can swim."

Duncan inclined his head, acknowledging her statement. "Aye, but did you ever test the theory?" Dina shook her head no.

"And that is why we both put hope in our idea." Duncan continued.

"We knew that a selkie's skin is special, sacred even, to the individual selkie, but we did not know that it was impossible to use another selkie's skin. Not until then.

"By that time, I had joined the crew of a fishing vessel. It turned out that I had an affinity with the sea, even having given up my past life. So, that brings us up to the start of the war. I'd been sailing with the fishing vessel for years, and I would have been happy to continue. But, when that bell was rung, Isla, when the news broke that we were at war, I knew I needed to keep you all safe. I felt... I felt like there was something wrong. Something stirring in the water. And it was big. And dark. It bore no goodwill towards us, the fisherfolk, nor, I believe, the land dwellers. I felt it grow, the sea bearing tidings of a mighty foe."

Isla nodded, slowly. It made sense. "Rhodric has said that there's a threat growing against the island. Against the selkies. He said it was in the water, and it's at their borders now."

Duncan's forehead furrowed, deepening the lines running along his browned skin. His mouth set into a grim line.

"That is why I joined the Navy. I wanted to feel like I was doing something. Even if I couldn't do anything in the sea, I could be of use to the war that was brewing on land. We were on the ship for months, and you cannot know what your letters meant to me, lass. Yours and your mother's. They kept me going."

He paused, thinking back to the night which had

brought him to the cell he was now sitting in.

"A storm was raging that night. We'd had word that enemies were near. In or on the water, we did not know. The whole crew were on high alert. All hands were on deck."

Isla leant forwards, in rapt attention. Her father had not ever included any details of the ship in his letters – not about any danger anyway.

Duncan continued, "We had evaded enemy ships before, even decommissioning some in our turn. Our mission was to keep the sea passage safe, to enable the pilots to fly overhead unscathed. But that night, it was strangely quiet. The storm was fierce, and the thunder deafened us; we were blind to the direction of the enemy's ships. I remember thinking that it was not a natural storm, it had arisen suddenly, and it seemed to target the ship we crewed. Even though I had abandoned the sea, up to that point I had felt it had not abandoned me. For we had always seen the tides and winds in our favour. Skies cleared in our path where they should have been heavy. Smooth sailing prevailed when we would have expected tumultuous waves. But this night, it was different.

"All were on the lookout when the sirens sounded onboard. But the sirens sounded too late. I had been on alert from the beginning of the storm, but I too was caught unawares. The ship was hit. A torpedo. And in the midst of the chaos, I was taken. I do not know by what, but something, some creature from the depths was there. A tentacle seized me. I was caught unaware; I managed to fight the creature off once it had me in the water. But it was a long, hard-won battle. To begin, it seemed that it was toying with me, trying to tire me. I didn't know what it was doing at first. It would advance, attack, and then retreat. It felt, to me, as if it were waiting for something. And then, I realised; it was waiting for me to assume my selkie form."

"You had your selkie skin with you?" Isla asked, surprised.

"I have had my selkie skin with me at all times. Not for my use, but it has served as a reminder of the choice that I made, and of the love that I have for my family."

"Oh." Isla thought for a moment. "So, you could have used your selkie skin to get away – to escape the sea creature!"

Duncan inclined his head. "I could have done, aye, I am sure. And if I had, I would have been able to draw on the sea's mighty power as was my birth right."

Dina's voice drifted across from the other cell, "You could have ended the threat to us, Lord Duncan. If you had taken up your mantle once again. You could have ended all of this."

Pain crossed Duncan's face. "Aye," he answered softly. "It is possible that I could have done. It is indeed possible that I could have harnessed the sea's power once again, wresting it from whoever had control of the sea monster – for I do not think the creature who had stolen me from the ship was the holder of that malevolent power. And yet, there was equally the possibility that the power of the sea was too far gone. And, once I had transformed back to seal form, I did not know if it was possible to return to my life on land. I am afraid... I could not bear the risk."

Isla's throat burned with unspoken emotion.

"Do you forgive me, child?" Duncan asked, not to Isla, but to Dina. Isla turned to look in her direction. Through the shadows, Isla could just make out Dina's still form. After a silence, which stretched for what seemed an age, Dina cleared her throat. "I understand, Lord Duncan. And there is nothing to forgive. You had chosen your family, as is right."

"Thank you. That means a great deal to me."

Isla looked back and forth between them. She could hold her silence no longer. "Father... Dina... I must tell you something. Dina, I've just found out something. Your mother... she didn't die in an ambush at sea. Your mother...."

"Father, Dina is your niece. Aunty Marion is your mother, Dina. But she doesn't know that you're alive. She was told that you died when she was first trapped on Arraway."

Isla didn't know what reaction she had been expecting, but she *had* rather thought to have received a slightly more surprised reaction. Her father and Dina both nodded, once.

Smiling at Isla's confused expression, Duncan replied, "I had guessed. Dina. You are remarkably like my sister. Not, perhaps in appearance. You favour your father's clan. But, your mannerisms, and your fierceness... they are from Marion, there is no doubt about it."

Isla was confused. The Marion she knew did not match that description. Perhaps, she thought, life on land had changed her.

Looking to Dina, Isla was surprised to see that the girl, her cousin, was nodding, slowly. "I knew." She said simply. "I figured it out years ago. There were holes in the story that Rhodric told me. I know why, of course. Easier to tell me that my mother was dead than that she could not return to the sea, to me."

"You're not angry?" Isla whispered. Somehow, Dina's ears caught the question.

"I have been angry," she answered. "At the person who

stole my mother from me. At the fact that I thought that she had not tried hard enough to return to me. At Rhodric for lying to me. But then I realised that perhaps, she too, had been lied to. That she may not know about me. And I knew that Rhodric was doing his best to keep the clan together. He did what he thought was right. So, I have been doing everything in my power to be the best that I can be; my battle skills, my tracking, and voyaging. I wanted to be ready when my mother returns. To show her that I am worthy of carrying her mark."

Dina touched her cheek, "Marion of the Calder Sea is a legendary warrior. If I can live up to her name, that is all I can do."

"She would be proud of you, lass," Duncan said gruffly. "And if I had known...if she had known...I do not know if it would have changed anything, if it *could* have changed anything, but she would have ensured she was in your life. There is no doubt about that."

Dina nodded. "But it would have been cruel. To show her I was alive. But not present. Always distance between us. One day, she will return. I know it."

Isla bit her lip. As soon as they got out of here, she would make sure Marion knew about her daughter. Patch... where was he? Isla hoped he would be quick in bringing help. She looked about once again, realising that she had not stopped to question their surroundings.

"The brownie hollow..." she whispered. "Surely the brownies are *good*? *They* can't be the ones to have captured you...not, not Hob?"

Duncan shrugged. "At times, we cannot know the true nature of those we think we can trust. But our instincts are to be trusted also. Use your gut. If you feel, in the depths of your bones, that somebody is to be trusted, usually it is so."

Isla looked around again. "I trust Hob. He *can't* have been part of this?" Then Isla cast her mind back. She'd told Hob that Dina was her cousin... well, that she had a cousin. And the next thing she knew, Dina had disappeared. That was just a coincidence... wasn't it?

"But - so, you didn't become a selkie again. So, how were you captured? What happened once you defeated the sea monster?"

"I was weary. The battle had taken much from me. I was in human form and had been in the water for a long time. Much longer than a human could survive. And yet, there I found myself. Weakened, exhausted, and still facing the onslaught of the sea, and the creatures which were sent to test me, and to beat me. And then... it was a long night. I knew the ship had gone down. And yet I could do nothing but pull some men to safety on the remnants of the ship. But I was not to join them in safety. When I was close to pulling myself onto a raft floating just above me on the surface of the water, I was struck from behind. I did not see what it was that struck me. My vision went black. And then, I found myself here alone. My selkie skin, gone. I did not even know where I was until Dina appeared. And then... well, here you are."

"You never saw *anything*, or heard anything whilst you were kept here?" Isla asked, trying desperately to work out who could possibly be behind her father's and Dina's capture. She could not imagine the type of being who would be so cruel, and so powerful.

"No lass. It was as Dina described. Whenever a morsel of food was brought, it was as if a band of sightlessness dropped over my eyes. And my ears were stopped, so I could hear nothing. But, you say, this is a broonie hollow? I have often heard that broonies are helpful folk. I have not met one myself, but they bear also a reputation for trickery and mischief if they are slighted. You know of a broonie?"

Isla said slowly, "Hob isn't unkind or mischievous. He's the brownie of Calder Cottage. He always wants to help us."

"And your mother? What does Tuppence think of the broonie?" Duncan asked.

Isla flinched. Her father did not know.

"Mother... Mother is sick." Isla whispered. Duncan greyed at her words.

"What do you mean?" He asked in a hoarse voice.

Hurriedly, Isla carried on and explained what had happened. "And... she hasn't been 'Mother'. Not really. But maybe... if Rhodric is right, then maybe she is, was, under a spell..."

"You said 'was'?" Duncan interrupted, pouncing upon her words.

"I... found a bag... just outside these cells. By the fire. It was hidden, but I found it. I think it was... a spell bag? It had a lock of Mother's hair in it." Isla paused, paling at the fury growing on her father's face. She took a deep breath and then continued.

"But... I was so angry. I thought it might be why Mother isn't, hasn't been, Mother. So – I burnt it. And then, it was like the lights came on, and I followed the sound of the sea here, and I found you."

Duncan exhaled. "You did well, Isla. Very well. It sounds to me as if you found a hex bag. Nasty things. Perhaps, lass, you have set your mother free."

"But why would this creature's power be impacted by a human... even if she is your wife? Forgive me, Lord Duncan, but I do not understand. Why should the power of the sea be influenced by any other than selkie?" Dina asked, her brow furrowed in confusion.

"Because I chose her." Duncan replied. "It was my choice which led me to give Tuppence my heart, and my life. The life of the sea. And, therefore, the power of the sea. It is my guess that once Tuppence had been weakened, my power, that of the sea, filtered through her and to the despicable creature which has done this," he gestured around them. "But I believe the sea yet gave her protection. She was not taken from us fully."

"So, Mother might be better?" Isla asked hopefully, heart racing.

"I hope so, lass. I certainly hope so."

"Shh." Dina's urgent whisper silenced them immediately.

In the quiet that followed, the trio could make out the hum of voices, far off, but drawing steadily closer.

"Isla, quick, draw to the shadows." Duncan mouthed hurriedly.

Isla did as directed, shrinking into the darkness beside her father's cell. Footsteps echoed around the passageway. Both light and quick-footed, Isla thought. Brownies!

Then, one footstep stumbled. "Ow!" came a voice. "That was a big rock! Hob, watch out."

Hamish's voice was unmistakeable. Isla shot out of the shadows like a dart, ignoring her father's motioned plea to stay where she was.

"Hamish!" she cried, swinging her brother around. "What are you doing here? And... Hob?" She faltered, all her doubts and suspicions rushing to the surface as she caught sight of the brownie a step behind her brother, eyes wide as he took in the sight around them.

"Patch got me," Hamish said proudly. "I understood

him Dina!" He smiled as he recounted his achievement, then suddenly realised where Dina was. "You're in a prison! Patch said you were in danger.... And Father!" Sobbing, Hamish ran forward as soon as he saw his father and pushed his arms through the bars to give his father a massive bearhug.

"Hamish! My boy! You have grown so much – I would not have recognised you!" Duncan proudly studied his son from the door of the cell, clutching him as tightly to him as he could.

"Patch said it was the Brownie Glen. So... I brought Hob. Hob has brownie magic. He brought us straight there! But how did you get here, Father?" Hamish's muffled voice drifted out from the region of Duncan's midriff.

"Brownie magic?" Isla rounded on Hob. "What do you know about this? Did *you* steal my father and Dina?"

Hob shrunk back a step beneath Isla's barely concealed anger. "No... no! Of course not!! Ah would never... ah had no idea. I did not ken Laird Duncan or Lady Dina were here... Ah swear!"

Under Isla's furious gaze, Hob drew back again. "Ah promise, lass. Ah swore an oath to protect ma broonie hoose, and all within and withoot the hoose. Ah could not do anythin' to cause ye, or yer family harm."

Isla remembered what her father had said. Deep in her heart, Isla felt that Hob was telling the truth. She trusted him, even if it did not make sense to do so.

Finally, she nodded and Hob's shoulders sagged in relief. Hamish spoke up, having listened to the exchange in confusion. "Why are you all in here? Isla, why didn't you get them out?"

Isla shook her head. "I couldn't. The doors won't

move."

Hob inched closer, craning his neck to take a closer look. Isla waved him forwards. "Hob, do you know anything about these locks?" she asked.

Hob examined the door, a nose breadth from the metal. "Ah have not seen these passageways before," he squeaked.

Isla's heart sank, and she began to turn away.

"But," Hob continued, "There be magic in these doors. Only a broonie can release them once they are locked. Let me see..."

Hob ran a long, knobbly, crooked finger over the hinge of the door.

Hopes rising, Isla watched as the brownie moved his hand from the hinge to the lock. His finger appeared to press in the lock, which sank slightly, leaving the imprint of Hob's fingerprint for a moment so fleeting that Isla thought she might have imagined it. And then, the door sprang open. Amazed, Duncan stepped out, looking in disbelief at his freedom.

"Now, Dina!" Hamish cried, running over to her cell. The selkie girl smiled at him, and Hob opened her cell door in turn.

"Come on, let's go!" Isla grabbed her father's hand, handing him his selkie skin, and waved Hamish, Dina and Hob to follow them.

"But I want to know what happened!" Hamish cried as they all sped down the passageway back to the centre of the brownie hollow.

"Aye. Ah would be extremely interested in learning that also."

A creaky voice stopped them dead in their tracks as they rounded the corner. They were faced with the sight of

Pealle, the brownie chieftain, standing in the entrance of the secret passageway. The fire of the Brownie Hearth flickered in between them, reflecting a malicious glint in the ancient eyes which surveyed them.

CHAPTER 21

THE MASK SLIPS

"Chieftain Pealle!" Hob squeaked, bowing low. "Yer chieftainship, we foond..." he stuttered to a stop as the stooped brownie before them raised an eyebrow.

"Och, aye. And what is it that ye think ye've foond?"

The whisper echoed and reverberated in the chamber. Through the firelight, a cruel glimmer of spite crept across the shrivelled face. The tongues of flame of the hearth gave light to the sinister smile which was snaking across the brownie chieftain's mouth.

Hamish clenched a fist involuntarily. "You were supposed to help us. You *did* help us!"

Dina growled, a low and menacing warning. Disgust and contempt were the only emotions Isla could read through the animalistic snarl she now wore.

"You are the creature that bested me?" she spat. "A broonie?!"

Duncan placed a heavy hand on Isla's shoulder, and drew Hamish behind him as he carefully stepped around them, placing himself in between the hearth and the others.

"I do not think that the creature we see before us is a broonie, niece." He said quietly. Isla noticed that his eyes did not stray from where Pealle was stood.

"That is Chief Pealle. Head of the broonies! Ah would ken if it wasnae he!" Hob interjected, indignantly.

"We met him before – that *is* the brownie chief." Isla said, although her voice lacked conviction.

"Aye, lass. I do not doubt you met this creature before, aye, and Hob, that you see this as your Chieftain. But I do not think, no I do not, that we are seeing the true guise of the creature that is standing there."

Duncan raised his head, sniffing the air. He addressed Pealle. "The sea. Can you feel it? Can you sense it? Its power is increasing. I fear your power over it is fading. Soon, there will be nothing left for you." Duncan said, quietly yet with authority.

"What do *ye* ken of the sea's power?" Pealle asked with a sneer. "Ye, who gave up, turned yer back on it. The power that should have been mine by right!"

"And what right does a broonie have to the sea?" Dina snarled.

"*Every* right. Ah was born of the sea, just as ye were child. But ma claim is aulder, stronger. Ah am the true bearer of the sea's power! And yet, ah have always been overlooked." The brownie chief straightened as he spoke, a menacing chill emanating from him even through the heat of the fire.

"Do ye ken how long ah have had to hide away? Pretend to be a lowly, snivelling broonie?" Lip curled, Pealle straightened even further. No, Isla realised. He wasn't straightening. He was *growing*. His shape was changing. No

266

longer hunched and sloping, he had become larger, stockier. His skin, although still mottled and creased with age was no longer the nut-brown of a brownie, but rather a greyish green. Green stringy hair hung unkempt from his head in patches, draping across his shoulders like pondweed. The creature smiled, coldly, and wickedly sharp yellow fangs protruded from his mouth. He waved a gnarled, webbed hand around himself.

"This is what you wanted to see?" He asked, stepping forwards, closing the gap of protection the Brownie Hearth afforded them. His voice had changed, deepening, intensifying, hinting at long-held knowledge and cunning.

"You're a water goblin!" Hamish cried. His voice trembled, and he squeaked as he said it, but the look of fear crossing his face was not unjustified Isla thought.

Giving a mocking, bobbing, bow, the creature applauded.

"Och, very good laddie. The young master has enlightened us all. You are quite correct my young friend. I am a water goblin. *The* water goblin. At your service." He paused and smiled sardonically. "Actually, at my service I think is the right thing to say. I have been on this island for two thousand years. It was my island. The sea gifted it to me after it made me. And then, humans came, and they stole it from me. Making promises, but always breaking them. And then. That *woman*. The sea gave her a present. A child. And then, all the sea cared for was that its blood was alive, in the water, part of it forever. I, who had been here from the first, I was cast aside. Forgotten, ignored. I lost my home.

"I crawled away when my home was overrun, living where I could find shelter in the pools and streams which had not yet been laid claim to by the unworthy, the interlopers. I stayed away and practised using and growing the scant power that had been gifted to me whilst I was still the favourite of the sea. Slowly, very slowly, it grew. Hundreds of years passed. And my opportunity did not come."

"What did you want?" Isla asked, unable to contain herself. "What *do* you want?"

"That is simple, little girl." The goblin's eyes glittered dangerously, as it drew another step nearer, its webbed green feet gaining ground.

"My birth right. The sea is mine. It always should have been. And yet... and yet... *selkies*." He spat. "Selkies were the favourite children. I vowed to make it my dominion once and for all. And then, after all my centuries of waiting, my chance finally came. Never would I have believed that the answer to my problems would be the same as the very cause of them. A woman. Brought to these islands by chance? Perhaps. But I think not. The sea had offered me the opportunity to reclaim my destiny."

"Tuppence." Duncan breathed. His voice was calm, but Isla saw how he moved, mirroring every slight movement the goblin made. Her father was on high alert. For the first time, Isla realised how dangerous her father appeared. She was glad he was here.

"Yes. Your darling 'Penny'." Pealle sneered. "The one thing to make you turn your back on the gifts you had been given. A foolish choice. But one which will give *me* the chance to finally take my rightful place. A whisper here, a whisper there, and everything was falling into place.

"Your sister, your heir presumptive, unable to access your power. *I* made sure of that. A simple spell, quite easy to master when you have nothing but time on your hands.

"A word in a mad king's ear, and a sister was sent to

retrieve her brother. A word whispered in the ear of a lonely lovelorn train conductor convinced him to steal away that sister's path back to the sea."

Dina hissed.

Pealle looked at the selkie girl, suddenly amused. "Quite one of the best-executed parts of my plan. And the result... delectable. Yes, selkies. Annoying. But predictable. A welcoming party sent by your clan, I believe, fell right into my lap. Quite delicious." A bead of saliva dripped from one of the goblin's fangs, as he recalled the day that had torn the selkie colony apart.

Duncan and Dina mirrored each other's horrified expressions.

"You see, the plan, my plan, was working. And yet, I did not account for the bonds of the sea being so tightly bound to you." A fixed stare from the goblin towards Duncan was menacing.

"So far away. Almost unreachable." The goblin held a faraway look in his eyes, allowing Duncan, for a fraction of a second, to motion to the children and Hob. Isla understood. She pulled Hamish softly but firmly to the left of their father. Dina and Hob followed suit. Now, Duncan was facing the goblin more or less alone. Pealle, his focus purely on Duncan now, did not notice.

"Even, to your sister. I had also not factored in the island getting in the way, giving its protection. It was my idea to get that fool to steal the selkie skin when your sister was on the land. So then she was stuck here, and I – I could go in to remove the power that so desperately wanted to be with her. But the selkie island's protection held, unfathomably, and the selkie got her house. Her safety. So, I waited.

"The stupidity of humanity helped, of course. Always

squabbling. It gave me the perfect opportunity to begin to call you home. It was so easy, once the pieces were in play. I had the ship where I wanted it. The sea was sufficiently under my control – I could manage it for short periods, but that was enough.

"I had you in my grasp. But you did not take up your selkie form."

"And why would that matter to you?" Duncan asked through gritted teeth.

Pealle looked very much as if he were having to explain a simple concept to a particularly dim-witted student. "Because," he answered, "once you are in your selkie form, I can kill you. And your power will be no more. The first step is you, of course, and then your sister, back in her selkie skin. I had hoped that that deed would already be done. It was I who gave that train conductor the idea to replace it back to where it was taken. I knew it would be found. But that plan was foiled. She chose to put it back, and she did not leave the island. Curious, but no matter. It will be dealt with."

The way he said it was matter of fact, as if announcing the weather. His calmness chilled Isla to the core.

Pealle began, "You are stubborn, I'll grant you that. So, when your offspring were shipped up to the island, well, things began to look up."

Isla thought back to the arrival at the train station, that first day. "You," she muttered. "*You* were there, on the platform."

"Very clever, child," the goblin sneered. "You did not see me, but I could tell you sensed something. That was my first indication that you may have something of the sea running in your blood, diluted though it may be. That, of course, would mean that the sea had offered you its protection also, unworthy as you are.

"And so, who else should I turn to but the lovely Penny. The answers to my problems once again."

Isla and Hamish gasped as the goblin before them changed shape in an instant, taking on the form of a distinguished-looking gentleman dressed in a white coat.

"It took mere moments to acquire what I needed for my spell; the respected Doctor Byrne was very simple to replicate." Pealle said, almost bored. "And yet, an enigma. A woman who did not die when she was supposed to. The sea - again, it surprised me. Astonished me, in fact, that the powers it had would be so wasted, providing protection for a nobody such as that."

Isla clapped her hand over Hamish's mouth before her brother had the chance to shout at the goblin in defiance.

"But never mind that. It was back to the original plan. And so here we are. A letter from the good doctor, a couple of visits from myself," Pealle transformed once again, shifting from doctor to the bad-tempered milkman Basil had seen off in a hurry, back to the brownie chieftain's form they were so familiar with.

Resuming his own, goblin, appearance, Pealle continued. "All so that I could persuade you to take on your selkie form. I almost didn't know how to bring your offspring *here*, until I overheard the lass tell Hob here about her cousin."

Hamish looked up questioningly at Isla.

"Later," she mouthed.

"With *that* disappearance, finally, I got their attention!" the goblin crowed, grinning exultantly.

"You do like to talk a lot, don't you, given that you want to kill me," Duncan said lightly. As he spoke, Isla saw he was inching closer to the goblin.

"A thousand years of nobody to talk to, nobody to listen. Well, maybe apart from a brownie or two. Why all of the chitchat now?" Duncan asked.

"Well, you see. It is very simple." The goblin ran a clawed nail through his teeth, picking out something long and spidery. Isla shuddered in disgust.

"Now that we are all together, all cosy-like, you have a very simple choice to make." Pealle stopped and leered at Duncan.

"Choose which of your bairns you'd like to see die first... or change into your selkie form and give me the power which is rightfully mine."

Hamish gasped, and Isla too reeled back as if she'd been struck. Dina, standing next to them, put herself in front of her cousins, forming a shield of her body. The goblin furtively advanced, his eyes locked onto the children with a sneer. Dina's teeth bared in challenge. She growled her anger, and Isla dared a glance away from Pealle up to her cousin. The sea's rage shone through Dina's eyes, and as she pushed Isla and Hamish behind her further, she took a step forwards towards the water goblin, propelled by the fury she could no longer contain.

Below them, the crashing of the waves could be clearly heard, the tempo increasing, a cacophony of sound rising with Dina's slow advance.

Pealle looked up when a roll of thunder sounded, mild interest in his eyes. He too advanced another step, selkie warrior and water goblin locked in position. Isla was horrified, she could see the murderous intent shining hungrily from Pealle's eyes. Another bead of saliva dripped delicately from his fangs. He inhaled deeply, in memory. "Ah. Selkie. You seek to use the power of the sea against me? You cannot. It is in my blood also. You may be fierce, but you are weak. You can do me no harm." He laughed, a cold note resounding in the chamber between them.

"I will reclaim the small holding of power you are trying to use against me. Yes, I remember your kin... they tried their best against me – I am sure you will be just as delicious as they were. A nice appetiser..."

Dina sneered in contempt. "You can try, river maggot."

"Oh, selkie. Your arrogance is a delight."

Dina and Pealle were mere feet away from each other now, the fire separating the space between them. Isla saw Dina's clenched fists and her measured gait and closed her eyes in terror. Just as she peeped through her eyelids, she saw just a hint of a glance between Dina and her father. Isla put an arm around Hamish, pulling him closer into her.

The goblin's eyes were now focused solely on Dina. Duncan coughed, reminding Pealle that he was waiting for an answer.

Hob looked terrified. Eyes darting around, he saw what Isla had spotted earlier – that Duncan had now moved directly in front of Pealle, away, even from the protection of the fire. In the flickering firelight, the goblin did not see the brownie's slight form inching closer towards him.

"By 'give you my power', you mean, you kill me, correct?" Duncan asked, as if weighing up his options.

The goblin smiled toothily. "Naturally."

Duncan nodded, appearing to have made his decision. "Then so be it, goblin."

"Father, no!" Isla screamed. Hamish turned and buried his face in his sister's shoulder.

To Isla, everything that happened next transpired in a blur.

Duncan said, smiling menacingly back at the goblin, "If

you wanted the selkie skin so badly, all you had to do was ask."

Pealle looked confused.

"Hob, now!" Duncan cried, and the brownie barrelled sideways from where he had moved to, straight into the goblin, knocking him into Duncan's waiting arms.

Duncan threw the selkie skin over the goblin's torso, seized the goblin by its shoulders, still wrapped and blinded by the selkie skin, and heaved the wriggling mass of goblin limbs straight into the fires of the Brownie Hearth.

The bundle of selkie skin and goblin shrieked and danced as it tried to evade the flames. But, to no avail. A single high-pitched keening note was the last noise that they heard, echoing around the Brownie Hollow, up through the passageway and finally it was taken up onto the wind and carried away.

A great sizzle sounded from the depths of the flames, and a whoosh of steam erupted from the firepit. It blew away as quickly as it had materialised, leaving behind only the lingering smell of scorched fur.

"He... he's gone," Hamish stuttered in disbelief, checking for himself that the goblin was really gone.

"Aye, that he is Hamish." Duncan said, wearily sinking down to sit on the stone next to the hearth. "It's over now."

"Your... your selkie skin, Lord Duncan," Dina murmured. She looked scandalised.

"Father!" Isla realised what her father had done. "Father, you threw it away. It's gone too. You'll never be able to go back!"

Shocked, Isla went over to her father, who grabbed her and reached for Hamish, and held them both tight to his chest.

"And I would do the same a thousand times," Duncan said gruffly, tears in his eyes. "I would take a life on land with my family, with *you*, over a lifetime of forever in the sea."

Dina cleared her throat. "You would have made a good king, Lord Duncan," she said eventually. As they looked at her expectantly, she broke into a grin. "But I suppose I will have to make do with a land-locked uncle."

Duncan chuckled and reached for his niece, pulling her into the embrace.

Hamish looked between the three of them, and then to Hob, who was hopping from one leg to the other, looking uncertain as to where he should be.

"Someone is going to have to tell me eventually, you know," Hamish said seriously.

His earnestness broke the tension that had remained in the room, and they fell about laughing as Hamish became increasingly infuriated. "Hey! *Somebody* tell me! What did I miss?!"

Duncan chortled, ruffling his son's hair. "Don't you worry. I'll tell you the whole story."

Dina smiled. "It is time that I found Patch. I think we will have our own news to tell when we get back. I have a feeling the borders will not be a problem any longer."

And with that, she turned and made her way to the secret passage.

Isla ran after her. "You'll need this!" she said, handing Dina back her selkie skin. "Oh, aye, that I will." Dina winked at Isla and Hamish, and grinned broadly, "I'll see you soon cousins. But not on land for quite some time I think."

Soon, in the distance, many feet below them, they heard the distant splash of the selkie entering the water.

Hamish's gaping face looked to his sister and father for an explanation.

"Come on," Duncan said, getting to his feet. "You too Hob. Let's go home."

CHAPTER 22

HOME

Outside, finally in the open air at the entrance of the concealed brownie glen, Duncan inhaled deeply, drawing in the brisk air.

"That's more like it!" He lifted his face to the sky.

Isla looked up. She smiled. The skies had cleared, and the calls of the gulls were drifting down to where they stood, carried on a gust of sea air.

Hob looked up at them, a look of consternation visible on his face. "Laird Duncan," he squeaked, wincing slightly as Duncan looked at him. "Ah... cannae ken hoo ah was hoodwinked by such a vicious creature. Ah never would have... Ah didnae ken what it was..." Hob fidgeted, kneading his long fingers together in dismay.

"Master broonie," Duncan replied kindly. "There is no blame to be placed upon you. We were all deceived. The goblin had hundreds, nay, a thousand years to plot his deviousness and trickery."

Hob looked stunned at the unexpected absolution he

was receiving.

"And besides," Duncan continued. "You did more than your part in vanquishing the goblin." He laughed, amused suddenly by a thought which had just occurred to him.

"I wager that soon, you will be known as 'Hob the Goblin Slayer'."

Hob blushed, the colour turning his cheeks a ruddy brown. He stuttered, laughing nervously, "Ah didnae do anythin' really. The goblin angered me... 'twas yer Lairdship as did the slayin'."

A smile played around the corners of Duncan's mouth. "Stories have a habit of growing beyond our control. I rather fancy having a goblin slayer be the house broonie of Calder Cottage."

He gave a sideways glance, noting a gorse bush rustling uncharacteristically in the absence of any breeze. With a twinkle in his eye, he suddenly threw an elaborate bow, calling out in a loud voice, "Hob, of the Broonie Glen, I am indebted to you for your great act of service to me and mine. You have liberated me, and you have vanquished the evil water goblin, discovering it to be masquerading as the chieftain Pealle. I am greatly in your debt."

Hob stood, open-mouthed, as he listened to Duncan's proclamation. "Wh... what?" he stammered, rather inelegantly. But Hamish too had spotted what Duncan had seen, and lightly punched the brownie on his wrinkled arm. "Shhh," he whispered.

Isla looked around, and saw, to her great astonishment, that from the undergrowth, a sea of brownies was emerging. Hesitantly, she looked to her father, unsure whether the silent army surrounding them was a threat or not. But Duncan merely stood quietly, having straightened from his bow. Hamish stood next to him, grinning as he watched Hob's face change colour dramatically. His brownie friend swivelled his head to take in the large audience they had just amassed.

Suddenly, the entire body of brownies began to applaud, and a cacophony of squeaks, whistles and cheering crashed over them. A wave of brownies rushed up to Hob, and he was soon being lifted aloft and paraded by the beaming brownie crowd.

A stooped brownie, advanced in years, bowed stiffly in front of Duncan, Isla and Hamish. "Ye have our thanks," the brownie rasped.

"It has been many years since the Broonie Glen has been open to us. We have been cast oot. Only young Hob has been permitted to see the chieftain. But, today, we have finally been able to return home. Thank you." Again, he bowed, and the trio bowed in return.

Awed, Isla watched the celebrations, joy rising in her. She hugged her father and brother, and whispered quickly in her father's ear, "Wait here, I'll be right back." She shot off, leaving Hamish and Duncan staring after her. She knew where she needed to go. Hob's celebrations had given her the perfect opportunity.

When she returned, she caught sight of the last few brownies disappearing out of sight as they dropped one by one through the entrance to the Brownie Glen.

Hob rejoined them, dishevelled and appearing to be utterly nonplussed at what had just happened.

"Someday, Hob, you'll have to tell us how the brownie world works," Hamish said, shaking his head over the unexpected antics which he had just witnessed.

"Aye, if I work it oot meself!" Hob replied shakily. He

looked around at them and laughed nervously, questioning, "Ah still have a little broonie magic left in me today...?"

Duncan shook his head, smiling. "I have not seen the island for some time. And the sea air is restoring my soul to me. Come, let's walk... No broonie magic required."

"Come on, then, let's go find Aunty Marion... and Mother!" Isla called, as she skipped ahead, leading them on a merry chase through the bracken and gorse; their feet leant speed by the hope of what they might find upon their return to Calder Cottage.

Their peals of laughter heralded their arrival long before they were in sight of the cottage. Marion stood at the gate, a beacon welcoming them home, her red hair blowing freely in the breeze. Her eyes were bright, and her skin glowed, reflecting the brightness of the sun. Her luminosity was dazzling. Isla knew instantly that something had happened.

Marion flung the gate open when she saw the children in the distance. "Isla, Hamish, come see! There is a change in the air, I can feel it!"

Hob melted away, unseen, as Isla hung back, curious though she was to find out what her aunt was talking about. She held Hamish back as well, and their pause caused Marion to look up, beyond them.

Duncan smiled, and opened his arms wide. "Hello sister." Marion gasped, and approached hesitantly, almost disbelievingly.

"Duncan!" She put a hand to the stubble on his cheek, touching the scar that criss-crossed his beard. "It is really you. You're alive! I knew that there was something different in the air. The sea... I feel it. It is free!"

Duncan nodded, the two flame-haired siblings caught in

a close embrace.

"Thank you for looking after my family, Marion." He said, releasing her. "It is true. We are free."

Smiling tearfully, Marion looked towards Isla and Hamish, who were waiting for her to speak. But then, Isla couldn't help herself. She had to tell her aunt.

"Aunty Marion... this is yours." From beneath her jacket, Isla pulled an elegantly beautiful bundle of fur, the unmistakeable grey of a selkie skin.

"You found it!" Marion exclaimed, raising a questioning eyebrow at her niece.

Isla flushed. "Yes, well... sort of. I followed you when you found it Aunty Marion... but it's yours Aunty Marion. It's time you use it." Isla rushed her words, stumbling slightly over them in her haste.

"I... I don't understand Isla, love." Marion's confusion was mirrored on Hamish's face.

"You said you didn't find it!" Hamish said accusingly.

Isla nodded, looking down at her feet shamefacedly. "I didn't want to lose you Aunty Marion. So, I hid it back again. I'm really sorry."

"Isla, lass. You know as well as I that I chose to stay. With you, with Hamish. It is alright, Isla, I'm not angry."

"But Aunty Marion. There's something you should know... your baby. Your daughter. Rhodric lied to you Aunty Marion. She's not dead, and she knows about you."

"My Murdina? She's - she's alive?" Marion paled, and clutched a hand to her throat.

Isla nodded. Hamish piped up, "But she gets called Dina."

Marion nodded, blankly. Isla could see the thoughts swirling in her eyes. "Dina," she murmured. "Alive." Suddenly, Marion looked up, tears welling in her eyes. She laughed exultantly. "I have a daughter! And now this." She looked down at her selkie skin, clutched tight in her hands.

"But I promised you all. I promised to stay." Isla winced at the stricken expression her aunt now wore.

"It's different now," Hamish said seriously. He reached up and hugged his aunt. "It's alright Aunty Marion. We'll be alright."

She smiled and blinked through the tears which were spilling down her cheeks as she clutched Hamish tightly.

"Tuppence?" Duncan asked cautiously. The question prompted Marion to nod, still smiling. "This way." She led them to the other side of the house to the bench that their mother was frequently to be found on in the sunny island days.

Isla and Hamish rushed forward, eagerly anticipating seeing their mother restored to the vibrant, vivacious mother they remembered.

Isla's heart leapt when she saw her mother's golden head turn as Hamish bounded over to her and pounced, throwing his arms around her.

"Mother!" he shouted. "You're back!"

Isla drew to a stop. She saw the confusion on her mother's face. She withdrew from Hamish's embrace, a fact which he did not seem to notice, but it was not lost on Isla.

Tuppence looked quizzically at her son, saying slowly, "Hamish?"

"Mother?" Isla whispered. She looked at Marion. "Why... why isn't Mother well again Aunty Marion? Why isn't she better? We broke the spell. We got rid of the water goblin. Why isn't Mother, Mother again?"

The questions tumbled out of her mouth, but they were spoken so quietly, Marion had to lean in to catch them. She pulled Isla close. "Isla, the spell has been broken.

Look, she's coming back to us. But it will take time, my sweet."

Duncan's voice broke through, "Tuppence... Penny, my love."

At his words, Penny's eyes brightened, and the fog which she still seemed to be immersed in, lifted, for a moment. A smile of pure warmth lit up her face, showing Isla the mother that she knew. "Duncan!" she said, pouring an ocean of love into her husband's name. "Isla, Hamish!" Isla stumbled forward and stroked her mother's hair as Duncan pressed his wife's hands to his lips.

Then, in an instant, the fog descended in Penny's mind once more. Her vitality faded.

Isla turned to her father in despair. Hamish, meanwhile, was lost in his mother's embrace, not paying attention to the fact that his mother had retreated once more.

"Father, what do we do?" Isla cried. Hamish looked up at her in surprise. "She's coming back Isla... I know she is, I can tell."

Duncan nodded, putting an arm around his daughter's shoulders. "You have a wise brother, lass. Your mother, she has been locked away inside of herself for a long time. The darkness that was forced upon her I believe yet lingers, but in her mind alone. I do believe she still thinks herself trapped. We can help her, love, come back to us, but it is your mother who must do the battling now. You see, she's in there, and she wants to come out, to be herself again. Look."

Isla looked at her mother - really looked. Her mother's blue eyes looked back. A slight tilt of her lips, and a fleeting glint of life and recognition snapped and flickered in the depths of her eyes. Then, the vacant expression returned.

"Will you help me?" Duncan asked of his children.

"Will you help me to help your mother regain who she is?"

Isla watched Hamish nod enthusiastically. "I will," she said carefully, looking up at her father.

"Good. My brave children. Do not doubt, she will come back to us."

Duncan looked to his sister. "You see, Marion. We will be fine. Penny is making her way back. It will not be our easiest adventure together, but we have weathered many storms. This one, I feel, is lessening."

Marion smiled, "I believe you are right. She will come back. She has already made great progress."

Isla had never seen her aunt look unsure of herself, and yet, as she held her selkie skin in her hands, and glanced down at it, uncertainty marked her every movement.

"You know, sister. The curse has been lifted. And my selkie skin, it is gone. What power was mine is now yours. I see the power of the Calder Sea is upon you."

Marion straightened, and looked at Duncan. She traced the form of the mark which she bore on her arm as she nodded, considering his words.

"I feel it," she replied. "I knew something had changed. But I did not think... but aye, here it is."

Duncan smiled again at his sister. "Wear it well," he said gently. "It has been rightfully yours these many years. It is time, Marion."

His words had a rousing effect on Marion. She drew herself to her full height. Raising her head high, Marion surveyed the sea before her. Isla saw, for the first time, the regal qualities which her aunt possessed. The Queen of the Calder Sea smiled.

"Aye. It is time."

Embracing Duncan, Penny, Isla and Hamish in turn, Marion bid them each farewell. "It is my privilege to be your aunt," she whispered to Isla. "Hamish, dear boy, never lose your sense of wonder."

"Duncan." Marion's words failed her. Duncan nodded, understanding. "All is well. Your home awaits you, my sister."

Nodding in reply, Marion inhaled sharply. "You are always most welcome, you know." She said to the children.

"And if you should ever have need of help, the sea will answer. Always remember that. And always, remember who you are. You are children of the Calder Sea."

Whirling around, she disappeared around the crest of the hill, leaving the reunited family in her wake. Isla put her arms around Hamish and their mother. With their father next to them, she felt at peace.

A flash of red drew Isla's gaze to the beach below. Her aunt's distant figure drew closer and closer to the sea. At the water's edge, Marion stood for a moment, and looked back at the land and life she was now leaving behind. Then, unwavering in her choice, she stepped into her selkie skin and dived into the sea's waiting embrace.

From the clifftop, Isla could just make out the selkie queen gliding away from shore. Out on the horizon, a second selkie patiently awaited her.

Brushing a tear from her eye, Isla smiled. Dina was finally meeting her mother. The sea had called her home.

EPILOGUE

FORESHADOWING

The boat drew up onto the shore with a thud. Isla threw her oars into the bottom of the boat and hefted the vessel onto shore. The motion came naturally to her, a quick, steady action made easy after a year's worth of practice.

Barefoot, she raced up the sand, her footprints lapped up by the waves chasing in her wake. Panting and laughing with exhilaration, she tumbled onto the sand at the feet of a statuesque, flame-haired woman. Her cousin followed seconds behind, scowling fiercely.

"You cheated!" Dina grumbled, flopping down beside her.

"It's not my fault if I can row faster than you can swim!" Isla playfully swatted Dina's shoulder. The friendly shove she got in return was meant in jest, but it also knocked her for six.

"Nice to see you again, Isla," Marion interrupted hurriedly, as she helped a dishevelled Isla back up from the sprawled heap she'd landed in.

"Sorry, Aunty Marion. Dina met me at the point. She told me I'd gotten soft, now I've been away at school for six months. But I showed her!" Isla stuck her tongue out good naturedly at her cousin.

"How is school on the mainland?" Marion asked. "Will you continue next year do you think? We've received your letters – Patch has done a marvellous job with marine postal delivery!"

Dina scoffed. "School. It sounds boring to me."

Isla couldn't disagree. "Well, it's not fun. Not really. But Mother says it's good for me. Hamish will go next year. At least, we can go from and come back to the island each day. That's not so bad."

"How is Penny?" Marion asked, surveying her niece seriously now. "I have not heard news in a while. It is strange. I am reacquainting myself with our selkie ways and customs, but it does not seem quite real that I cannot simply walk up to the cottage to look in on your mother and father!"

"Mother is doing... much better. She still has days when she is lost, or has trouble coming back to herself. But those days are becoming much fewer. Father is with her always, taking her for walks, making her laugh, helping her to remember. And Hamish, Hamish is feeding us all. With Hob's help of course. Although, Hamish said that he thinks the brownies want to make Hob the new brownie chieftain. He's famous now in the brownie world! I don't know if he will do it – he's too shy really.

"But there's nothing much new. Father is finishing off a boat he's made. For Mother. He says that the last step is the sea. So, he's going to give it to her."

Marion nodded, smiling. "He has some good ideas at times, does my brother. Sometimes."

"Oh, he didn't think of it," Isla said, embarrassed but proud all at once. "I... the sea told me so."

Dina suddenly looked significantly less disinterested in the conversation. "You've been practising," she said. "Good. About time, my cousin caught up with the pups in their sea-speak."

She smiled as she spoke, Isla rolled her eyes. Dina's sense of humour still had a long way to go.

"What's new here?" Isla asked, looking around. They had not yet gone through the cave to the colony. All seemed to look as it always had, out here at least, Isla thought to herself.

Dina scowled. "Nothing. No water goblins to make life more interesting."

"Hush Dina!" Marion scolded her daughter, laughing as she did so.

Isla regarded them with interest. Mother and daughter appeared to have fallen into a friendly to-and-fro. Isla realised they were still testing the waters of their newfound relationship.

"Are the borders still clear?" she asked.

Marion nodded. "Yes, we've had little movement. No threats since our warriors chased off the last of Pealle's allies. That was months ago now. It's been hard work clearing up the mess that was left, but I think we've managed it."

Dina grimaced. "It's boring now."

Marion shook her head in exasperation. "Boring is often better my daughter, particularly when you have charge of an entire selkie colony."

"Well, lucky I don't have that responsibility, isn't it?" Dina replied lightly, brushing off Marion's reproach.

"One day, my dear, you will."

Dina rolled her eyes away from Marion's line of sight and scrunched her face up in distaste. Hurriedly, she changed the subject.

"So, you have all decided to stay?" she asked Isla. "Lord... Uncle Duncan, he does not want to move you all back to the city?" She spoke the unfamiliar word, slowly trying out the sound of it. It sounded strange in her ears.

"Father thinks staying here is the safest place for us," Isla replied. "Technically, he's still classified as 'Missing, presumed dead', so he's not in any rush to re-join. And, he says, London is going to become less safe. We've heard stories. Many of my friends are being sent out from the city, to the countryside. Some are even leaving the country altogether!"

Marion nodded. "Times are difficult for the land. Dark are the days ahead. But you will be safe here. Duncan is right about that."

Dina sprang to her feet, dusting sand off herself, and sent it flying all over Isla.

"Come on, let's go in. I'm sure there'll be many selkies looking forward to greeting you again Isla. They've all... we've all, missed you," she qualified with a shy smile.

Isla grinned back and nodded, "I'm ready. Aunty Marion? Are you coming?"

Marion inclined her head. "You go on ahead, I will join you soon."

As the girls raced each other to the cave front, Marion Calder, Queen of the Calder Sea, looked out over the waters towards the land she had once called home.

"Aye," she whispered. "Very dark are the days ahead." Marion stood there, watching, until the sun began to wend its way down, until it sank beneath the waves of the horizon. Then, she turned and walked towards the cave entrance. Her people were waiting for her. Perhaps, she thought, perhaps they would yet have a part to play.

ABOUT THE AUTHOR

Fiona Torsch lives in Derby with her husband and kooky cocker spaniel. She dearly loves a good story. She hopes you enjoyed this one.

Made in the USA
Columbia, SC
24 November 2023

27064022R00178